Praise for
Anne Perry's Christmas Mysteries

A Christmas Journey

"One of the best books to brighten up the joyous
season."
—*USA Today*

A Christmas Visitor

"Perry creates excellent winter atmosphere in the
wild, snowy lands of northern England."
—*The Arizona Republic*

A Christmas Guest

"[A] satisfying tale."
—*The Wall Street Journal*

A Christmas Secret

"Anne Perry has crafted a finely written Christmas
puzzle that has a redemptive seasonal message
woven within its solution."
—*The Wall Street Journal*

A Christmas Beginning

"Intriguing . . . Perry's use of period detail is, as-
always, strong and evocative."
—*The Seattle Times*

BY ANNE PERRY

FEATURING WILLIAM MONK

The Face of a Stranger
A Dangerous Mourning
Defend and Betray
A Sudden, Fearful Death
The Sins of the Wolf
Cain His Brother
Weighed in the Balance
A Breach of Promise

The Twisted Root
Slaves of Obsession
Funeral in Blue
Death of a Stranger
The Shifting Tide
Dark Assassin
Execution Dock

FEATURING CHARLOTTE AND THOMAS PITT

The Cater Street Hangman
Callander Square
Paragon Walk
Resurrection Row
Bluegate Fields
Rutland Place
Death in the Devil's Acre
Cardington Crescent
Silence in Hanover Close
Bethlehem Road
Farriers' Lane

Hyde Park Headsman
Traitors Gate
Pentecost Alley
Ashworth Hall
Bedford Square
Half Moon Street
The Whitechapel Conspiracy
Southampton Row
Seven Dials
Long Spoon Lane
Buckingham Palace Gardens

THE WORLD WAR I NOVELS

No Graves as Yet
Shoulder the Sky
At Some Disputed Barricade
Angel in the Gloom
We Shall Not Sleep

THE CHRISTMAS NOVELS

A Christmas Journey
A Christmas Visitor
A Christmas Guest
A Christmas Secret
A Christmas Beginning
A Christmas Grace
A Christmas Promise

Anne Perry's Silent Nights

Anne Perry's Silent Nights

Two Victorian Christmas Mysteries

A CHRISTMAS BEGINNING

A CHRISTMAS GRACE

Anne Perry

BALLANTINE BOOKS TRADE PAPERBACKS
NEW YORK

2009 Ballantine Books Trade Paperback Edition

A Christmas Beginning copyright © 2007 by Anne Perry
A Christmas Grace copyright © 2009 by Anne Perry

Published in the United States by Ballantine Books, an imprint of The Random House Publishing Group, a division of Random House, Inc., New York.

BALLANTINE and colophon are registered trademarks of Random House, Inc.

Originally published in hardcover as two separate works entitled *A Christmas Beginning* and *A Christmas Grace* by Ballantine Books in 2007 and 2008.

ISBN 978-0-345-51729-6

Printed in the United States of America

www.ballantinebooks.com

2 4 6 8 9 7 5 3 1

Text design by Julie Schroeder

A Christmas Beginning

To all those who
dream impossible dreams

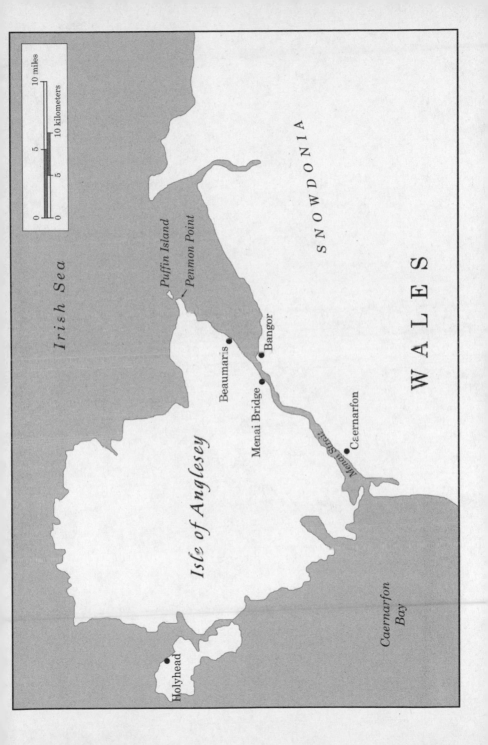

*S*O THIS WAS THE ISLE OF ANGLESEY. RUNCORN stood on the rugged headland and stared across the narrow water of the Menai Strait towards the mountains of Snowdonia and mainland Wales, and he wondered why on earth he had chosen to come here, alone in December. The air was hard, ice-edged, and laden with the salt of the sea. Runcorn was a Londoner, used to the rattle of hansom cabs on the cobbles, the gas lamps gleaming in the afternoon dusk. Every day he was surrounded by the sing-song voices of costermongers, the cries of news vendors, drivers of every kind of vehicle—broughams to drays—and the air carried the smell of smoke and manure.

This isolated island must be the loneliest place in Britain, all bare hills and hard, bright water, and silence except for the moan of the wind in the grass. The black skeleton of the Menai Bridge had a certain grace, but it was a cold elegance, not the low, familiar arches across the Thames. The few lights flickering on in the town of Beaumaris behind him indicated nothing like the vast city he was used to, teeming with the passions, the sorrow, and the dreams of millions.

Of course the reason he was here was simple. Runcorn had nowhere else in particular to be for Christmas, no family. He lived alone. He knew many people, but they were colleagues rather than friends. He had earned his promotions until he was now, at fifty, a senior superintendent in the Metropolitan Police, separated by office from those he had once worked beside. But he was not a gentleman, like those of his own rank. He had not the polish, the confidence, the ease of speech and grace of movement that comes with not having to care what people thought of you.

He smiled to himself as the wind stung his face. Monk, his colleague many years ago, one of his few friends, had not been born a gentleman either, but somehow he had always managed to seem like one. That used to hurt, but it did not anymore. He knew that Monk was human too, and vulnerable. He could make mistakes. And perhaps Runcorn himself was wiser.

The last case in which they had worked together had been difficult and in the end ugly. Now Runcorn was tired of the city and he was due several weeks of leave. Why not take it somewhere as different as possible? He would refresh his mind away from the familiar and predictable, take long walks in the open, think deeply for a change.

The sun was sinking in the southwest, shedding brilliant, burning light over the water. The land was dark as the color faded and the headlands jutted purple and black out of the sea. Only the uplands, ribbed pale like crumpled velvet, still caught the last rays of light.

How long was winter twilight here? Would he soon find himself lost, unable to see the way back to his lodgings? It was bitterly cold already. His feet were numb from standing. Turning, he started to walk towards the east and the darkening sky. What was there to think about? He was good at his job, patient, possibly a little pedestrian. He never had flashes of brilliant intuition, but he got where he needed to. He had succeeded far more than any of the other young men who had started when he had. In fact, his own success had surprised him.

But was he happy?

That was a stupid question, as if happiness were something you could own and have for always. He was happy at times, as for example when a case was closed and he knew he had done it well, found a difficult truth and left no doubts to haunt him afterwards, no savage and half-answered questions.

He was happy when he sat down by the fire at the end of a long day, took the weight off his feet, and ate something really good, like a thick-crusted ham-and-egg pie, or hot sausages with mashed potatoes. He liked good music, even classical music sometimes, although he would not admit it, in case people thought he was putting on airs. And he liked dogs. A good dog always made him smile. Was that enough?

He could only just see the road at his feet now. He thought about the huge bridge behind him, spanning the whole surge and power of the sea. What about the man who built that? Had he been happy? He had certainly created something to marvel at, and changed the lives of people far into the future.

Runcorn had untangled a few problems, but had he ever built anything, or did he always use other people's bridges? Where did he go, anyway? No more than home to bed. Tonight it was to be an unfamiliar lodging house. It was comfortable. He would sleep well, he usually did. Certainly it was warm enough, and Mrs. Owen was an agreeable woman, generous in nature.

*T*he next morning was sharp and cold, but a pale sun struggled over the horizon, milky soft through a fine veil of cloud, which Mrs. Owen assured him would burn off soon. The frost was only a dusting of white here and there, enough to make the hollows stand out on the long, uneven lawn stretching down to the big yew tree.

Runcorn ate a hearty breakfast, talked with Mrs.

Owen for a little while because it was only civil to appear interested as she told him about some of the local places and customs. Afterwards he set out to walk again.

This time he headed uphill, climbing steadily until nearly midday when he turned and gazed out at a cloudless sky, and a sea shimmering unbroken into the distance.

He stood there for some time, lost in the enormity of it, then gradually descended. He was on the outskirts of Beaumaris again when he turned a corner in the road and came face-to-face with a tall, slender man of unusual elegance, even in his heavy, winter coat and hat. He was in his mid-thirties, handsome, clean-shaven. They both stopped, staring at each other. The man blinked, uncertain except recognizing Runcorn's face as familiar.

Runcorn knew him instantly, as if it had been only a week ago they had met. But it was longer than that, much longer. It had been a case of suicide suspected to be a murder. John Barclay had lived in a house backing onto the mews where the body had been found. It was not Barclay whom Runcorn remembered; it was his widowed sister, Melisande Ewart. Even standing here in the middle of this bright, windy road, Runcorn could see her face as clearly as if it were she who were here now, not her arrogant, unhelpful brother.

"Excuse me," Barclay said tensely, stepping around Runcorn as if they had been strangers and walking on up the road, lengthening his stride. But Runcorn had seen the recognition in his face, and the distaste.

Was Melisande here too? If she was, he might see her, or at least catch a glimpse. Did she still look the same? Was the curve of her hair as soft? The way she smiled and the sadness in her had continued to haunt him in the year since they'd last met.

It was ridiculous for him to think of her still. If she remembered him at all, it would be as a policeman determined to do his job regardless of fear or favor, but with possibly a modicum of kindness. It was her courage, her defiance of her brother Barclay in identifying the corpse and taking the witness stand, that had closed the case. He had always wondered how much that had cost her afterwards in Barclay's displeasure. There had been nothing he could do to help.

He began walking again, around the bend in the road and past the first house of the village. Was she staying here also? He quickened his step without realizing it. The sun was bright, the frost nothing more than sparkling drops in the grass.

How could he find out if she was here, without being overeager? He could hardly ask, as if they were social acquaintances. He was a policeman who had investigated a death. It would be pointless to see her, and much too painful. Chastising himself, he thought what a fool he was to have even thought about it.

He hurried on towards his lodgings, the safety of Mrs. Owen's dining room table and the cheerful conversation of strangers.

*B*ut Runcorn did not stop thinking of Melisande. The weather grew a little milder, and for the first time it was well above freezing. He saw more than a hundred birds pecking over a field, and a farmer told him they were redwings. There were plenty of yellow gorse in bloom and the occasional cowslip. He walked in the sun and the wind, once or twice in the rain, and over a couple of days learned his way along the shore to east and west of Beaumaris. He found favorite places, hollows out of the wind, orchids that caught his breath with sudden pleasure, intimate rock pools where strange shells and seaweeds could be found.

On Sunday he dressed in the one decent suit he had brought with him and went to the morning service at the church nearest to the place in the road where he had encountered John Barclay. It was a solid stone building with stained-glass windows and a bell that rang out in the gusty air, the rich sound carrying across the town and into the fields beyond.

Runcorn knew why he was here, drawn as if by the pull of a magnet. It had nothing to do with the worship of God, even though he entered through the great, carved wooden doors with head bowed, hat in his hand, and a mixture of reverence and hope that made his heart beat faster.

11

Inside the old church was a stone floor and a high ceiling crossed with massive, carved hammer beams. The light was hazy and the sound hushed. Colors in the great illuminated windows showed the stations of the cross and what looked like a woman following after the figure of Christ in the street. She knelt to touch his robe, and Runcorn remembered a biblical story about healing. He could not recall the details.

The congregation was already seated as he slipped into a pew along one side. He watched with interest, bowing his head as Barclay passed by him, then lifting it again with a sudden pang of disappointment that Melisande was not with him. But there was no reason for her to be on this wind-scoured island in its barren glory, with its wild coast, its birds, and the roaring sea. What was there for a beautiful woman to do here?

Then another, entirely different woman, perhaps in her mid-twenties, walked past the end of his pew and continued on up the aisle. She moved with a unique grace, almost fluid, as if she were not touching the hard stone of a church floor with her boots, but were barefoot on grass, or the smooth sand of a beach. Her head was high, and when she turned, her pale face was quickened by a secret laughter, as if she understood something no one else did. She was wearing a green so somber it appeared almost black, and her cloud of dark hair escaped the rather rakish hat she seemed to have put on at the last moment, without thought. Her eyes were peat-brown, and wide. Runcorn noticed that, even though she looked at him for only an instant.

She went on up to the very front row, and sat down beside a woman perhaps fifteen years older, who turned to greet her with a quick, warm smile.

Runcorn suddenly noticed the movement of a man a couple of rows in front of him who quickly turned to stare at the younger woman with an intensity unsuitable in church. His features were regular and he had an excellent head of hair, thick with a slightly auburn tone to it. He was almost handsome, but for a tightness about his mouth that gave him a look of meanness. He was perhaps approaching forty.

If the young woman were aware of the man's attention, she showed no sign of it at all; indeed, she seemed indifferent to any of the people around her except the vicar who now appeared. Middle-aged, he had a pale, ascetic face with a high brow and the same peat-dark eyes as the girl in green. Almost immediately the service commenced, with the usual soothing and familiar ritual. The vicar conducted the proceedings somberly and somewhat as if it was a habit he was so accustomed to that it required far less than his full attention. Runcorn began to wonder if there were any way in which he could escape before the sermon without his departure being rudely obvious, and concluded that there was not. Instead, he decided to occupy his thoughts by looking at the people.

The man in front of Runcorn was turning to look at the young woman again. There was too much emotion in his face to believe he was simply admiring her. He had to know her, and there had to have been conflict between them, at least on his part.

What of her? Runcorn could not see her now because she was facing forward, her attention on the vicar as he began his sermon. His subject was obedience, an easy matter for which to find plenty of reference, though not one so simple to give life to or warmth, or to make seem relevant to Christmas, now less than two weeks away. Runcorn wondered why on earth the vicar had chosen it, for it was singularly inappropriate. But then, Runcorn reflected, he did not know the congregation. There could be all kinds of passions running out of control that obedience might hold in check. The vicar might be the good shepherd trying every way he knew to lead wayward sheep to safe pasture.

Barclay was also looking at the young woman in green, and for a moment there was a hunger in his face that was quite unmistakable. Runcorn was almost embarrassed to have seen it. Two men courting the same woman? Well, this must happen in every village in England.

He had not been paying attention to the service. He had no idea what the curate had risen to do, only that his face was in every way different from that of the vicar. Where the older man was studious and disciplined, this man seemed mercurial and full of dreams. Though barely into his twenties, there was a keen intelligence in him. He looked at the girl and smiled, then as if caught in a minor offense, quickly looked away. She turned a little, and Runcorn could see, even in the brief profile of her face, that she was smiling back, not wistfully as a lover, but with life and laughter, as a friend.

Runcorn would never know what tangle of emotions bound those people together. He had come to church because he thought Barclay would be here and, in spite of the absurdity of it, there might be a chance he would see Melisande. He would like to think she was happy, whatever it was that had saddened her in London. The thought of her still facing some sort of darkness was so heavy inside him he felt tight in his chest, as if a physical band prevented him from taking a full breath. Where was she? He could not possibly ask Barclay if she was well. And any answer he gave would be no more than a formality. His ilk did not discuss health or happiness with tradesmen, and he had made it abundantly clear that he regarded Runcorn, and all police, as the refuse collectors of society. He had said as much.

The congregation rose again to sing another hymn. The organist was good and the music pealed out with a powerful, joyous melody. Runcorn enjoyed singing, his voice was rich and he knew how to carry a tune.

It was as he started to sit down again, a moment or two after the people to the left of him, that he saw Melisande. She was nowhere near Barclay, but it was unmistakably her. He could never forget her face, the gentleness in it, the clear eyes, the laughter and the pain so near the surface.

She looked at him now with sudden, wide amazement. She smiled, and then self-consciously turned away.

Runcorn's heart lurched, the room swayed around him, and he sat down in the pew so hard the woman in front turned to glare at him.

Melisande was here! And she remembered him! That smile was far more than just the acknowledgment of a stranger caught staring at her. It was more than civility, it had had warmth. He could feel it burn inside him.

The rest of the service passed by him in a blur of sound, beautiful and meaningless, like the splashes of color the sunlight painted through the windows.

Afterwards he stood in the bright winter stillness

as the congregation came outside again, talking to each other, shaking the vicar by the hand, milling around exchanging gossip and good wishes.

Someone recognized him as a stranger and invited him to be introduced. He moved forward without thought as to what he was going to say, and found himself shaking the hand of the vicar, Reverend Arthur Costain, and offering his name but not his police rank.

"Welcome to Anglesey, Mr. Runcorn," Costain said with a smile. "Are you staying with us over Christmas, or perhaps we may hope you will be with us longer?"

In that instant Runcorn made his decision. Melisande and Barclay already knew his profession, but he would tell no one else. He was not ashamed of it, but knowledge that he was a policeman made many people uncomfortable, and their defense was to avoid him.

"I will stay as long as I can," he replied. "Certainly until the New Year."

Costain seemed pleased. "Excellent. Perhaps you will call at the vicarage some time. My wife and I

would be delighted to make your better acquaintance." He indicated the woman beside him, who had
turned to welcome the girl in green during the service. Upon closer inspection, she was more interesting than he could have guessed from several rows
behind. She was not as beautiful as her younger
companion, but there was a strength in her face
which was unusual, full of both humor and patience.
Runcorn found it instantly pleasing, and accepted
the invitation, only then realizing that the vicar,
at least, had said it as a matter of form. Runcorn
blushed at his own foolishness.

It was Mrs. Costain who rescued him. "Forgive
my husband, Mr. Runcorn. He is always hoping for
new parishioners. We shall not press you into staying beyond your pleasure, I assure you. Is this your
first visit to the island?"

He recognized her kindness with surprise. As a
member of the police, he was not used to such accep-
tance from her social class. He had lost his sense of
where Melisande was in the crowd, but he knew precisely where Barclay was standing, only yards away,
looking at him with distaste. How long would it be

before he told Mrs. Costain that Runcorn was a policeman?

But Barclay was not actually looking at Runcorn, he was staring at the girl in green, his eyes so intent on her face that Runcorn knew she must be aware of it, even uncomfortable. There was a brooding emotion in Barclay that seemed a mixture of longing and anger, and when the man with auburn hair who had also watched her approached, his face tight and bitter, for an instant the tension between her and Barclay was so palpable that others were momentarily uncomfortable as well.

"Morning, Newbridge," Barclay's voice was curt.

"Morning, Barclay," Newbridge replied. "Pleasant weather."

Everyone else was silent.

"I doubt it will last," Barclay responded.

"Do you imagine we will have a white Christmas?" Reverend Costain put in quickly. "It is in little over a week now. It would be nice for our party."

Barclay's eyebrows rose. "White?" he said sarcastically, as if the word held a dozen other, more pungent meanings. "Hardly."

The girl in green glanced over at him with amusement and then a sudden little shiver, hunching her shoulders as though she were cold, although she was well dressed and there was no wind.

"Olivia?" Costain said anxiously, as if to distract her. "Come meet our visitor, Mr. Runcorn. Mr. Runcorn, my sister, Miss Olivia Costain."

"Don't fuss," his wife's voice was soft. Had Runcorn not been standing so close he would not have heard her.

The vicar was visibly disconcerted. He looked from Barclay to Olivia and clearly did not know how to address the deeper meaning that was understood between them. The attempted introduction was lost in the tension between them.

Barclay nodded curtly and walked over towards Melisande, who was waiting for him on the path by the lych-gate. Runcorn watched him go, and then for a moment his eyes met Melisande's and he was unaware of anyone else. Newbridge brushed past him, breaking the moment. He reached Olivia and said something to her. She replied, her voice cool and light. Her words were courteous, her face almost

21

empty of expression. Then she turned and walked away. Runcorn was certain in that instant that she disliked Newbridge.

He thanked Mrs. Costain for her kindness, glanced briefly at the others in acknowledgment, then excused himself. He made his way across the graveyard between the headstones, the carved angels, and the funeral urns and into the shadow of the yew trees beyond. He walked out of the farther gate into the road, his mind still whirling.

It was his profession to watch people and read reactions. There was so much more to investigating than attending to the words given in an answer. It was as much the way these words were said, the hesitations, the angle of the head, the movement and the stillness that told him of the passions beneath. That small group in the churchyard had been torn by emotions too powerful to control except with intense effort. The air was heavy, tingling on the skin like that before the breaking of a storm.

In spite of his separateness, his observation of it so intellectually cool, he was as much a victim as any of them. He was just as human, as vulnerable and every bit as absurd. What could be more ridiculous than the way he felt about Melisande, a woman to whom he could never be more than a public servant that she had been able to assist, because she had had the courage to do the right thing in spite of her brother's disapproval?

He went back to Mrs. Owen's house because he knew she had cooked Sunday dinner for him and it would be a graceless thing not to return and eat it, despite already feeling as if the comfortable walls of the house would close him in almost unbearably. And the last thing he wanted was trivial conversation, no matter how well meant. But he was a man of habit, and he had learned the cost of bad manners.

At least he had an excuse to leave quickly. The weather being exceptionally pleasant for December, he was determined to walk as far as he could and still return by dusk. The wild, lonely paths along the shore with the turbulent noise of breaking water and screaming gulls fit his mood perfectly. It was nature eternal and far beyond man's control. It was an escape to become part of it, simply by hearing the sounds, feeling the wind in his face, and looking at the limitless horizon. It was big and impersonal, and that comforted him. He saw in it a kind of truth.

❧

*T*he next day Runcorn walked the shore all the way from Beaumaris north and east to Penmon Point. He stood and stared at the lighthouse and Puffin Island beyond. The day after he went in the other direction, all the way past the Menai Bridge until he could see the great towers of Caernarfon Castle on the opposite shore, beneath the vast, white-crowned peaks of Snowdonia. The following day he walked aimlessly in the hills above Beaumaris until he was exhausted.

Even so, he did not sleep well. He rose at seven, shaved and dressed, and went outside into the winter dawn. The air had a hard edge of ice on it, so sharp he gasped as he breathed it in. But he found a perverse pleasure in it, also. It was clean and bitter, and he imagined he could see the distances it had blown across, the dark, glimmering water and the starlight. Eight days to go. Perhaps they would have a white Christmas after all.

Without realizing it he had walked uphill towards the church again. Its tower loomed massive against the lightening sky. He went in through the lych-gate and up the path, then around through the graveyard, picking his way across the grass crisp with frost. The dawn was sending pale shafts of light up in the east and throwing shadows from the gravestones and the occasional marble angel.

Perhaps that was why he was almost upon the body before he realized what it was. She was lying at the base of a carved cross, her white gown frozen hard, her face stiff, her black hair spread out in a cloud around her like a shadow. The only color was the blood drenching the lower half of her body, which flooded scarlet with the strengthening daylight.

Runcorn was too horrified to move. He stood staring at her as if he had seen an apparition, and if he waited, his vision would clear and it would vanish. But the cold moved into his bones, the fingers of light crept further around her body, and she remained as terribly real. He knew who she was, Olivia Costain, the girl in green who had walked up the aisle of the church as if on a grassy lea.

He moved at last, going forward to bend onto one knee and touch her freezing hand. It was more than cold, the fingers clenched and locked in place. Her eyes were wide open. Even here, like this, something of her beauty remained, a delicacy to the bones, which wrenched inside him with pity for what she had been.

He looked down at the terrible wound in her stomach, clotted with thick blood, the flesh itself hidden. She must have been standing close to the grave, with her back to the cross, facing whoever it was that had done this to her. She had not been running away. He studied the ground and saw no damage to the grass except what he himself had done, bending over her. There was nothing to say she had fought, no marks on either of her hands, or on her arms or throat. Her killer could not have taken her by surprise from behind, they had stood face-to-face. The attack must have been sudden and terrible.

From such an injury she would have bled to death

very quickly, he hoped in just moments. It was bright, arterial blood, the force of life. Surely it would not be possible to stand close enough to someone and inflict such a blow without being stained by blood oneself?

He stepped back and automatically cast his eyes about for the weapon. He did not expect to find it, but he must be certain. He could see nothing, no trace of red in the white daylight, no irregularity in the frost-pale grass, except the way he himself had come, as both she and her killer must have also, before the dew was iced hard.

People would pass this way soon. He must find someone to watch the body, keep anyone else from disturbing it. He must report it to the local police. At the very least he must prevent Costain from seeing her himself.

Who'd be closest? The sexton. But where to find him? He turned slowly, seeking a well-worn path, another gate. There was nothing. He went a few steps to the east, but there was nothing but more graves. Increasing his pace, he went in the opposite direction, around the corner of the church tower, and saw a more trodden way and a path at the end. Running now and slipping a little, he turned to the wall and the small cottage beyond nestled in its apple orchard. He banged on the back door.

It was answered by an elderly man, clearly in the middle of his breakfast.

"Are you the sexton, sir?" Runcorn asked.

"I am. Can I help you?"

Runcorn told him the harsh facts and asked him to stand guard over the body, then he followed the man's directions to the cottage of Constable Warner, who would still be at home at this hour.

Warner was just finishing his breakfast and his wife was reluctant to disturb him until she saw Runcorn's face in the inside light, and the shock in his eyes. Then she made no demur. She passed him a cup of tea, and insisted he drink it while he explained his profession and his errand to Warner himself, a large, soft-spoken man in his early forties.

"I suppose you'll be used to this, coming from London, an' all," he said a little huskily, after Runcorn had described the scene to him, and the little he had deduced from it. "I never dealt with murder before, 'cepting as you'd call a fight that ended badly murder." His face was filled not only with sorrow but with a kind of helplessness as the enormity of his own task dawned on him. Runcorn could see his fear.

"If I can help," he offered, and immediately wondered if he had trespassed already, implying however obliquely, that the local force was inferior. He regretted it, but it was too late.

Warner swallowed. "Well, we'll be getting someone from the mainland, no doubt," he said quickly. "Maybe the chief constable, or such. But I'd be mighty grateful if you'd lend a hand until then, seeing as you have the experience."

"Of course," Runcorn agreed. "First thing, someone'll have to tell her family, and as soon as possible, get a doctor to look at her. Then we should have her put somewhere decent."

"Yes." Warner looked bewildered. "Yes, I'll do that. Poor vicar." He pushed his hand up over his brow, blinking rapidly. "What a terrible thing to happen." He glanced at Runcorn hopefully. "I suppose it couldn't be an accident of some kind? Could she have . . . fell, somehow?"

"No," Runcorn said simply. He did not bother to go over the details again, or even mention the absurdity of Olivia Costain walking alone at night in the graveyard carrying a knife large enough to cause an injury like the one he had seen. She had not tripped, she had fallen backwards from the weight of the assault. The blade had not been found.

Warner sighed, his face pale but flushed unnaturally across the cheeks, his eyes downcast. "Sorry, I just . . ." He looked up again suddenly. "We aren't used to this kind o' thing here. Known Miss Olivia since she were . . . little. Who'd do this to her?"

"We have to find that out," Runcorn said simply. "It's where our duty gets hard and ugly, and it matters we do it right."

Warner rose to his feet, scraping the kitchen chair on the floor as he pushed it back. "I'll go an' tell the vicar, an' Mrs. Costain. She'll be torn to bits. They were very close, she an' Miss Olivia, more like real sisters they were, not just in-law, like. Will you . . . will you go and find Dr. Trimby? His house is hard to find, my wife'll take you. Then I'd better get a message to the inspector in Bangor, and no doubt he'll be sending for Sir Alan Faraday from Caernarfon."

Runcorn accepted without further discussion. A few moments later he was walking beside Mrs. Warner as she led him through a hasty shortcut across the road and through one back street after another until they arrived at the door of Dr. Trimby's house. It was now nearly nine o'clock on a gusty morning, the streets were busy, and there were three or four people already waiting in his surgery.

Trimby's name did not suit him. He was short and stocky with flyaway hair, a shirt that defied the iron, and a cravat as unfashionable as it was possible to be. Nothing of his apparel matched anything else. However, his attention was instant and complete. Once Mrs. Warner had told him who Runcorn was, he listened with a mixture of grief and total concentration. He made no notes at all, but Runcorn had no doubt that he remembered every detail. His blunt, asymmetrical face was heavy with sadness.

"I suppose you'd better take me to her," he said, hauling himself to his feet. On the way out he picked up his bag, good leather once, but now bearing the scars of twenty years of service in all weathers.

They walked back up to the graveyard more or less the way Runcorn had come with Mrs. Warner, and found the sexton still standing guard alone and shivering with cold.

Trimby looked past him at the body and his face bleached so pale Runcorn was afraid for a moment that he was going to collapse. But after a painfully intense effort, he regained his composure, then bent and began to make his professional examination.

Runcorn excused the sexton and waited quietly in the rising wind, growing colder and colder as the minutes passed.

Finally Trimby stood up awkwardly, his legs stiff from kneeling, his balance a little uncertain.

"No later than midnight," he said hoarsely. He coughed and began again. "Far as I can tell from the rigor mortis. But you can see that yourself with the frost, I expect. Cold, exposure makes a difference. Look for whoever saw her last, if you can trust them. Can't . . . can't make a wound like that without getting blood on yourself. She didn't fight." His voice broke and he took a long, difficult moment to regain his self-control. "Nothing much else I can tell you. Can't learn anything more from this. I'll get her out of here, get her . . . decent." He turned to go.

"Doctor . . ." Runcorn called out.

Trimby waved a hand at him impatiently. "You can see as much as I can. This is your business, not mine." He continued to walk rapidly between the gravestones.

Runcorn's legs were longer and he caught up with him. "It's not all you can tell me," he said, matching his step to Trimby's. "You know her, tell me something about her. Who would have done this?"

"A raving madman!" Trimby snapped back without turning to look at him or slacken his pace.

Runcorn snatched his arm and pulled him up short, swinging him around a little. It was a thing he had never done before in all the violent and tragic cases he had ever dealt with. His own emotions were more deeply wrenched than he had imagined. "No, it was not a madman," he said savagely. "It was someone she knew and was not afraid of. You know that as well as I do. She was facing him, she wasn't running away, and she didn't fight back because she wasn't expecting him to strike her. Why was she here anyway? Who would she meet in a graveyard alone, late at night?"

Trimby stared at him, angry and defensive. "What kind of world do you live in where a man who would do that to a woman is considered sane?" he asked, his voice trembling.

Runcorn saw the profound emotion in him, the bewilderment and the sense of loss far deeper than what he must have felt from the expected deaths he encountered in his practice from time to time. Olivia had presumably been his patient and he might have known her all her life. Runcorn answered honestly. "When we say 'madman,' we mean someone unknown to us, who acts without reason, attacking at random, someone outside the world we understand. This wasn't someone like that, and I think you know it."

Trimby lowered his gaze. "If there were anything I could tell you, I would," he replied. "I have no idea who it was, or why this happened. That is your job to find out, God help you." And he turned and strode away through the last of the gravestones, leaving Runcorn alone, cold, and spattered by the first heavy drops of rain.

*I*t was a miserable day of small duties before Runcorn finally met again with Constable Warner and told him what Trimby had said. The medical evidence, such as it was, confirmed his own deduction, but added nothing that was of help. Olivia Costain had been stabbed in the stomach with a broad blade. The single thrust had severed the artery and she had bled to death within moments, falling backwards from where she had been standing. As Runcorn had supposed, there were no defensive wounds on her hands or arms, or anywhere else on her body.

"She probably died before midnight," he finished.

Warner looked tired, his eyes red-rimmed as if he had been sleepless far longer than one interminable day. They sat at the same kitchen table as they had in the morning, again with a pot of tea between them.

"I told the vicar," he said miserably. "Poor man was shattered. I think Mrs. Costain took it even harder. Very close, they were."

"Did you find out who was the last to see Miss Costain alone?" Runcorn asked, bringing him back to the facts. He had seen constables profoundly shaken by death before. The first few times were the hardest, especially when the victim was particularly vulnerable, young, old, or in some other way helpless. It helped to concentrate on the little they could do now that was of use.

Warner looked up. "Oh. Yes. Housekeeper saw her leave at about ten, or a few minutes after. Said she was just going for a walk. Seems she did that quite often, walked alone, even after dark. Didn't go far."

"So there are two hours during which she could have been killed?"

"Yes, seems like it," Warner agreed. "I asked everyone where they were. Not a lot of help. The vicar was in his study, Mrs. Costain was in the library reading until she went to bed at about eleven. Their neighbors in the big house up the road would be Mr. John Barclay and his sister, Mrs. Ewart, widow so they say. He went out to visit a friend, but he walked home alone and didn't disturb the servants when he got in. So there's no proof where he was after about half past ten. She was in bed, but she dismissed her maid, so we've only her word." Warner looked more and more unhappy. "And the curate, Kelsall, lives alone in a little cottage half a mile away. Mr. Newbridge, who had been courting Miss Olivia until recently, lives about two miles away, and he was working in his study until eleven. But he dismissed his manservant after dinner, so we have only his word also."

"Reasonable," Runcorn admitted reluctantly. "I couldn't account for myself either. A late walk on a clear winter evening is a natural thing to do. Have a look at the stars. You can really see them here. And most people who have servants let them go if there's no need to keep them up. Anybody see her after that? See anybody about, or hear anything? What about servants, courting maybe? Any neighbors up?"

Warner shook his head. "Asked anywhere I knew of, Mr. Runcorn, and not a thing I can see as helps us at all. All the other neighbors so far can say where they were, 'cos they all have families, or servants as saw them. Not that they all knew Miss Olivia that well, except in passing, as it were. Terribly shaken up, they were. We've never had anything like that here. It's . . ." he stopped, lost for words.

He shook his head slowly, avoiding Runcorn's eyes. "Got a message, chief constable's going to be here sometime late tomorrow. He'll take over then. Can't say as I'm sorry. This is not the kind of thing I know how to handle, Mr. Runcorn. The odd robbery now and then, even a barn burning or a real bad fight I can deal with, but this is different. Got everybody frightened, and sick with grief, it has. Glad enough to have Sir Alan take charge of it. But I'm obliged to you for your help. We'll hand over a tidy investigation, evidence all straight and done right, thanks to you." He smiled very slightly, his shoulders easing a little, his color ashen as if at last he could let go of some of the burden which he had carried today. Only yesterday he could not have even thought of it in his worst nightmare. "I'm sure Sir Alan would want to thank you himself, but for us here, I'm grateful, Mr. Runcorn."

Runcorn knew it would be this way, he had no jurisdiction in Anglesey, no standing beyond that of any other responsible citizen. And yet he felt absurdly disappointed. It was not that he wanted work. The case was tragic, nothing about it was obvious, and he certainly had no idea who could have done it, or why. But he wanted to see it to the end, he wanted to find out who had destroyed a young woman who had been uniquely alive and full of grace. And perhaps also he had wanted to be of value, here so very close to Melisande, not merely another onlooker. Dealing with violence and fear was the one thing he was good at. It was where his skills were truly valued.

But of course the chief constable was coming. It was too grave a case for him not to. It was not even twenty-four hours since the murder, and panic was already rising, fear cold and dark, wakening like the wind rattling at the windows. Except that the wind could be shut out, and fear entered in spite of all the locks and bars in the world.

"Glad to help," he said quietly. "Sorry it wasn't more."

Warner held out his hand suddenly. "Very glad you were here, Mr. Runcorn. Very glad."

Runcorn took it. There did not seem any more to add, and now he would leave to be alone, to face the fact that he did not belong here as he walked down the incline towards Mrs. Owen's house, and another night before an empty day.

*B*ut in spite of his resolution, by early evening Runcorn walked back towards Warner's house, past the field where the redwings were still busy. He was hungry for information, though he knew it was foolish because they could not tell him anything. It was no longer his concern, he was not one of them. The reminder was painful. It forced him to realize more vividly an emptiness inside himself, a growing need for something more than he had.

As he passed the entrance to the churchyard, memory and grief clenched inside him again, making him even colder. He was surprised to see John Barclay ahead of him, walking beside a man almost his own height, a man who was bare-headed even in this wind, his hair thick and fair. He had an almost military precision to his step, and even at a distance Runcorn could see the elegance in the cut of his clothes. It had to be Sir Alan Faraday, the chief constable. But why was he talking so closely to Barclay, as if they were friends?

Runcorn stopped, and perhaps the unexpected action caught Barclay's eye, because he put his hand on Faraday's arm and said something, and both of them turned towards Runcorn. Barclay took the first step forward, and there was something obscurely threatening to his action.

Runcorn stood his ground.

"Good evening," Barclay said quite loudly, speaking when they were still several yards distant. "Runcorn, isn't it?"

"Good evening, Mr. Barclay," Runcorn replied, still not moving.

Closer to, the other man was good looking, his eyes were steady and remarkably blue.

"This is the London fellow I was mentioning," Barclay told him. "Runcorn gave us a hand before you could get here." He looked at Runcorn. "Sir Alan Faraday, chief constable of the county. Obviously this is in his hands now. Very serious case, indeed. Warrants the highest attention, I think, before the horror of it can cause public fear and unrest. But we're obliged to you for your help in the beginning."

"Indeed," Faraday affirmed, watching cautiously. "Very good of you to step in so professionally. It seems you've left all the evidence well ordered for us. Very nasty case, and of course people are terrified. It looks as if we have a lunatic on the island. We must do all we can to reassure them, and see that panic does not take hold."

Runcorn was at a loss to know how to respond graciously and without allowing his emotions to betray him. It was at times like this he wished desperately that he had more polish, more of the assurance of a gentleman, which would allow him to assume he was in the right and demand others to assume it also. Instead, he felt like a good servant being dismissed for the night. And yet to resent it would make him look absurd.

But he was absurd. It stung, it was humiliating.

Monk would have known how to carry it off with such flare that Faraday and Barclay would have been the ones to feel foolish. But he was not Monk, he was not clever with words. Above all, he had no grace, no elegance.

"You are welcome to such help as I can give, Sir Alan," he replied instead, and heard himself sound as if he were indeed a servant asking for approval.

Faraday nodded. "Good of you," he said briefly. "We should be able to find the fellow soon enough. Small place, and all that. Decent people. Terrible tragedy, just before Christmas."

Barclay looked at Faraday. "I'd like a word with Runcorn, if you don't mind. I'll meet you up at the vicarage in a moment or two."

The chief constable acknowledged Runcorn with a brief nod, and within moments he was fifty yards away, walking easily as if miles would have meant little to him.

"Good man," Barclay observed with satisfaction. "Ex-army, of course. He'll sort this out, calm people's fears, and get us back to something like normal. Can't undo the memory or the loss, but no one could do that. You can't help any more, Runcorn. These are not your people, not the class you are used to dealing with. I'm sure you mean well, but you won't understand them, or their ways."

Runcorn wished to say something, but everything that came to his mind sounded to him as if he were trying to defend himself. He remained standing silently in the wind, the grief of the churchyard, the reality of death and loss overwhelming. He should not give even a passing thought to his own feelings.

"As long as you find who killed Miss Costain, it hardly matters who assists you," he retaliated.

"My dear fellow, of course it matters!" Barclay said hotly, but with a continued smile on his face, more of a pulling back of the lips to show perfect teeth. "We cannot help the dead, but the feelings of the living matter very much. Our conduct can make an enormous difference to their fear, their sense of danger and disorder. But what I really wanted to say to you, privately from Faraday, is that he is an excellent man, and very soon to become engaged to marry my sister, Mrs. Ewart, who as you may recall is widowed." His eyes did not waver from Runcorn's face. "It is a most fortunate match and will offer her everything she wishes. I hope I do not have to spell out in detail how unfortunate it would be if you were to mention your past professional involvement in London, however innocently intended. It can only raise questions and require explanations that would be wiser to leave unsaid. So please do not force yourself to anyone's attention by making apparent that you have a past acquaintance, however superficial."

Runcorn felt as if he had been slapped so hard the breath was momentarily knocked out of him. He drew in his breath, and found nothing to say in return, not a word that could touch the wound in him.

"I knew you'd understand," Barclay said blithely. "Hope this wretched matter is all ended rather faster than you dealt with the other business. What a mess! Still, this seems clearer. I'm obliged to you. Good day." And without waiting for Runcorn to think of a reply, he turned and followed after Faraday.

*T*he next two days passed in a chaotic unhappiness as Faraday took over all that Runcorn had left, of course with the help of Warner, who had no choice in such matters. Warner's position reminded Runcorn a bit of his own when Monk had been in the Metropolitan Police with him, years ago. Monk was always cleverer, always so sure of himself, at least on the surface. Runcorn had not known then of the private ghosts and demons that haunted him, for his own blindness had seen nothing but the iron-hard grace of the mask with which Monk protected himself. But if Faraday had anything of Monk's complexity, Runcorn found no trace of it in his smooth face, no vulnerability in the eyes, no leap of the mind to understand more passionately than others.

Runcorn would have been glad if at least Faraday had had Monk's skill. More than any personal rivalry, it mattered that they find who killed Olivia Costain. And he realized with a rising sickness in his stomach, they must also prevent the murderer from killing anyone else who might threaten him in any way. Runcorn's mind turned immediately to another unique and lovely woman—Melisande. That was the core of his fear, and for that he would sacrifice any dignity or personal pride, any ambition whatever.

But two days went by, and as far as he could tell, or hear from a fearful Mrs. Owen, no progress at all had been made. It was now less than a week until Christmas. Parties were canceled. Whenever they could, people remained in their homes. After dark the streets were deserted, even though there was no snow yet, and the wind no fiercer or colder than before. There were whispers of madness, even of something loose that was less than human, some creature of the dark that must be destroyed before the light of Christmas and hope returned to the world.

In the street a little before noon, Runcorn passed Trimby, still looking as untidy as before. He was striding out, his coattails flying, his hat abandoned and his hair streaming out like a wind-blown banner, and he went by without speaking, consumed in his own thoughts.

Runcorn could bear it no longer. He went to the vicarage where he knew Faraday would be, and found him speaking to writers and journalists from the island, and from mainland Wales as far away as Denbigh and Harlech.

No one took any notice as one more man pushed his way into the crowded withdrawing room, and he stood at the back and listened while Faraday did his best to dispel the fear rising with every new question. What kind of a lunatic was loose among them? Had there been sightings? When? Where? By whom? Could somebody be sheltering this creature? Did the vicar have any opinions? Why had Olivia Costain been the victim?

Faraday kept on trying to soothe the fear. At the end, he answered so decisively that Olivia was an exemplary young woman, known and loved in the community and of an unblemished reputation, that his very vehemence suggested doubt.

And when Runcorn spoke to him later, alone, his words reinforced that impression. They were in the room Costain had set apart for Faraday's use, a cozy study with a good fire burning, and walls crowded with books and hung with an odd jumble of paintings, cartoons, and drawings. There were papers spread over the table and a pen and inkwell beside them.

"Thank you for coming," Faraday said rather abruptly. "As long as you're here, I might as well ask if you have anything to add. You seem to have interested yourself rather much." It was a graceless turn of phrase, but he was asking for help.

"It wasn't a madman," Runcorn said grimly. "You know that, sir. The evidence says it was someone she knew." He remained standing, too angry to sit, although in truth, he had not been invited to do so.

"No," Faraday agreed unhappily. "At least, I appreciate that she knew him, but I think it's not wise to say so." He looked up at Runcorn intently. "I hope you will have the decency not to speak irresponsibly? It will only increase the fear there is already. As long as people think it is someone they don't know, at least they are not turning upon each other." He seemed to be concerned that Runcorn understood. "There is a sense of unity, a willingness to help. That is why I am not saying that she was a difficult young woman with some very unsatisfactory ideas, even dangerous in a way. Poor Costain had his troubles with her. She appeared to be unwilling to settle down. She refused several very good offers of marriage, and it looked as if she was not prepared to become adult and accept her role in society. She expected her brother to keep her indefinitely, while she drifted from one rather foolish dream to another. Her virtue had not yet been questioned openly, but it was only a matter of time before that happened, which is hard for any man, but especially one in his profession."

Thoughts raged through Runcorn's mind, memories of Olivia walking up the aisle of the church with the same careless grace she might have displayed on the beach, the foam breaking around her, the wind off the sea in her face. Why should she marry to suit her brother's social or religious life? Then Runcorn realized he was actually thinking of Melisande marrying Faraday to suit Barclay's ambition, and to free him from responsibility for her.

He looked at Faraday, straight-backed, good-looking, unimaginative, comfortable. Did he love Melisande? Did he adore her, see in her unique courage and grace? Certainly she possessed a will strong enough to defy convention and risk her own safety to give witness to a crime, as she had done in London for Monk and Runcorn when they had been pursuing a dangerous assassin. Did Faraday care desperately that she was happy, that nothing in her was forced, crushed, distorted into duty rather than belief? Or was she just a lovely and very suitable wife, one of whom he need never be anxious or ashamed, one who would fit all his social and political ambitions?

That was what Barclay wanted for her, never to be in want or need in the conventional sense, to be respected, even envied, to be secure for the rest of her life. In many ways perhaps that was more than most women could expect. And yet Runcorn, who could offer her nothing but admiration, was incensed for her. He wanted her to have so much more than that.

It was impertinent of him, and arrogant. Perhaps she was realistic, and for her such a marriage would be sufficient.

He finished the rest of his conversation with

Faraday hardly knowing what he was saying, except that at the end he was dismissed knowing little more than he had when he came in. There was fear and confusion everywhere, and Faraday was, so far, at a loss to know where to proceed next. His knowledge of men and events, his ability to command, did not extend to anything like this.

*T*he following morning, Runcorn set off alone. He followed the south shore of the island, over rocks and sand, always watching the tide, aware of its danger. The sea was both provider and destroyer, it granted no mercy to anyone. He had read that somewhere. Looking at its constantly shifting surface, its blind power, its beauty and deceit, he believed that absolutely.

He walked until he could see the towers of Caernarfon across the strait, then he rested a short while and walked back again through occasional rain, with the wind behind him. He was exhausted and it was late in the day when, without thought, his feet took him back to walk up towards the church-yard. He knew why, Barclay and Melisande were staying in the big house beyond the green. If there was anywhere he might catch a glimpse of her, it was here.

It was a quarter of an hour later as he was watching the light fade on the hills that he heard her voice behind him. Her footsteps had been soundless on the grass.

"Mr. Runcorn?"

He swung around, his breath catching in his throat. He had difficulty answering her. She was wearing a dark gown with a hooded cloak over it to protect her against the wind. The amber light from the last of the sun was soft on her face, accentuating her cheekbones and the line of her chin. He had never seen anyone so beautiful, or so able to hope, to care, and to be hurt.

"Good evening, Mrs. Ewart," he said hoarsely.

"I am glad you are here," she answered. "Sir Alan is a good man, and I suppose John was right to send for him . . ." she hesitated. "But I don't believe he has the experience of . . . of a terrible crime like this, to be able to learn quickly enough what happened, and who is responsible."

Should he try to comfort her? He could see the fear in her eyes. She was right, Faraday had no idea how to investigate a murder. It was not really what chief constables were for. He was doing it because Melisande was here, and perhaps because the crime had raised such terror on the island that people were close to panic. The brutality of it was something they had never experienced before.

Should Runcorn lie to her, he wondered.

"Quickly enough?" he questioned. "Do you fear it will happen again?" Why had he asked her that? It was no comfort at all.

"Won't it?" she said softly. "You know about these things. Does somebody do this once and then stop? Won't they defend themselves if we get close to them, if we seem to be about to tear the mask off and show who they really are?"

He shivered in spite of himself. Her fear touched him more sharply than the dusk wind. She was right, the only safety lay in swiftness, in striking before the victim knew the direction of the blow, and striking fatally. He longed to be able to protect her, but he had no duty, no place here at all.

"Won't they?" she repeated. "Have I put you in an impossible position?" She looked away from him. "I am very afraid that we are out of our depth. Sir Alan is speaking as if it is some random beast come out of the wild places in the center of the island, the hills beyond our climbing." She stopped abruptly, biting her lower lip, afraid to say the rest of what was crowding her mind.

He said it for her. "But you think the beast comes from within someone here in the houses and streets you think you know?"

Her eyes opened wide and there was a warmth in them, even a kind of relief. "Don't you? Please be honest with me, Mr. Runcorn. This is too terrible for us to be exchanging lies because we think they are easier. Olivia deserves better than that, and for our own sakes we can't afford to keep looking the other way."

Why did she think so? She had not seen the body as he had. What had she heard or felt that she understood this? Who was she afraid for? Did she know who it was, or perhaps suspect? She knew Costain and his wife, and of course she knew her brother Barclay. She had been fond of Olivia, so it was possible she had learned from her something of Newbridge, or even of the curate Kelsall. Was she afraid the investigation would expose things that were ugly in any of them, or all?

Everyone has actions, wounds they are ashamed of, secrets they will fight to protect. Someone might even lash out to protect the memory of Olivia herself. Grief can cause many violent things no one could foresee, even in those most affected. Sometimes it deepens love, other times it breaks it.

"Have you told Sir Alan your fears?" He hated even mentioning the man's name.

She shook her head fractionally. "No. I think he has enough to worry about, with the feeling that's growing among people, and their demands for help, and for a solution. Nobody can just . . . produce it because it's needed. We are not children to have all our fears soothed away. Something terrible has happened, and Alan cannot undo it for us, or provide the answers we want." Distress, and something like pity, touched her face. "I don't suppose anyone can."

Runcorn wondered if she meant only what she said—that they must all endure it because there was no other way, and it was unfair to expect it. Was she defending Faraday, or saying he could not handle the task, or both? Runcorn struggled to read her eyes, the line of her lips, but it was too dark to see clearly anymore, and he did not understand anyway.

He knew she was afraid, but then only a fool would not be. Whatever the truth was, it would bring pain. Their lives would never heal over the things they would hear of each other, the shortcomings, the secrets ordinary life could have left decently covered. Murder swept all that away.

Did she love Faraday? The helplessness and the mercy of it was that one did not have to be perfect to be loved, one did not even have to be especially good. Love was a gift, a grace. He had never tested it himself. He was clumsy, ungenerous, never knowing how to respond.

He longed now to say something that would comfort her, be of more help in the days ahead, which would hold pain for her, but all he could do was tell her the truth. Of course he wanted to protect her, most of all from the actual danger. It was the one skill he had, but he was unable to use it because this was not his jurisdiction. He had no more authority here than the postman or the fishmonger—less, because he did not belong.

"Mr. Runcorn . . ." she said tentatively.

"Yes?"

"You found Olivia's body, didn't you." It was not really a question. She was leading to something further.

"Yes." The misery of it was in his voice.

"Do you think she was killed by a madman, someone none of us know?"

He hesitated.

"Please?" she said urgently. "This is no time for comfortable lies. Do not treat me as if I were foolish. Olivia was my friend. I really cared for her very much, even though I knew her well only a short time. We . . . we had much in common.

"I would like to know the truth, and Alan will not tell me."

"Then . . ." he started, and stopped. She was inviting him to tell her something that the man she was going to marry had refused her.

"Your silence is answer." She turned away from him, her voice tight with disappointment.

He could not bear it. "No, it was someone she knew," he admitted. "She was facing him, not running away."

She looked at him again, her expression filled with grief. "Poor Olivia. Can you think of anything more terrible? I want to ask you if she felt much pain, but I am not sure if I can endure the answer."

"No," he said quickly. "It can only have been a few moments at most."

"Thank you." Her voice was soft. "I'm sorry to have . . . Mr. Runcorn, will you please help us? I don't think we know how to deal with this. We are not used to such . . . discomfort of the mind, such feelings of pain and fear when we don't know what to do."

He was stunned, and yet this was exactly what he

had wanted, to help! Had she any idea what she asked of him? He had no authority, no rights here at all. Faraday would resent it. Barclay would be furious. He should tell her that, explain all the reasons why he could not do it. Instead, he simply said, "Yes, of course I will."

"Thank you." The faintest smile softened her mouth for a moment. "I am very grateful. I should not have kept you standing here in the cold so long. Good night, Mr. Runcorn." And slowly, with intense grace, she turned and walked away.

He was too overwhelmed to reply. He remained where he was, shivering in the wind until he could no longer see her figure in the shadows, then at last he turned to go back to Mrs. Owen.

*T*here was only one obvious place to begin, and that was with Constable Warner.

Runcorn arrived at Warner's kitchen the next morning at eight o'clock, having risen when it was still dark and walked up the incline so as to know exactly when Warner turned his light on.

"Doing everything we can think of," Warner said, offering Runcorn fresh, hot tea, which was accepted gratefully. The day was bitter, a raw wind edged with sleet blowing in from the east. "Hard to know what to do next," he went on, bending to open up the stove so the heat spread out into the room. He did not look at Runcorn. "Porridge?" he asked.

"Thank you." It had been too early to expect breakfast from Mrs. Owen, and actually he had barely thought of it.

"I feel helpless," Warner added, his voice full of misery.

Runcorn recognized it as an oblique way of telling him that Faraday was making no progress, and possibly had little idea what to do next. He had painted himself into something of a corner with his assumption that it was a madman. It was easy enough to understand why he had done so, faced with the brutality of the crime and the horror it had awoken in everyone, family and stranger alike. The whole town suffered under a weight of shock as if life had been darkened for all of them. Something irreparable had been destroyed.

Warner was too loyal to say outright that Faraday was floundering; in fact, he would not even look Runcorn in the eye as he tried to find the right words, but that was what he meant.

"He's going to have to acknowledge that it was someone she knew," Warner said aloud. "Nobody'll want to think so, but you can't get away from it." He stirred the porridge a final time. "Then you can start asking the questions that'll lead us to the truth." His voice carried more confidence than he must have felt.

Warner ladled the porridge into two bowls and brought it to the table, along with milk and spoons and both salt and sugar. "But what kind of questions?" He faced Runcorn fully now, the awkwardness of pretending he was not really looking for help had been negotiated.

They both started to eat while Runcorn thought carefully of how to reply. The porridge was thick and smooth and the more he ate, the more he liked it. He wondered what he could say that was honest and still kept a remnant of tact? Or did tact matter any more at this point? Surely now it was harsh and dangerous enough that only the truth would serve? If he were taking over this case from someone else, what would he do, were he able to have complete control of it?

Warner was waiting for him to speak, his face pale with the deep exhaustion of fear.

"I'd be plain," Runcorn told him quietly. "There's not a lot of use going back over where everyone was because they've already said, and no one's going to admit to a lie. I suppose you haven't found the blade?"

Warner shook his head.

"It would have come from someone's kitchen," Runcorn observed.

"We could see who's missing one?" Warner suggested doubtfully. "But that'd mean pretty well saying as we thought it was one of them, or we couldn't even look."

"And for all we know, it could've been washed and put back," Runcorn added.

Warner winced, his face clearly mirroring his racing imagination, the Sunday joint carved with the weapon of murder.

Runcorn clenched his teeth. This was difficult, but he had promised Melisande that he would help, which meant that he must do so, wherever the truth led him, even to angering Faraday and possibly making an enemy of him. Nobody would welcome the sort of questions that must be asked, but to investigate other than honestly would serve no purpose. However painful the truth of why Olivia had been killed, and by whom, it must be found. And, inevitably, other secrets, follies, and shames would also be uncovered. Perhaps even Melisande would be forced to see things she might have preferred to overlook. Runcorn had a strong feeling that very little would be the same afterwards.

Should he have warned her of his prediction? Should he do so now? Of course he knew the answer in his heart. In the past he had sometimes done what was expedient, said the right things, turned the occasional blind eye. It had won him the promotion Monk had never received. It had also earned him Monk's contempt, and if he were honest, his own as well. He could never have Melisande's love—it hurt to say so—but he would keep the integrity which made him able to look at her without shame.

"I don't know whether Sir Alan will look into the weapon more closely or not," he finally said to Warner. "But what I would do, were it with me, is to learn more about Miss Costain herself, until I knew everything I could about who really loved her, hated her. Who might have seen her as a threat, or a rival? And to do that I would also have to learn a lot more about her family and all those others who were part of her life."

"I see," Warner said slowly, thinking about what that could mean. He searched Runcorn's face, and saw there was no pretense in it, and no way of evading the truth. "Then that's what we'll have to do, isn't it." It was a statement. "I've only dealt with robberies before, and a little bit of embezzlement, a fire once. It was ugly. I expect this is going to be far worse. We'll need your help, Mr. Runcorn." This time there was a lift of doubt in his voice. He was asking as openly as he dared to.

For Runcorn the die was already cast, he had

promised Melisande. Warner could add nothing to that. But he realized now that to investigate with any honesty he would have to go to Faraday and ask for his permission, which the chief constable had every right to refuse. Even the thought of facing him, pleading to be allowed to have a part in the case, clenched his stomach like a cramp. But as an investigator he would be useless without Faraday's approval. The simplest solution might be to ask and be refused. Melisande would have to accept that. She would see Faraday's inadequacy and recognize it for the pride it was, and excuse Runcorn.

But would he excuse himself? Not even for an instant. Part of honesty would be using his skill to ask Faraday in such a way that he could not refuse. He had made enough mistakes in the past with clumsiness of words, lack of judgment, selfishness, that he ought to have learned all the lessons by now. If he wanted to badly enough, he could place Faraday in a position where it would be impossible for him to refuse help. This was his one chance to become the man he had always failed to be. He had let pride, anger, and ambition stop him.

"I'll have to have Sir Alan's permission," he said to Warner, and saw the constable's face cloud over instantly. "I couldn't do it behind his back, even if I would like to."

Warner shook his head. "He'll likely not give it."

"He might if I ask him the right way," Runcorn explained. "It'd be hard for him to say no in front of you, and whatever other men he has on the case, and perhaps the vicar as well? Even Mrs. Costain. She was very close to Olivia. It would be hard to explain to her why he refused help."

Warner's eyes widened with sudden understanding, and a new respect. "Well, I'd never have thought of that," he said slowly. "Maybe I'll just have a word with Mrs. Costain, and see as how that can be done. You're a clever man, Mr. Runcorn, and I'm much obliged to have you on our side."

So it was that evening that Runcorn walked up the incline through heavy rain beside Warner and they knocked at the vicarage door a few moments after Sir Alan Faraday had gone inside to inform Mr. and Mrs. Costain of his progress on the case. Warner was due to report also, so the housemaid did not hesitate to take their wet coats and show them both into the parlor where the others were gathered close to the fire.

Naomi Costain looked years older than she had a week ago. Her strong features were deeply marked by grief, her skin so pale she seemed pinched with cold, although the room was warm. She wore black, without ornament of any kind. Her appearance did not seem an ostentatious sign of mourning but simply as if she had not thought about it since the tragic events. Her hair was pinned up and kept out of her way, but it did not flatter her.

Costain himself sat in one of the armchairs, his clerical collar askew, his shoulders hunched. Faraday stood with military stiffness in front of the fire, successfully blocking it from anyone else, but apparently unaware of it. He stared at Warner with a look of hope, then seeing Runcorn behind him, his expression closed over.

"Good evening," he said tersely. "Is there something we can do for you, Mr. Runcorn?" He did not use Runcorn's police rank, although he knew it.

Runcorn assessed the situation. There was no room for prevarication. He must either explain himself, or retreat. He felt foolish for having allowed Warner to do this in front of Costain and his wife. Now his humiliation would be that much more public. Faraday could not afford to lose face in front of others; this had been a tactical error, but it was too late to mend now. He chose his words as carefully as he could, something he was not used to doing.

"It appears to be a far more difficult case than it looked to begin with," he began. "I imagine that this close to Christmas, like everyone else, you are short-handed, especially of men used to dealing with crime."

The silence was deafening. They were all staring at him, Costain with bewilderment, Naomi with hope, Faraday with contempt.

"This is an island where there is very little crime," Faraday replied. "And even that is mostly the odd theft, or a fight that's more hot temper than cold violence."

"Yes," Costain agreed quickly. "We . . . we've never

had anyone killed . . . so long as I've been here. We've never dealt with anything like this before. What . . . what do you advise?"

Faraday glared at him. His question had been peculiarly tactless.

Runcorn knew to retreat. A word of pride or the slightest suggestion of professional superiority, and he would be excluded in such a way that there would be no room for Faraday to change his mind and ask him back.

"I don't know enough to advise," he said hastily. "All I meant to do was offer whatever help I can, as an extra pair of legs, so to speak."

Faraday moved his weight from one foot to the other, still standing directly in front of the fire.

"Thank you," Naomi said sincerely, breaking the uncomfortable silence.

"To do what?" Faraday asked with an edge to his voice.

Runcorn hesitated, wondering if Faraday's question was a demand that he explain himself, or an oblique and defensive way of asking him for advice. He looked at Faraday, who, as usual, was immaculately dressed, his thick hair neat. But there were hollow shadows smudged around his eyes and a tension in the way he stood which had little to do with the cold. He was in an unenviable position, and with a sudden surge of pity that startled and disconcerted him, Runcorn realized just how out of his depth Faraday was. He had never faced murder before, and people who were frightened and bewildered were looking to him for help he had no idea how to give.

"Ask some of the questions that may lead us towards whoever attacked Miss Costain," he answered. He chose the word "attacked" because it was less brutal than "murdered."

Outside, thunder rolled and the rain beat against the windows.

"Of whom?" Faraday raised his eyebrows. "We have already spoken to all those who live anywhere near the graveyard. Everyone in Beaumaris is appalled by what has happened. They would all help, if they could."

"No, sir," Runcorn spoke before he thought about it. "At least one would not, and maybe many others." He ignored Faraday's scowl, and Costain's wave of denial. "Not because they know who is guilty," he explained. "For other reasons. Everyone has things in their lives they would not share with others: mistakes, embarrassments, events that are private, or which might compromise someone they care for, or to whom they owe a loyalty. It's natural to defend what privacy you have. Everyone does."

Costain sank back in his chair. Perhaps as a minister he was beginning to understand.

Faraday stared. "What are you suggesting, Runcorn? That we dig into everyone's private lives?" He said it with immeasurable distaste.

Again Runcorn hesitated. How on earth could he answer this without either offending Costain and his wife or else retreating until he lost whatever chance he had of conducting a proper investigation? He knew the answer was to be brutal, but he loathed doing it. Only the thought of Olivia lying in the churchyard, soaked in her own blood, and his promise to Melisande, steeled him.

"Until you find the cause of this crime, yes, that is what I am suggesting," he answered, meeting Faraday's blue eyes steadily. "Murder is violent, ugly, and tragic. There is no point investigating it as if it were the theft of a pair of fire dogs or a set of silver spoons. It's the result of hatred or terror, not a moment of misplaced greed."

Costain jerked back as if he had been hit.

"Really!" Faraday protested.

"Mr. Runcorn is quite right," Naomi said softly, her voice sounding with a trace of hesitancy in the quiet room. "We must all put up with a little inconvenience or embarrassment if it is necessary to learn the truth. It is very good of you, Alan, to wish to protect us, and I appreciate your thoughtfulness, but we must face . . . whatever we must to put this behind us."

Faraday waited only a moment, then he turned again to Runcorn. He had no choice but to concede. He got it over with quickly. "Yes. Yes, I regret it, but that does seem to be the situation. Perhaps it would be helpful if you were to give us some of your time, and it is most honorable of you, when I assume you are on holiday. Naturally I shall require you to report to me regularly, not only anything that you may feel you have learned, but also, of course, your intentions for the next step. I had better advise you what we have done so far, and where you should proceed."

"Yes sir," Runcorn said quietly. He had no intention whatsoever of taking instructions from Faraday, who was obviously as concerned with appearances and order as with the darker sides of truth.

Faraday turned to Costain. "If I might speak alone with Runcorn for a few minutes?" he requested. "Is there somewhere suitable?"

"Oh . . . yes, yes, of course." Costain rose wearily to his feet. He looked like an old man, confused, stumbling in both mind and body, although he was barely over fifty. "If you would come this way."

Runcorn excused himself to Naomi, thanking her for her support, nodding to Warner, then he followed Faraday and Costain across the hall to a small study. The fire in this small room was only just dying, still offering considerable warmth, since Faraday didn't resume a position in front of it. Heavy velvet curtains were drawn against the night and the spattering of rain on the glass was almost inaudible here. The walls were lined with bookshelves. Runcorn had a moment to spare in which to notice that, predictably, a large proportion of them were theological, a few on the history or geography of biblical lands, including Egypt and Mesopotamia.

As soon as the door had closed behind Costain again, Faraday turned to Runcorn.

Outside the thunder cracked again.

"I appreciate your help, Runcorn, but let me make this perfectly clear, I will not have you taking over this investigation as if it were some London back-street. You will not cross-question these good and decent people about their lives as if they were criminals. They are the victims of a hideous tragedy, and deserving of every compassion we can afford them. Do you understand me?" He looked doubtful, as if already he was seeking a way to extricate himself from his decision to allow Runcorn to help.

"Even in London, people are capable of honor and grief when someone they love is murdered," Runcorn said hotly, his good intentions swept away by a protective anger for the people he had known, and for all the other victims of loss, whoever they were. The poor did not love any less or have any different protection from pain.

Faraday flushed. "I apologize," he said gruffly. "That was not what I meant to imply. But these people are my responsibility. You will be as discreet as you can, and report to me every time you make any discovery that could be relevant to Miss Costain's death. Where do you propose to begin?"

"With the family," Runcorn replied. "First I would like to know far more about her than I do. Ugly as it is, she was killed by someone who was standing in front of her, and she was not running from him. She must have known him. Had a stranger accosted her alone at night, in the churchyard, she would have run away, or at the very least have fought. She did neither."

"For God's sake, what are you suggesting?" Faraday said hoarsely. "That someone of her family butchered her? That is unspeakable, and I will not have you . . ."

"I am stating the facts to you," Runcorn cut across him. "Of course I will not put it in those terms to her family. What are you suggesting, sir? That we allow whoever it was to get away with it because looking for him might prove uncomfortable, or embarrassing?"

Faraday was white-faced.

Runcorn had a sudden idea. "If you allow me to ask the ugly questions, Sir Alan, it will at least relieve you of the blame for it. You may then be able to be of some comfort to these families afterwards." He did not quite say that Faraday could blame Runcorn for any offense to their privacy, but the meaning was plain.

Faraday seized it. "Yes, yes I suppose that is so. Then you had better proceed. But for heaven's sake, man, be tactful. Use whatever sensitivity you have."

Runcorn bit back his response. "Yes, sir," he said between his teeth. "I shall begin immediately with Mr. Costain, as soon as you have finished speaking with him yourself."

"For God's sake!" Faraday exploded. "It's already nearly eight o'clock in the evening. Let the poor man have a little peace. Have you no . . ."

"No time to waste," Runcorn concluded for him. "It will be no less upsetting tomorrow."

Faraday gave him a look of intense dislike, but he did not bother to argue any further.

It was no more than quarter of an hour before the door opened and Costain came in alone.

"Please sit down, sir," Runcorn indicated the armchair opposite the desk.

Costain obeyed. The angle of light from the gas lamp on the wall showed the ravages in his face with peculiar clarity.

"I'm sorry to pursue this, Mr. Costain," he began, and he meant it honestly. The vicar's emotions vividly revealed themselves on his aging face. "I will make it as brief as I can."

"Thank you. I would be obliged if you did not have to trouble my wife with this. She and Olivia were . . ."—Costain's voice caught and he needed a moment to regain control—"were very close, more like natural sisters, in spite of the difference in their ages," he finished.

For a moment there was life again in Costain's face as memory flooded back. "They both loved the island. They would walk for miles, especially in the summer. Take a picnic and spend all day away, when duties allowed. My sister was especially fond of wild-flowers. We have many here that one does not find anywhere else. And of course birds. Olivia loved them, too. She would watch them ride the wind."

For an intensely vivid moment Runcorn remembered her face as she had passed him in the aisle of the church, and he found it easy to believe her heart had flown with the birds, her imagination far beyond the reach of earth. No wonder she had been killed with passion. She was the kind of woman who would stir uncontrollable feelings in others: inadequacy, failure, a sense of blindness and frustration, perhaps envy. Not love; love, however unrequited, did not destroy as Olivia had been destroyed.

Costain had overcome his feelings again, at least enough to continue. "But I cannot see how that is of help to you, Mr. Runcorn. Olivia was . . . good-hearted but . . . I regret to say it, undisciplined. She had great compassion, no one was more generous or more diligent in caring for the needy of the parish, whether in goods or in friendship, but she had no true sense of duty."

Runcorn was confused. "Duty?" he questioned.

"Of what is appropriate, of what is . . ." Costain hunted for the word. His face showed how acutely aware he was of their social difference as he searched for a way to explain what he meant without causing offense. "It was already late for her to marry," he said with a slight flush in his cheeks. "She refused many perfectly good offers, without reason except her own . . . willfulness. I had hoped that she would accept Newbridge, but she was reluctant. She wanted something from him quite unrealistic, and I failed to persuade her." The edge of pain in his voice was like a raw wound. "I failed her altogether," he whispered.

"I believe Mr. Barclay also courted her?" Runcorn asked, longing to fill the silence with something more than pity.

"Oh yes. And he would have been an excellent match for her, but she showed no inclination to accept him, either." Costain's shoulders bowed in confusion and defeat.

Runcorn saw Olivia as a beautiful creature refusing to be bound by the walls of convention and other people's perception of her duty. He remembered

Melisande standing in the doorway of her brother's house in London, wanting to help, because she had seen a man leaving the nearby house where a murder had taken place, and Barclay had ordered her inside because he was unwilling that either of them should become involved in something as ugly as murder. He did not care about the bruising to her conscience that she hid. It had probably not even occurred to him. Had he been thinking of her more practical welfare, trying to protect her from dangers she did not see? Or merely protecting himself?

He saw in Costain a man imprisoned in his calling and his social station, bound to duties he had no capacity to meet. Perhaps no one could have. He was too filled with misery to offer Runcorn much more practical help.

"Thank you, sir," Runcorn said as gently as he could. "Would you please ask Mrs. Costain to spare me a few minutes."

Costain looked up sharply. "I asked you not to disturb my wife any further, Mr. Runcorn. I thought you understood that?"

"I wish I could oblige you, sir, but I cannot. She

may be able to tell me of things Miss Costain confided in her, a quarrel, someone who troubled her or pursued her . . ."

"You are suggesting it was someone my sister knew! That is preposterous." He stood up.

Runcorn felt brutal. "It was someone she knew, Mr. Costain. The evidence makes that clear."

"Evidence? Faraday said nothing of that!"

"I will describe it if you wish, but I think it is better if you do not have to hear it."

Costain closed his eyes and seemed to sway on his feet. Perhaps it was only a wavering of the lamplight. "Please do not tell my wife this." His voice was no more than a whisper. "Is this why you think Faraday inadequate to the investigation?"

Runcorn was caught off guard. He had had no idea his opinion was so clear. He certainly had not meant it to be. Should he lie? Costain deserved better, and he had already seen far more of the truth.

"Yes sir."

"Then do what you have to." Costain turned and made his way to the door, fumbling with the handle before he could open it.

Naomi Costain came in a few moments later and closed the door behind her before she sat down. Her face was pale, and in the lamplight the stain of recent tears was visible, even though she had done her best to disguise it. There was a kind of hopelessness in her more eloquent than all the words of loss she might have spoken.

"I will be as brief as I can, ma'am." Runcorn felt a deep sense of intrusion.

"There is no need to," she replied. "Time is of no importance to me. What can I tell you that would help?"

"Mr. Costain said that you and your sister-in-law were very close." He hated his own words, they sounded so trite. "If I knew more about her, I might understand the kind of person who would wish her harm."

She stared into the distance for so long he began to think she was not going to answer, possibly even that she had not understood that it was a question. He drew in his breath to try a different approach when at last she ended the silence.

"She had imagination," she said slowly, testing

each word to be certain it was what she meant. "She would never be told what to think, and my husband found that . . . willful, as if she were deliberately disobedient. I don't believe it was disobedience. I think it was a kind of honesty. But it made her difficult at times."

Runcorn knew little of society, especially on an island like this. He needed to understand the jealousies, the ambitions, the feelings that could escalate into the kind of savagery he had seen perpetrated against her.

"Was there anyone she challenged?" he asked, fumbling for a way to ask what he wanted without hurting her even more. "She was beautiful. Were there men who admired her, women who were rivals?"

Naomi smiled. "You knew her?"

He felt as if some opportunity had passed him by. "No. I saw her once, in church."

The smile faded.

"Oh. Yes, of course. I expect people were envious. It happens, especially against those who do not conform to the way of life expected of them. She did not

have many friends, she grew very impatient sometimes. It is not a good quality. I used to hope she
would learn to curb it, in time." She sighed. "She
liked Mrs. Ewart. At first I thought it was just because she was from London, and brought a touch of
glamour with her. She could speak of the latest plays
and books, music, and that sort of thing. But then I
saw it was deeper than that. They understood something that I did not." A sadness filled her face again,
a kind of loneliness that Runcorn found, to his
amazement, that he understood. It was a knowledge
of exclusion, as if someone had gone and left her
alone in the dark.

"Was she happy?" he asked impulsively.

She looked at him with surprise. "No." Then instantly she regretted it. "I mean that she was restless, she was looking for something. I . . . no, really,
please disregard me, I am talking nonsense. I have
no idea who could have been so deranged by envy or
fear, as to have done such a thing."

He had the overpowering feeling that she was
lying. She knew something she was not prepared to
tell him. "The best thing you can do for her, Mrs.

Costain, is to help us find who killed her," he said urgently.

She rose to her feet, her face weary, her eyes very direct. "Do you believe that it would be best, Mr. Runcorn? How little you know us, or perhaps anyone. You are a good man, but you do not know the wind or the waves of the heart. Landlocked," she added, walking to the door. "You are all landlocked."

It was too late for Runcorn to see anyone else that night, and his mind was in too much confusion to absorb any more. He thanked Costain, and went out into the darkness to walk back to Mrs. Owen's lodging house. The rain had stopped and the wind was bitter, but he was thankful to be alive. He liked the clean smell of the sea, wild as it was, and the absence of human sounds. There were no voices, no clip of horses' hooves, no rattle of wheels, only the hoot of a tawny owl.

❊

*I*t was difficult to gain an interview with Newbridge and it took Runcorn the best part of the morning before he finally stood face-to-face with him in his withdrawing room. The house was old and comfortable. Possibly it had stood in those grounds for two centuries or more, occupied by the one family in times both fat and lean. There were portraits on the walls that bore the same cast of features back to the times of Oliver Cromwell and the Civil War. They were dressed in the ruffles and lace of the Cavaliers. There were no grim-faced, white-collared Puritans.

Some of the furniture had been magnificent in its time, but it now bore marks of heavy use—legs were uneven, one or two surfaces were stained and needed refinishing. But Runcorn had time to notice no more than that before he was aware of Newbridge's impatience.

"What is it you want, Mr. Runcorn?" There was a thickness to his voice and he moved his weight from one foot to the other as though he were anxious to be elsewhere. "I have nothing I can tell you about poor Olivia's death. If I had, I would have told Faraday, for God's sake! Is it not bad enough that we have to live with this tragedy without having to drag out all our memories and our grief over and over again for strangers?" He stood leaning against the mantelshelf, an elegant man, tall and a little lean, with thick wavy hair that grew high from his forehead. His eyes were hazel, deep set, and there was the thin, angry line to his mouth that Runcorn had first noticed in church.

Runcorn found his tolerance already stretched. Loss had different effects on people, and most of them were not attractive. In men it often turned to anger, a kind of suppressed fury as if they had been dealt a blow.

Runcorn bit back his own emotions. "In order to have some better idea of who might have killed her, sir, I need to know more about her. Her family are overweighed with grief just now, and of course they see only one side of her. It is very difficult to speak anything but good of loved ones you mourn. And yet they were also human. She was not killed by accident. Someone was consumed by an unholy rage, and stood face-to-face with her, and even at the last moment, she did not run away. That needs explaining."

Newbridge was very pale and his chest was rising

and falling as if he had climbed to a great altitude and was struggling for breath.

"Are you saying that something in her nature provoked the act, Mr. Runcorn?" he said at last.

"Do you think that impossible?" Runcorn kept his voice low, as though they were confiding in each other.

"Well . . . it's . . . you place me in a terrible situation," Newbridge protested. "How can I observe any decency, and answer such a question?"

"There was no decency in the way she was killed, or indeed, that she was killed at all," Runcorn pointed out.

Newbridge sighed. His face was even paler. "Then you force me in honor to speak more frankly than I would have wished. But if you repeat it to her family, I shall deny it."

Runcorn nodded very slightly.

"She was charming," Newbridge said, looking somewhere away from Runcorn into a distance only he could see. "And beautiful, but I imagine you know that. She was also childish. She was twenty-six, an age when most women are married and have children, and yet she refused to grow up." His body stiffened.

"She would not take any responsibility for herself, which placed an unfair burden upon her brother. I think she took advantage of the fact that he is childless, to remain immature herself, and charge him with her care long past the time when she should have accepted that burden herself."

"Do you think Reverend Costain resented this?"

"He is too good a man to have refused to care for her," Newbridge answered. "And frankly, I think he indulged her. His sense of obligation as a Christian minister was out of proportion. She knew that and took advantage of it."

That was the harshest thing Runcorn had heard said of Olivia, and he was startled how it hurt him. For all he knew, it might be true. Yet he felt as if it was Melisande of whom it had been said. He could think of no reply. He kept his own emotion tightly in check, unaware that he was clenching his muscles and that his nails dug into the palms of his hands.

"Indeed?" he said the word between his teeth.

"Did she make use of anyone else's goodwill in such a way?"

The silence weighed heavily for several moments. Somewhere outside a dog barked, and a gust of rain beat against the windows. The urgency of it brought Newbridge back to the present as if some reverie had been broken. An anger within him came under control, or perhaps it was grief. Runcorn found it impossible to tell, no matter how carefully he watched. He felt intrusive. This man had wanted to marry Olivia. How hard it must be for him to govern his emotions in front of an inquisitive stranger who had seen her hideously dead, but never known or loved her alive.

"She did not, so far as I am aware," Newbridge said finally. "Mrs. Costain was very fond of her, and she had other friends as well. Mrs. Ewart. And Mr. Barclay was courting her. But I imagine you know that. She was friendly with the curate, Kelsall, and various young women in the town, at least in a casual way. Most of them were married, of course, and not free to waste their time in pursuit of dreams, as she did." He looked away from Runcorn again, as if trying to imagine he was not there. "Or to spend hours reading," he went on. "They may have met in charitable work. She was always willing to help those less fortunate, whether they were deserving or not. There was a generosity in her . . ." He stopped abruptly, his head still turned. "Look, I really cannot help you. I have no idea who would want to hurt her, or why. The only possible suggestion I can make is to look more closely at John Barclay. He came to the island only lately. He's a Londoner. Perhaps he lost patience with her indecision. On the other hand, perhaps I merely dislike the man." He faced Runcorn at last. "Now, if you will excuse me, I have nothing further to add. My butler will show you to the door."

*R*uncorn had no choice but to see Barclay next. It was an interview he was not looking forward to, but it was unavoidable. Was it really possible that he had lost his temper with Olivia and faced her in the churchyard with a carving knife? Runcorn disliked the man, but he found that difficult to believe. Runcorn didn't doubt that the man had a hot temper, even that he was capable of delivering a physical blow to another man, but premeditated murder of such bloody violence was beyond even Runcorn's imagination.

Nevertheless, as he walked up the driveway of the great house, sheltered by laurels, his feet crunching on the gravel, he felt a distinct flutter of fear in the pit of his stomach. He did not imagine for an instant that Barclay would attack him, but even if he did, Runcorn had never been a physical coward. He was tall and powerful, and had fought many battles in the streets of the East End in his earlier years. It was the ugliness of misery and hate that frightened him, the brutality of Melisande learning that her brother was capable of such acts, and then having to face the public shame of it. The scandal would follow her as long as she lived, not from any guilt of hers, but by association.

But if Runcorn were to evade it now, even for her sake, then he betrayed himself, and the principles he believed in and had sworn an oath to uphold. He was a servant of the law and the people, and as he stood on the front step of this beautiful house on the Isle of

Anglesey, as if it were a crossroads in the journey of his mind, this was more important than pleasing anyone else. If he foreswore that, then after he had parted from Melisande and left Anglesey, he would have nothing left.

The butler answered the door and invited Runcorn to go into the morning room, saying he would inform Mr. Barclay of his presence.

Runcorn accepted and followed the man's stiff figure across the parquet floor to the faded, comfortable room facing onto a side garden. A fire was lit and several armchairs were pulled into a ring around it. Two bookcases were filled with volumes that looked as if they had seen much use. A bowl of holly leaves and berries sat on a low table. Runcorn knew it was a house taken only for the season, but it had an air of being lived in with ease and a certain familiarity.

Barclay appeared after nearly quarter of an hour, but he seemed in an agreeable mood and made no objection to Runcorn having called without prior appointment.

"Learn anything yet?" he asked conversationally, coming in and closing the door.

Runcorn found himself relaxing a little. He realized Melisande must have prepared the way for him, at least as much as she could. He should respond with tact, for her sake.

"It appears that Miss Costain was a more complex person than we had at first assumed," he replied.

Barclay shrugged. "One always wishes to speak well of the dead, particularly when they have died violently, and young. It's a natural kind of decency, almost like laying flowers." He did not sit, or invite Runcorn to, so they both remained standing at opposite sides of the fire.

It was Runcorn's turn to speak. He tried to frame his questions as if he were asking for assistance. "I am trying to find out as much as I can about where everyone was, leading up to the time she was killed. Something must have caused it to happen . . ."

Barclay's face registered a quick understanding. "You mean a quarrel, or a discovery, that kind of thing?"

"Exactly." Runcorn was glad to be able to agree. "Constable Warner has already done a great deal in that line, but I was wondering if you could help any further. You knew Miss Costain. Were you aware of any events that day, anyone she saw, or anyone who was angry or distressed with her?" He was not sure what he expected. For the time being, simply to talk was good. He could move slowly from small facts to larger passions.

Barclay gave it some thought. "She could be a difficult woman," he said after a while. "A dreamer rather than a realist, if you know what I mean?" He met Runcorn's eyes. "Some women are a trifle impractical, especially if they have always been cared for by a father or elder brother, and never had to consider the real world. Olivia . . . Olivia was spoiled. She was charming and generous. She could be an excellent companion. But there was in her a streak of willfulness, a clinging onto childhood dreams and fancies which could become tedious after a while. I felt for Costain." He gave a slight shrug, as if confiding an understanding better implied than spoken.

"Did they quarrel?" Runcorn asked.

"Oh for heaven's sake, not to the point where he would take a knife and follow her up to the graveyard and kill her!" Barclay looked appalled. "But I'm sure she tested his patience sorely. It is not an easy thing to be responsible for one's sister. You have a father's distress and obligation without a father's authority." He spread his hands in a gesture of futility. "I don't doubt for an instant that he did the best he could, but she was flighty, unrealistic, apparently unaware of her own responsibilities in return."

He gave a slight smile. "Made me grateful that my own sister is so much more sensible. Faraday will make an excellent husband for her. He has every quality one could desire. He is of fine family, he can provide for her both financially and socially. He is of spotless reputation, good temperament, altogether a thoroughly decent fellow. And fine looking as well, which is hardly necessary, but it is very agreeable. Melisande is a beautiful woman, and could take her pick from quite a few. I'm most grateful that she has more good sense than Olivia had, and does not entertain absurd fancies." He held Runcorn's gaze and smiled steadily and coldly.

Runcorn's head was crowded with an avalanche of thoughts and feelings, bruising him, crushing sense and rational meaning. He struggled to think of something to say that was sensible, purely practical, and would remove that smirk from Barclay's lips.

"You are right," the words were thick and clumsy on his tongue. "A sane man does not murder his sister because she is disinclined to marry the suitor he has chosen for her. But have you ever had a suggestion that Costain may not be entirely sane?"

Barclay's smile vanished. "No, of course not. Olivia could at times try the patience of even a good man, but her brother is beyond reproach. If he were a man less devoted to decency, less governed by the affections of a brother and more of a lover, or would-be lover, then he might be less . . . sane." He lifted his shoulders very slightly. "Thank God it is not my trade or my duty to find out who killed her. I cannot think of anything more unsavory than hunting through the sins and griefs of other people's lives in search of the final depravity, but I appreciate that someone has to do it if we are to have the rule of law. If I can be of assistance to you, then naturally I shall do what I can."

"Thank you," Runcorn said bleakly.

Barclay dismissed his thanks with a gesture of his hand, and before Runcorn could frame the next question, he continued. "I would be obliged if you did not harass my sister with this any more than is absolutely necessary. She was fond of Miss Costain. They had certain situations in life in common, and Melisande is a soft-hearted woman, at times a trifle naïve. She was inclined to believe whatever Olivia told her, and I fear it was not always the truth. Olivia was not a good influence." His smile returned.

"I am glad that Melisande is committed to Faraday, and will soon be settled. Perhaps she would have been able to prevail upon Olivia, had she lived. But that is tragically of no importance any more. If I can think further, I shall certainly inform you." He turned the corners of his mouth down. "Unpleasant word, inform. Sounds as if it were clandestine, somehow deceitful, but then, to defend someone guilty of such a crime would be even worse, wouldn't it?" It was half a question, the answer assumed.

Runcorn found the words sticking in his throat, but he had to force himself to agree. "Yes sir, I regret that murder frequently exposes many smaller sins that can change the quality of our lives forever afterwards."

Barclay stared at him, an expression in his eyes that was impossible to read: anger, triumph, a knowledge of his own power, an uncertainty.

"Thank you, Mr. Barclay," Runcorn said quietly. "I appreciate your assistance. I wish everyone were as honorable in their duty."

If Barclay detected any sarcasm, he did not show it even by a flicker.

*T*he curate, Thomas Kelsall, was utterly different. His slender figure was bent forward as he walked and there was tension in the angle of his shoulders. Runcorn caught up with him as he strode doggedly through the pounding rain on his visits to the parish's old and needy. Some of them would normally be Costain's duty, but considering the circumstances, young Kelsall had taken it upon himself.

"You may think it arrogant of me," he said to Runcorn as they kept pace with each other. "Some people might prefer to see the minister himself, but just now not only is he spending time with poor Mrs. Costain, but he does not know how to answer people. What can they say to him? That they are sorry? That she was the most charming, the most vividly alive person they ever knew, and her death is like God taking some of the light from the world?" He kept his face resolutely forward. "And what can he say, except agree, and try to keep from embarrassing them with his pain? It is better I go. At least they do not feel as if they have to comfort me. I can address their problems, which is what I am there for."

"But you did know her well, and feel her death very hard." Runcorn knew it was brutal, but stretching it out with euphemisms would be like pulling a bandage off slowly. And it was less honest.

"We were friends," Kelsall replied simply. "We could speak to each other about all manner of things, without having to pretend we felt differently. If something was funny we laughed, even if sometimes people like the vicar thought it was inappropriate. He was her brother, and my superior, but our eyes would meet and we would each know the other thought the same. We both understood what it was to have dreams . . . and regrets." His voice trembled a little. "I cannot imagine I will ever like anyone else quite so much, so fully."

Runcorn looked sideways at him, plunging forward into the wind and rain, and did not know for certain whether it was tears that wet his cheeks or the weather. They reached the house of one elderly parishioner, and Runcorn waited outside shivering in the lee of the porch until Kelsall returned. They set out walking again.

"Is it true that she refused Mr. Newbridge's offer of marriage?" Runcorn asked after forty or fifty paces.

Kelsall hunched his shoulders and walked more intently forward. Thunder rumbled around the horizon. "She was a woman of deep feelings," he said, shaking his head a little and fumbling for the right words. "Visionary. You could never have tied her down to petty things. It would have broken her. He couldn't see that. He didn't love her, he liked what he thought she was, and did not look closely enough to see that he was utterly wrong. I don't think he even . . . listened." He looked suddenly at Runcorn. "Why do people marry someone they don't even listen to? How can they bear to be so lonely?" He was shuddering, waving his hands as he strode. "Of course she refused him. What else could she do?"

Runcorn did not reply. In his mind for a moment he saw the face of the girl in green as she had passed him in church, then he saw Melisande, and the bland, handsome features of Faraday, and he was filled with the same helpless despair that he heard in Kelsall. Had the curate loved Olivia? Would it have been infinitely more than friendship if he could have chosen? Was there a completely different kind of hunger beneath the grief he displayed in his young, vulnerable face?

They walked together without speaking again, and he left Kelsall at his next parishioner's house.

Making his way back up the incline again to find Warner, he did not change his mind. He still thought Kelsall a friend, but perhaps a closer one, more observant, more of a confidante than he had at first assumed.

The redwings were gone from the field. He hoped they would be back after the rain.

He spent the afternoon with Warner, but the only thing that emerged from their efforts was that Kelsall's alibi was finally confirmed by the absent-minded old gentleman he had been visiting, who had been up late with the croup.

In the late afternoon, just before dusk, there was a sudden lifting of the clouds and the air was filled with the soft, warm light of the low sun, already touching the high ground with a patina of gold. Suddenly the sea was blue and the Menai Strait a shining mirror barely wind-rippled as the icy breath of the sky whispered across it and disappeared.

Runcorn started to walk again, drawn towards the shore. It was cold, but he did not mind. There was a simplicity to it, a perfect melting of solid earth with the living, changing sea, a boundlessness of one into the other.

He turned and craned his neck upwards as he watched gulls soaring inland on the invisible currents, careening sideways and slipping down and then up, looking effortless as they mounted into the light and were lost to view.

It was almost silent, a faint whisper of water behind him. London had never offered him such infinite peace. There was always noise, some kind of clatter of human occupation, an end to vision, to possibility.

He began climbing upwards, away from the shore. Perhaps he was wrong, and he had allowed himself to believe in limits where there were none, except those he made for himself. He thought of the past with a different view, almost as if he were regarding someone else. He saw in himself a man of practical common sense, one whose judgment of character was usually right but without empathy. He lacked a passion, an understanding of dreams. Had he guarded himself from such things, afraid to face his own smallness? He had hated Monk's anger and his fire, his impatience with stupidity, his arrogance. Or more truly, was he afraid of it, because it challenged the conformity that was so much less dangerous?

Was that what Olivia had done, too, challenged

conformity? She had climbed these hills, he knew that from Naomi Costain. She might even have stood on this level stretch of the path and stared at the fire of the setting sun, as he was doing, and looked at the horizon where the sky and the sea became one.

Thinking of Olivia, Runcorn realized that small people like himself who want to be safe, who have no driving hunger, are afraid of those who upset their world, remove the boundaries that close them in and excuse their cowardice. He had hated Monk for that. Who had hated Olivia? Not Naomi. But what about Costain? Did she question this edifice of his faith, the daily justification of his status, his income, his reason for being? Could he forgive her for that?

Or was he simply a good man who did not understand a difficult sister who was his responsibility to feed and clothe, and keep within society's bounds, for her own sake?

The sun was a scarlet ball on the horizon, and even as he watched, it dropped below the rim, spilling fire across the sea. He decided he would stand here

as darkness gathered and closed in, wondering what
Olivia had felt. What visions had she seen, and perhaps died for? Was Melisande anything like her, except in his imagination? But he was a practical man,
trained from years of making himself fit the mold of
necessity, and the only real service he could perform
now was to discover the truth. It might help no one
to name the guilty, but it was surely a necessary service to free the innocent from blame, of others and
their own.

In the morning Runcorn rose early and ate the
rich breakfast Mrs. Owen cooked for him. She
seemed to enjoy filling the plate to overflowing with
bacon, eggs, and potato cakes, then watching him
make his way through it. He did not really want so
much, and initially he ate it only to satisfy her sense
of hospitality. But in succeeding days, as he worked
his way through the meal he had talked to her and
learned with growing interest her opinions of vari-

ous people in the village and involved in the case. Her perception was simple, but sometimes surprisingly acute.

"Just the right man for the vicarage here, Mr. Costain is," she said. "Poor soul, his wife. Lonely I think. No children. Doesn't know how to talk without really saying anything, if you know what I mean? People don't always want to think. Like Miss Olivia, she was."

Runcorn had his mouth full and was unable to ask her to explain further, and he worried that if he did, she might think that perhaps she had said too much, and be more discreet in the future.

"Like some more tea, Mr. Runcorn?" she offered, the pot in her hand.

"Helps a lot of things, from a headache to a broken heart. Lovely girl, Miss Olivia was. Quick to sorrow, and quick to joy, God rest her. Never found anyone for herself, that I know of, in spite of what they said."

Runcorn swallowed his mouthful whole and nearly choked himself. "What did they say?" he asked huskily, reaching for the tea to wash it down.

"Just silly gossip," she replied. "Nothing to it. Would you like another piece of toast, Mr. Runcorn?"

He declined, finished his tea, and set out to look for Kelsall. This time he found the curate in the church, tidying up.

"Do you know something new?" he asked, striding towards Runcorn, black cassock swinging.

Runcorn felt a twinge of failure, as if he should have done better. "Not yet."

"Perhaps if we leave, we will not be interrupted," Kelsall suggested. "Here I am always 'on duty,' as it were. It's cold outside, but at least it's not raining." He suited his actions to the words without waiting to see if Runcorn agreed. In the graveyard he matched his steps to Runcorn's and guided their way out of the gate and onto a road leading out of the village towards the open hillside.

"Why do people kill others, Mr. Runcorn?" he asked. "I have been thinking of it all night. If any man knows, it is surely you. It is such a . . . a barbarous and futile way to solve anything."

Runcorn looked at his earnest face and knew that the question was perfectly serious. Perhaps it was one he should have asked himself in more detail days ago. "Several reasons," he said thoughtfully. "Sometimes it is greed, for money, for power, for property such as a house. Sometimes for something as trivial as an ornament or a piece of jewelry."

"Not Olivia," Kelsall said with certainty. "She had no possessions of any note. She was entirely dependent on her brother."

"Ambition," Runcorn continued. "It can drive people to violence, or betrayal."

"Olivia's death helps no one," Kelsall responded. "Anyway, there is nothing around here to aspire to. It is all predictable, small offices, of no great power."

Runcorn turned over all the past cases he could think of, particularly those of passion. "Jealousy," he said grimly. "She was beautiful, and from what people say, she had a quality unlike anyone else, a fire and a courage different from others of her age and position. That can also make people feel uncomfortable, even threatened. People can kill out of fear."

Kelsall walked on in silence. "What kind of fear?" he said at last.

Runcorn heard the change in his voice and knew that suddenly they were treading delicately, on the edge of truth. He must act slowly, he might be about to rip the veil from a pain that the young man had been keeping well covered.

"All kinds," he said, watching Kelsall's face in profile, his eyes and the lines of his mouth half hidden. "Sometimes it is of physical pain, but more often it is fear of loss."

"Loss," Kelsall tasted the word carefully. "What sort of loss?"

Runcorn did not answer, hoping Kelsall would suggest something himself.

They walked another fifty paces. The wind was easing off, although the clouds were low and dark to the east.

"You mean fear of scandal?" Kelsall asked. "Or ridicule?"

"Certainly. Many victims of blackmail have killed their tormentors." Was this what had happened? Perhaps Olivia had learned a secret that somebody was afraid she would use against them. He looked at

Kelsall as closely as he dared, but he could see no change in the curate's expression. He still looked hurt and confused.

There was no sound but the wind in the grass and, far away, the echo of waves breaking on the rocks.

"Olivia wasn't like that," Kelsall said finally. "She would never repeat anyone's secrets, still less would she use them. What for? The things she wanted could not be bought."

"What did she want?"

"Freedom," he said without hesitating to think. "She wanted to be herself, not the person convention said she should be. Perhaps we all want it, or think we do, but few of us are prepared to pay the price. It hurts to be different." He stopped and faced Runcorn. "Is that why she was murdered, because she made other people aware of how ordinary they were, how easily they denied their dreams?"

"I doubt it," Runcorn said gently. "Wouldn't someone able to see that quality in her also know that killing her would make no difference whatever to their own . . . futility?"

"Not if she laughed at them," Kelsall replied.

"Some people cannot bear to be mocked. Ridicule can hurt beyond some people's power to bear, Mr. Runcorn. It strikes the very core of who you believe yourself to be. One can forgive many things, but not being made to see yourself as ridiculous, a coward at life. That kind of rage is acid in the soul."

Was he speaking of himself? Runcorn almost wondered for a moment if he was on the brink of hearing a confession. It would hurt. He genuinely liked the young man. He had seen his gentleness with the frail and old, help given as a privilege, not a duty.

"What do you know, Mr. Kelsall?" he asked. "I think it is time you spoke the truth."

"I know that Newbridge and Barclay were at daggers drawn over her, but I don't know if either of them really even wanted her, or simply hated each other because the battle was public. Some people do not take to losing with grace."

Runcorn struggled to follow. "If that were so, would they not kill each other, rather than her?"

Kelsall shrugged, and started walking again. "I suppose so. Or even Faraday. Although it's a bit late for that now."

"The chief constable?" Runcorn caught up with him. "What has he to do with it?"

"Oh, he courted her too, a while ago," Kelsall replied. "The poor vicar thought that would have been an excellent match, even though he was quite a few years older than she. He thought it would settle her down a bit. But she gave him no encouragement at all, and he soon grew tired of it."

"Faraday?" the word burst from Runcorn in amazement, and a kind of dull and momentary anger. He had courted Olivia, and now he was going to marry Melisande. Olivia had refused him. And Melisande had been obliged to accept him.

Runcorn was being ridiculous, he knew it, and still his thoughts raced on. He might have lost interest in Olivia because she was flighty, a dreamer, irresponsible. He might love Melisande because she was gentler, a visionary still capable of loving the real, the human and fallible. A woman not only beautiful but brave enough to accept an ordinary man, and perhaps in time make of him something greater.

Kelsall was still talking, but Runcorn had stopped

paying attention. He had to ask the curate to repeat himself, and to drag his own attention back to the one thing he was good at, the skill that gave him his identity.

"You said something about Mr. Barclay," he prompted.

Kelsall shook his head a little. "I think the vicar envies him."

"Why?" Although he feared that he knew the answer.

Kelsall smiled without pleasure. "Barclay's sister does not argue with him. He has a way of making her understand what has to be done, what life requires of us, if we are to survive. I think Barclay would have persuaded Olivia as well, only he stopped wishing to, just before she died. I have no idea why, or I would have told you. The vicar thought Barclay a fine match for her. Only Mrs. Costain did not care for him." He gave a slight shrug. "But then, she did not care for Newbridge, either, so far as I could see. The vicar accused her of wishing Olivia to remain single because she was such a good companion. But of course it was no good for her. She should marry and have her own home, and children, like any other woman. And to be honest, it is something of an expense on a clergyman's stipend to dress and provide for two women." He looked deeply unhappy. "Fear of poverty is not the same thing as greed, Mr. Runcorn. Really, it is not."

"No," Runcorn said quietly. "No, it is a very human and natural thing. Perhaps Miss Costain was not aware of the drain she was on his resources."

"No. I think she was not always very practical," Kelsall conceded. "It takes a long time for a man of the cloth to earn enough to keep a wife, never mind a sister as well." There was loneliness and self-mockery in his voice, and he did not meet Runcorn's eyes.

"Or a policeman," Runcorn responded. "But then a policeman's wife would expect far less." There was self-mockery in his words too. On his salary he could not keep a woman like Melisande for a month, let alone a lifetime. It was not only social class that divided them, or experience and beliefs—it was money and all it could buy, the comforts a woman of Melisande's background accepted without even noticing them.

Kelsall caught the shadow of Runcorn's pain, and looked at him with new intensity and a sudden flame of gentleness in his eyes. He was tactful enough to say nothing.

*R*uncorn reported to Faraday just before dark as he had been commanded to do. It was an uncomfortable interview, and largely fruitless. He was leaving the vicarage and walking across the churchyard when Melisande caught up with him. She had come out of the house hastily and had no cloak with her. The wind blew her hair off her face and whipped long strands of it out of its pins. It looked soft, giving her a dark, wild halo and showing the pallor of her skin. She was frightened, he could see it in her eyes, but he did not know if it was for herself, or for the ugly things she could see unraveling before her, pulled at by the fingers of violent death.

He longed to be able to comfort her, and found himself wordless, standing there among the grass in the wind.

"Mr. Runcorn," she said urgently. "Forgive me for following you, but I wished so much to speak with you without my brother knowing. Might we go into the lee of the church?"

"Of course." He wondered whether to offer her his arm over the uneven ground. He would like to feel her touch, even through the thickness of his jacket. He could imagine it. But what if she refused? She might think it was impertinent. It was asking for humiliation to assume more than plain politeness, even for an instant. He kept his arm by his side and walked stiffly over to the shelter of the church walls. The silence was so painful that he started to speak as soon as they were there.

"I am learning a great deal more about Miss Costain." He told her most of what Kelsall had said, but more gently phrased, and he did not mention that Faraday had courted her, too, although he wondered if perhaps she knew. "It seems she was unwilling to accept any marriage her brother recommended for her," he finished. "And it was causing some ill-feeling, and a degree of financial stress."

"You mean Mr. Newbridge?" she said quickly.

He did not know how to answer. He had been clumsy. In trying to tell her something of meaning he had put himself in a position where either he had to lie or admit that it also meant her brother, and her own suitor.

Too quickly she understood. Her smile was self-mocking. "And John," she added. "It is no secret that he courted her as well, although I think he became a little disillusioned with her some short time before her death. I think he requires in a woman more sense of the practical than she was willing to give." She looked away from him and sighed in exasperation. "I'm sorry, that is such a foolish euphemism. Olivia was an individual, she had the courage at least to attempt to live her dreams. They were not so very unreasonable. She wanted to travel, but she would have worked to achieve that. Of course a vicar's sister is not supposed to work at anything. What is there that a respectable woman can do?" There was an ache of longing in her voice, as if she were speaking of herself, not a friend she understood too well.

"She had no real skills, and not a great deal of practical knowledge of the world," she continued.

"One cannot survive without at least some money. If one had been born poor one might at least have learned to do something useful. Sometimes I wonder if necessity might not be a better spur than dreams, don't you think?" Without warning she turned to look at him, meeting his eyes with fierce candor. "Do you like what you do, Mr. Runcorn?"

He was at a loss to answer her. He could feel his face flaming, as if she would see his emotions drowning him. "I . . . not always. I . . . it . . ." This was his one chance to be honest with her. "Sometimes it is terrible, painful, you see awful things, and cannot help."

"Isn't that better than seeing nothing at all?" she demanded. "And at least you can try!"

She was so vivid he almost felt as if he were touching her in the sharp air. Suddenly the words came easily.

"Yes. And at times I succeed. I can't bring back the dead, and catching the guilty doesn't always make sense, or justice, but it eases, and it explains. Understanding gets rid of the sense of confusion, the helplessness to know what happened and why."

She smiled. "You are fortunate. You have something worth doing, even if you don't always manage to complete it, at least you know you have tried."

He had never thought of it like that. Barclay had defined his job as clearing up the detritus of other people's crimes and follies, a sort of sweeper-up of dirt. Melisande clearly saw something more. "Is that how you see it?" he asked uncertainly.

She shook her head. "Oh, don't think of John. Sometimes he takes pleasure in being offensive. He denigrates what he doesn't understand. It's a kind of . . . fear. We are all afraid of something, if we are honest."

"What was Olivia afraid of?" He hardly dared ask. Were they even speaking of Olivia, or of Melisande herself?

She looked away again. "Of loneliness," she answered. "Of failure. Of coming to the end of your life and realizing all the passionate, beautiful things you could at least have tried to do, but you didn't have the courage. And then it's too late . . ." She stopped, not as if she had no further thought, but as if she could not bear to speak it aloud.

Perhaps he should have turned to the stark outline of the church, or even to the carved and orna-
mental gravestones beyond, but he did not. Her grief
filled the air, and he knew it was not only a compassion for Olivia but also an acute awareness of her
own suffering and emptiness. He had never so intensely wanted to touch anyone, but he knew he
could not, not even the cold, ungloved hand at her
side. There was no comfort he could offer except his
skill, and now he was increasingly afraid that what
he might learn further of Barclay would prove uglier
than she could imagine.

But he, too, had to follow the truth, wherever it
led. This wide, clean land with its endless distances
had awoken a disturbing awareness of his own defi-
ciencies, the narrowness that Monk had so despised.
Suddenly he wanted to change, for himself, not even
for dreams of Melisande, however sweet or hopeless.
He was aware of a gaping hole, of a loss he could feel
but not name. The silence of the air was a balm, but
something inside him ached to be filled.

"I'll find him," he said aloud to her. "But it will not
be comfortable. It will show hatred you did not know

was there, and weakness you had not had to look at before. I'm sorry."

"I know," she accepted. "It is foolish, like a small child, to imagine it is something out there, a piece of madness that just happened to strike us. It comes from inside. Thank you for being so honest." She hesitated a moment as if to add something else, then simply said good night, and with a brief smile, was gone.

He took a step after her, not knowing if he should walk beside her at least back to the gate of the big house. Then he realized the foolishness of such an act. She had sought him in the tumble of gravestones, and then the lee of the church, precisely not to be seen.

He turned and made his way back to Mrs. Owen, and something hot to eat and drink.

*I*n the morning he reported again to Faraday, who received him with a look of hope that he had at last found some concrete evidence. His expression died as soon as he saw Runcorn's face.

"I think you misunderstood me, Runcorn," he said tartly. "There really is no need to keep coming here to tell me that you have learned nothing."

Runcorn felt the chill and, for an instant, the thoughtless, ill-expressed temper he would have exhibited a year ago was hot inside him. He choked it down.

"I had a long talk with Kelsall, sir, and he clarified a great many things in my mind."

Faraday gave him a sour look of disbelief, but he did not interrupt. His expression said vividly what he considered Runcorn's mind to be worth, if a conversation with the curate could improve it.

Runcorn felt himself coloring. He knew his voice was tart, but it was beyond his control. "He asked the nature of motives for murder. They are generally simple: greed, fear, ambition, revenge, outrage . . ."

"Get to your point, Runcorn. What does that tell us that we did not already know? She was hardly threatening to anyone."

"Not physically, sir, but in reputation or belief, in challenge to authority, in threat to expose what is private, shameful, or embarrassing," Runcorn explained.

"Oh. You think perhaps Miss Costain was privy to someone's secrets? She would not have betrayed such a thing. If you had known her, you would not even suggest it."

"Not even if it were illegal?"

Faraday frowned. "Who? Whose secrets would she know? I shall have to ask Costain."

"No, sir!"

"Surely he is the most likely to know who . . . Good God!" Faraday's eyes inclined. "You don't think he—"

"I don't know," Runcorn cut him off. "But that is not the only kind of fear. There is the dread of humiliation, of being mocked, of having one's inadequacies laid bare."

"That seems a bit fanciful," Faraday said, but the color in his cheeks belied his words.

"Newbridge courted her, and she rejected him," Runcorn observed, making it a statement. "So, apparently, did John Barclay."

Faraday chewed his lips. "Do you think he is capable of such violence?"

"Did she reject him also?" Runcorn continued.

"Yes, I believe so. Surely he couldn't . . ." His eyes widened, the question already answered in his mind.

Runcorn saw it and anger burned up inside him for Melisande. This man was going to marry her, and yet in order to solve a murder he was willing to believe that her brother could be guilty. Or did it reflect a closer knowledge of Barclay than Runcorn had, especially during the time of his acquaintance with Olivia? Was he finally facing a grief he had tried to avoid, but could not any longer?

"You know him better than I do," Runcorn said with a greater gentleness. "How did he accept her rejection? Did he love her deeply?"

Faraday looked startled.

It raced through Runcorn's mind that what he dreamed of as love was not something Faraday even considered. There was no understanding of the passion, the hunger, the tenderness, the soaring of the heart or the plunge of despair. He was thinking of an arrangement, an affection. Runcorn was harrowed up with a rage so intense he could have struck Faraday's smug, bland face and beaten his assumptions out of him. He wanted to feel blood and bone under his fists.

Were these the feelings Olivia's murderer had felt? Only they had used a carving knife? Why? Was the killer a woman? Someone with no physical power to strike, but the passion nevertheless?

"It doesn't have to be a man," he said aloud. "Who else did Newbridge court? Or John Barclay? Who could have loved or wanted them with such fierce possessiveness?"

"A woman?" Faraday was stunned. "But it was . . . violent! Brutal."

"Women can be just as brutal as men," Runcorn said tartly. "It happens less often, simply for opportunity and perhaps schooling, but the rage is just as savage, and when it breaks through the years of self-control, it will be uglier."

"Jealousy?" Faraday tasted the idea. Now he was meeting Runcorn's eyes and there was no evasion in him, no weariness. "Over Newbridge? I don't think so. Although to be honest, I hadn't considered it. I'll have Warner look into it more closely. John Barclay, that seems possible. He can be very charming, and he has a high opinion of himself. He would not take rejection easily."

"I heard from Kelsall that it was he who rejected Miss Costain," Runcorn corrected him.

Faraday shrugged with a slight smile. "That may be what she told him," he replied. "They were friends. She might not wish him to think she had been rebuffed. She was a difficult young woman, Runcorn. If you intend to solve her murder, you must recognize that. She was a dreamer, impractical, selfish, very willful in certain matters. She steadily refused to be guided by her brother, a patient and long-suffering man where she was concerned, and I regret to say, not always best supported by his wife. John Barclay is much more fortunate, and I daresay wiser, even if he has a certain vanity."

With the very reference to Melisande, Runcorn felt the iron vise close around her as if it were around himself. In his mind he stood with her again in the churchyard and heard her voice speaking of Olivia, the emotion trembling in it, and he knew this fear was also for herself. But Melisande was a woman who obeyed necessity, understanding there was no choice. Olivia had rebelled. Were they connected? How? It still formed no pattern he could read to be certain of innocence or guilt.

"Thank you," Faraday said briskly, cutting across his thoughts. "The fact that it might have been a woman would explain why Miss Costain was not at first afraid of her. Also, of course, all those we have questioned would have been thinking in terms of men." His shoulders eased and he smiled momentarily. "Thank you, Runcorn. I am obliged for your expert opinion, and of course for your time."

*R*uncorn was unsatisfied. He had raised questions to Faraday; he had not given answers. How much was he seeing of the woman Olivia Costain had been, and how much was his picture of her colored by Kelsall's feelings for her? How much was his feeling for Melisande? He was not doing his job. He had in the far distant past criticized Monk for emotions, usually impatience and anger, and now he was guilty of them himself. How Monk would mock him!

And then with surprise, a lurch into freedom—he realized that he did not care. He could be hurt by other people's opinions of him, but he could no longer be twisted or destroyed by them.

Moreover, he realized that he could learn more of Olivia Costain's life from those less close to her, those who could see her with clearer eyes. And in doing that, he would also discreetly learn a great deal more about Alan Faraday as well. If there really was a violent and terrible envy, it could as easily be over him. And that might even mean that Melisande was in danger, too.

Should he warn her? Of what? He had no idea.

Just then, as he walked down the steep, winding road towards the town, he realized that in fact he did not believe it was a woman jealous of Olivia, so much as a woman afraid of her. She challenged the order of things. She was a disruption in the midst of certainty, the old ways mocked and the rules broken.

But who cared about that enough to kill the trespasser, the blasphemer? That could be a woman. Or a man whose power and authority was vested in the rules that do not change. Whoever he was he could even feel himself justified in getting rid of her, before she destroyed even more.

The vicar, Costain? The chief constable, Faraday? Or Newbridge, the lord of the manor, with roots centuries deep in the land.

He paused before a house where he had never stopped before, then finally knocked. The woman who answered was white-haired and bent nearly double over her cane, but her eyes were unclouded and she had no difficulty hearing him when he spoke. "Miss Mendlicott?"

"Yes I am. And who are you, young man? You sound like a Londoner to me. If you're lost, no use asking me the way, all the roads are new since I went anywhere."

"I'm not lost, Miss Mendlicott," he replied. "It is you I would like to speak to. And you are right, I am from London. I'm in the police there, but it is about the death of Miss Costain I want to ask you. You taught her in school, didn't you?"

"Of course I did. I taught them all. But if I knew

who had killed her, you wouldn't have had to come looking for me, young man, I've had sent for you. Don't keep me standing here in the cold. What's your name? I can't go on calling you 'young man.'" She squinted up at him. "Not that you're so young, are you!"

"Superintendent Runcorn, Miss Mendlicott. And thank you, I would like to come in." He did not tell her he was fifty. That made him twenty years older than Melisande.

She led him into a small sitting room with barely space for two chairs, but pleasantly warm. On the mantelshelf there was a small jug with fresh primroses and a spray of rosemary. Anglesey was always surprising him.

He told her without evasion that he wished to learn more of the men who had courted Olivia, and whom she had refused.

"Poor child," the old lady said sadly. "Understood everything, and nothing. Could name most of the birds in the sky when she was fourteen, and had no idea how few other people even looked at them. Blind as a bat, she was."

Runcorn struggled to keep up with her. "You mean she was naïve?"

"I mean she couldn't see where she was going!" Miss Mendlicott snapped. "Of course she was naïve. Nothing wrong with her eyesight. Didn't want to look."

"Did Sir Alan Faraday court her seriously, do you know?"

"Handsome boy," she said, staring beyond him into the winter garden with its bare trees. "Good at cricket, as I recall. Or so someone told me. Never watched it myself. Couldn't make head nor tail of it."

"Did he court Miss Costain?" he repeated the question.

"Of course he did. But she had no patience with him. Nice man, but tedious. She used to tell me about him. Came to see me every week. Brought me jam." Her eyes filled with tears, and unashamed, she let them slide down her cheeks.

"She talked about Sir Alan to you?"

"Done well for himself," she said, shaking her head a little. "Grew up here, then went south to the mainland."

"England?"

She gave him a withering look. "Wales, boy! Wales!"

He smiled in spite of himself. "But Olivia refused him."

"Course she did. Liked him well enough. Kind man, when you get to know him, she said. Good horseman, patient, light hands. Need that on a horse. Heavy hands ruin a horse's mouth. Loves the land. Best thing about him," she said.

"But she refused his offer of marriage?" He did not want to see Faraday as part of this wide, beautiful land with its wind and its endless distance, when Runcorn himself had to leave it and go back to the clatter and smoke of London. But he did want to think that there was a better side to him, a man who could love and give of himself, who could be gentle, handle power with a light touch.

"Was he angry that she refused him?" he persisted.

She looked at him as if he were a willfully obtuse student. "Of course he was. Wouldn't you be? You offer a beautiful and penniless young woman your name and your place in society, your wealth and your loyalty, and she says she does not wish for it!"

He tried to imagine the scene. Had he loved her? He certainly had not shown it when he spoke of her after her death. Had he forgotten her in his new love for Melisande? That was too raw in his mind to touch. "Why did she refuse him? Was there someone else she preferred?"

Miss Mendlicott smiled. "Not in any practical way. Sometimes she had very little sense. She could see the flowers in front of her, count their petals, and she could see the stars, and tell you their names. But she was fuzzy about the middle distance, as if there were mist over the field." There were tears in her eyes again and she did not brush them away. She was not going to dissemble or excuse herself to a man from London, probably not to anyone else, either.

"There was someone impractical," he concluded aloud. Had that been Kelsall after all, a young man who could still barely afford to keep himself, let alone a wife?

"A poet," she replied. "And explorer." She snorted.

"Of all the romantic and ridiculous things to be. Off to the Mountains of the Moon, he was."

"What?" He was jolted out of courtesy by shock.

"Africa!" the old lady said witheringly. "Some of these explorers have very fanciful minds. Heaven knows where they would have ended up, if she had gone with him."

"She wanted to?" It was surprisingly painful to ask, because he could imagine the loneliness of being left behind. He had always been a practical man, the whole notion of dreams was new to him. He had reconciled himself to a solitary life, his friendships and his time and effort were absorbed in his increasingly demanding work. Now he was torn apart by impossible dreams. How could he criticize Olivia for a similar longing?

The old lady was watching him with sharp, amused eyes. The age difference between them was enough that she could have taught him as a schoolboy, and that might well be how she was regarding him now.

"She did not confide that in me," she responded. He knew it was her way of avoiding answering. And that meant that Olivia had loved the man as well as the adventure, but many things had made it impossible. Perhaps she had not even been asked.

How could the reality of Faraday, kind, honest but predictable, have matched the dream? It did not matter now, because Olivia had not gone, and she had refused Faraday, Newbridge, and John Barclay, and no doubt worn out her long-suffering brother.

He thanked Miss Mendlicott and left.

*F*ollowing the visit to Miss Mendlicott's, Runcorn went back to the vicarage, where he disturbed Costain preparing the next Sunday's sermon. The vicar looked tired and grieved, more as if he were searching for some thread of hope for himself than for others.

Runcorn felt a pang of compunction about disturbing him with questions that had to be painful, but such awareness had never hindered him before, and he could not allow it to do so now. There was a kind of comfort in duty.

"I don't know what further I can tell you," Costain said wearily. "Olivia could be exasperating, heaven knows, but I cannot imagine anyone being driven to such a rage as to do that to her. It was somebody quite mad. I just cannot think that anyone we know is so depraved."

"Such things are always hard to understand," Runcorn agreed. "But it is inescapable that someone did this." He had no time to spare on re-treading old ground, and there were no words that would change or heal anything. "I believe there was a young poet and explorer she was fond of," he said.

Costain frowned. "Percival? Interesting man, and knowledgeable, but hardly a suitor for Olivia. He spoke well. But that was two years ago at least. And he went to Africa, or maybe it was South America. I don't recall."

"Mountains of the Moon," Runcorn supplied.

"I beg your pardon?" Costain's voice was sharp, as if he suspected Runcorn of a highly insensitive flippancy.

"In Africa." Runcorn blushed. It was just the kind

of clumsiness Monk accused him of. "At least that is what I heard. Could such adventure have caught Miss Costain's imagination, and perhaps made her compare more realistic suitors with something unattainable?"

"Probably!" Costain ran his hands over his brow, pushing his hair back. "Perhaps. But what does that have to do with her death? They grew impatient with her. Faraday is now going to marry Mrs. Ewart, so I understand. Newbridge was annoyed because Olivia turned him down, but that is hardly a reason to lose his sanity altogether. He is a perfectly decent man. I've known him most of his life. His family has lived here for generations. He could find any number of other suitable young women. If you'll forgive me saying so, Mr. Runcorn, you are looking for violent passion where there is only irritation and inconvenience or, at the very worst, disappointment. I cannot help but think you are looking in the wrong places."

Runcorn had a deep fear that Costain was right. He was drawn to the emotions around Olivia and her betrothal, or lack of it, because he felt that was where the seat of much violence lay. Perhaps he only saw so much in it because he had fallen in love for the first time in his life.

But of course nothing would make him kill anyone over it, least of all Melisande. He wanted her happiness, he wished her to be loved and to marry a man worthy of her, which he did not consider Faraday was. But then, maybe he would never think any man worthy of Melisande.

He thanked Costain and asked to see his wife. With deep reluctance, permission was granted. Runcorn found himself in the sitting room opposite Naomi.

"Are you any closer to the truth, Mr. Runcorn?" she asked almost as soon as the door was closed. She spoke very quietly, as if she did not wish her husband to overhear her questions, or possibly Runcorn's answers.

"I am not sure," he replied honestly. "Miss Costain was not afraid of whoever killed her, until the very last moment, when it was too late. That suggests it was someone she knew, possibly even cared for. And it was a crime of great violence, so profound emotion was involved." He watched her face and saw the pain in it, so deep that guilt twisted inside him.

"You are saying it was someone who knew her well, and hated her." She stared out at the bare, winter garden and the tangled branches of the trees outlined against the sky. "She did awaken strange feelings in other people, sometimes unease, and a sense of loss for the unreachable. She was not content to be ordinary, but is that a sin?" She turned now to look at him, searching his eyes for a response. "She reminded us of the possibilities we have not the courage to strive for. We are too afraid of failure. Does one kill for that?"

"One can kill for safety," he answered, surprised at his own words. "Did she threaten someone's comfort, Mrs. Costain?"

She walked to the farther side of the window. "Not at all. It was a foolish thing to have said. I'm sorry. I don't even know what she was doing outside at that hour on a winter night. She must have quarreled with someone."

"Over what?" he asked. "Who would she meet in the churchyard? He came with a knife, as if he intended harm."

She winced and shivered, holding her arms around herself. "I have no idea."

He had a sharp sense that she was lying. It was nothing obvious, only a subtle tightness in her shoulders, an altered tone in her voice. Was she protecting her husband? Or even herself? Was the threat that Olivia posed far closer to home than anyone had previously thought? Had Olivia, in desperation, tried to force her brother into keeping her for the rest of his life, and had he found the endless, draining expense too much to endure? Had his tortured self-control broken, and had he seized a terrible escape? This situation answered every fact they knew.

But what secret? What did this quiet, sad, seemingly conventional house hide?

"I think you have an idea, Mrs. Costain," he told her. "You knew your sister-in-law as well as anyone did. You cared for her, and you understood her. You also must know the expense of her remaining unmarried, and refusing offer after offer for no reason she was prepared to give, unless it was to you?"

She turned around to stare at him, anger flaring in her eyes, her mouth hard. "If I knew who murdered Olivia, I would tell you. I do not. Nor do I know anything that would be of use to you. I have admitted that she was a disturbing person, and hard for many to understand. I can tell you nothing new. Please do not waste any more of your time, or mine, in asking me such things. Good day, Mr. Runcorn. The maid will show you out."

*H*ow dare you behave with such crass insensitivity?" Faraday accused him that evening when he answered his summons to the big house. They were standing in the library. The gas lamps were lit and a good fire roared and hissed in the grate.

"You will not approach Mrs. Costain on the subject again," Faraday went on. "If anything should be necessary to ask, I will do it. Have you no sense at all of how the poor woman must be feeling?" His face was red and his features pinched with anxiety and perhaps a sense of panic as failure crept closer around him. They knew nothing more than they had the morning after Olivia was found. Every thread they pulled came loose in their hands. But this was not Runcorn's jurisdiction, no one was going to blame him if Olivia's murder went unsolved. Faraday was the only one with something to lose.

"She is lying," he said aloud. "She knows something that could have provoked the kind of rage we saw in that murder."

"Dear God!" Faraday exploded. "Tell me you didn't say so to her!" He closed his eyes. "You did! Don't bother to deny it, it's in your face. You oaf!" Suddenly he was shouting, his voice raw. "This may be the way it is done in the alleys and brothels you usually police, but these are decent people, gentry, people of class and Christian values. Runcorn, the man's a vicar! Have you really no . . ." He drew in his breath and let out a heavy sigh. "No. I suppose you haven't. It was my failure that I even let you in at the door."

Runcorn felt as if the fire had burned out of the

grate to scorch him. Perhaps Faraday was right. He was clumsy, and had always lacked the grace of someone gifted like Monk. He had achieved his rank by plodding patience, determination, the will to succeed, and perhaps now and then a flash of understanding of how the poor and the frightened had found ways of retaliating. He kept his word, so people trusted him, but he was not a gentleman; he had never known how to be.

"I did not tell her she lied," he said quietly. "I said I believed she knew something relevant that she had not said. I think she is complaining so hard because that is true."

"Don't make it any worse!" Faraday begged. "Man, you are like a cart horse in the dining room. Just get out of it! God alone knows who killed Olivia Costain, but we aren't going to find out your way." His voice was rough with the edge of defeat. He must be hot standing in this room, so close to the fire, wearing his beautifully tailored jacket. It was of the best tweed, and cut with the casual elegance of one who does not need to impress.

And yet he did need to. The whole island was

watching him, waiting for him to take away the burden of fear and tell them it was over, and justice would be done. And he had no idea how to do it, that much was clear to Runcorn, even if not yet to anyone else.

And begrudgingly, Runcorn felt sorry for him. Not much is expected of ordinary men. There is room for failure. It costs, but it is a familiar part of life. In the extraordinary, the men of Faraday's privilege and office, it was crippling. The chief constable would not know how to deal with it. Nothing had prepared him for the bitterness or the shame of defeat. Probably all his life he had been expected to fill a certain mold, to win, to take pain or loss without complaint.

Did Faraday imagine that Melisande needed him to be faultless or she would not love him? Was that some legacy from his love of Olivia, or was it woven into his life and upbringing, inherited from his father, and his father before him? Did he think that if someone close to him, like a wife, were to know his weaknesses as well as his strengths, then they would use them to some kind of advantage, to manipulate or mock him?

No one can always be right. Every man has his flaws, the places where he is desperately vulnerable. Never to attempt anything that may cause pain, or defeat, is to be a coward at life. One loves those brave enough to try. Runcorn had seen women sometimes love the defeated far more tenderly, more passionately than the victor. To love is to protect, to nurture, to need, and in turn be needed.

How did he know that, and Faraday did not?

The silence had lengthened and Runcorn had not yet even tried to defend himself. "Then you had better look into the Costains yourself, sir," he said aloud. "Because there is much that she knows but will not tell me."

"Nonsense," Faraday replied. "Thank you for your help, but it is not proving of any use. You are free to leave Anglesey whenever you wish. Good day."

Runcorn was beyond the gates of the drive and into the road when Melisande caught up with him.

"Mr. Runcorn!"

He turned. They were level with the hedge now and hidden from the windows of the house. Maybe he would not see her many times more, certainly not alone. He stopped and faced her, trying to imprint on his mind every line of her brow, cheek, lips, the color and light of her eyes, so he would never forget.

"I heard Alan tell you to go," she said anxiously. "He does not realize how his voice carries. Please don't listen to him. He is frightened that none of us will solve this murder, and he will be blamed for that. He takes his responsibility very hard."

"He doesn't wish me to stay," he pointed out.

"Does that matter?" she asked. "He needs you to, we all do. Someone killed Olivia and we cannot turn away from that as if it were some force of nature, and not one of us. We will suspect each other, until we know."

"Do you know anything about the explorer she met about two years ago?" he asked. "Could she have loved him?"

She thought about it for several moments. "She never said anything to me, but then why should she? We spoke often. I liked her right from the first time we met, but we talked more of books, ideas, places, far more than of people we knew, and never of men."

Another darker thought occurred to Runcorn, but he could not mention anything so indelicate to Melisande, much less suggest it of a woman who had been her friend. He felt the heat on his skin even as he pushed the idea from his mind, although he could not dismiss it altogether.

"Do you think it is something to do with Reverend Costain?" Melisande asked. "Is that why you spoke to Naomi so bluntly?" She was trying to read Runcorn's face, perhaps judge from it what he was unprepared to say.

"I think Mrs. Costain may be trying to protect both her husband and Olivia," he replied, navigating a tenuous path between truth and lie. If Olivia were one of those rare women who prefer their own sex to the other, then it was an excellent reason why she would not wish to marry, and at the same time, it would be impossible for her to admit to it to anyone.

But what if someone had learned? Any man might feel unbearably betrayed to be rejected for another woman. It would be seen as the final insult. It would be unendurable if anyone else found out. Was that what the quarrel with John had been?

"Oh," she said softly, sensing the movement of his thought. "You do not need to be so delicate with me. I am aware of such things, in women as well as in men. But I had no sense that it was so with her."

Now the blood scorched up his face and he felt ridiculous. If Faraday, not to mention Barclay, knew that he had even entertained such a thought in Melisande's presence, let alone discussed it with her, they would be appalled.

She was smiling, a flicker of real amusement in her eyes. "I liked Olivia," she told him. "I felt comfortable with her, and very free to be honest, perhaps not only with her but with myself. And that is not always true for me. If I can bear the way she died, and think of the brutality, and the passion that caused it, then surely I can look at a little human frailty without turning away with thought only for myself? She deserved better than that of me. Moral queasiness is rather a cheap escape, don't you think?"

He looked at her, and for a moment the pity and the honesty in her face made her infinitely beautiful to him. Faraday, with his lumbering imagination and his simplistic judgments, was a clod, bitterly unworthy of her.

He wondered again if she knew that Faraday had once courted Olivia also? Should he tell her? Was it just a grubby and horribly obvious attempt to spoil her happiness because he envied any man who could spend time in her company, let alone marry her? Or was it the only real honesty, because Faraday might be involved in Olivia's death?

He had no idea. The only answer would be to learn more about Faraday and then judge what to say. It must be the truth, and it must be fair. It was Melisande's safety that mattered, not whether she liked Runcorn's actions and certainly not whether Faraday did.

His face was still hot as he crafted his reply. "I don't like finding weaknesses in people, even if they help to solve a crime, but I can't afford to ignore them or lie to myself or others. I would like to have protected you from having to think of this."

"Thank you, Mr. Runcorn," she acknowledged. "I do not wish to be protected from life. I think we might miss a great deal more of the good, and the bad would find us anyway. At least the sense of emptiness would. I think I would rather eat something unpleasant now and then, than perish of starvation sitting at the table because I was afraid to try. Please find out what really happened to Olivia." She turned and walked away before he could find the words to answer her, and repeat his promise.

*H*e had no choice now but to look more deeply into Faraday's life and character. He began where Miss Mendlicott had ended and, through conventional methods, was able to look up the man's days in Cardiff University where he was moderately successful in gaining a degree in history, even though he did not need to earn his living by it. He had traveled in Europe on and off for a year or two in all the expected places. He did not see Venice or Capri. He did not venture as far as Athens, which Runcorn had read about, and would have leapt at the chance to see. He did not visit the beautiful city of Barcelona, named after Hannibal Barca, who had crossed the Alps with elephants, to attack Rome, before the days of Julius Caesar. That was one history lesson from school days that had fired Runcorn's imagination and he had never forgotten it.

Runcorn left the library in Bangor and walked out into the wind with his mind in a whirl. He had visited a different world where all the privileges of class and money did not buy the magic he had assumed. If Faraday had dreams at all, they were not of legendary places and the ghosts of the past. They seemed to be of the good opinions of others, perhaps domestic certainty and investment in the next generation of all that he had been bequeathed by his forebears.

As Runcorn walked down to the railway station he felt a sad, strange closeness to his subject. Faraday was in his early forties, and yet he wanted only safety, peace, and things to remain as they were.

Runcorn took the train to Caernarfon and continued his inquiries. He knew from long experience how to be discreet, to ask one thing while appearing to ask another. All he learned about Faraday confirmed the opinion that he was a decent man, but pedestrian, a man of likes and dislikes rather than of passions.

Runcorn remembered with a jolt that this was exactly how Monk had described him: half-hearted, lacking the fire or the courage to grasp for more than he could safely reach, a man who never dared the boundaries or stepped into the unknown as his bridges crumbled behind him. And Monk had despised him for it.

Did he now despise Faraday? Oddly, he did not. He pitied him and felt as if he were looking into a distorted mirror. There was something of himself in the man he saw, a man imprisoned in the expectations of others, too afraid of being disliked to follow his own vision, not hungry enough.

Did it take the face of one woman to stir a man deeply enough to abandon comfort and follow impossible dreams into the cold infinity? Then why was Faraday half-heartedly in love with Melisande, not absurdly and hopelessly as Runcorn was?

The following day he stayed in Beaumaris and asked more questions, seemingly idling his time with local gossip and trivial pieces of information about the past.

To aid in this, he pretended to have come originally to Beaumaris to look at property, inventing a brother who had done well in trade in order to seem wealthy enough to do so.

He was shown a house in the neighborhood of Faraday's handsome home, which added little to his knowledge, but he learned more of Newbridge, since his house was within view across a stretch of sloping valley.

"Can't see it so well in the summer time," the estate agent, a Mr. Jenkins, pointed out.

"Yes. I see what you mean," Runcorn agreed. "Looks like quite a decent place. Might that be for sale, Mr. Jenkins?"

"Oh no, sir. That belongs to Mr. Newbridge. Been in his family for years."

"Big family, has he?" Runcorn asked innocently. "Good place for children, I imagine."

"No, not married yet," Jenkins replied.

"Betrothed, then?"

"Not as I know." Jenkins was keen for a sale. "Courting the vicar's sister, the poor young lady that was killed."

Runcorn looked skeptical. "Do you think Mr. Newbridge might sell, if the offer were good enough?"

"No sir, I don't. Money isn't everything."

"Looks like a lot of land for one man to handle, and in none too good repair." Runcorn squinted across the valley, the wind in his face. "Cause resentment, will it, if an outsider buys old land?"

"Yes sir, it could," Jenkins said candidly. "Newbridges've been here since the Civil War. Big thing to keep up, a position like this, being the last in the male line of the family an' all, but he'll soon find the right wife, and then there'll be sons to carry on."

Runcorn was struck with a sudden horror at the weight of such responsibility, the need to marry, the burden of expectation. Too many people cared what he did, were watching and needing him to produce sons and fill the demands of the future.

Was some of that why he responded badly to Barclay, and why he had taken Olivia's rejection with anger as well as disappointment? Had she said something about him that might make it even harder for him to find a wife who was willing and able to take up this enormous responsibility? Newbridge had no title, no hereditary office, not even great wealth—just a family name and land he was tied to by history. Was he always trying to keep up with other men he felt had more to give, more charm, more heritage, more hope of office in the future?

It would make him an easy mark for Barclay's cruelty.

"I think I'll wait until I've been in touch with my brother, thank you," Runcorn said to Jenkins. "I'll let you know."

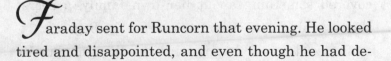

Faraday sent for Runcorn that evening. He looked tired and disappointed, and even though he had demanded Runcorn's presence, he paced the carpet in front of the fire and seemed reluctant to broach the subject.

They spoke of trivialities. Outside the rain lashed at the windows and the wind was rising steadily, roaring in off the great sweep of the Celtic Sea.

Runcorn grew impatient. "If you've learned something, sir, and I can be of help, perhaps you'd tell me what it is."

Faraday winced at Runcorn's lack of polish, and instantly Runcorn felt gauche. He had a hideous vision of doing something appalling that he did not even understand until too late, and Melisande being ashamed of him. Except that that was absurd. She might be disgusted. But to be ashamed one had to care, to feel some kind of kinship with the one at fault.

Faraday was still pacing back and forth, lost in his own inabilities.

"You suggested that Miss Costain might have discovered something about her own family, a secret that was shameful or embarrassing," he began.

Runcorn was unhappy with the thought, but its

ugliness did not invalidate it. He was afraid that it could be true, and Naomi's strong, weary face filled his mind. "I thought of it as unlikely but not impossible," he conceded.

Faraday's voice was heavy. "I'm grateful for your professional skill, and glad I don't have to share the kind of experience that has given it to you."

In spite of the fire, Runcorn felt colder.

"You recognized a crime committed with intense hatred," Faraday continued. "I used to assume all murders were, but you exposed the difference for me to see. I should be obliged to you for that also, but I'm not sure that I am."

"Do you know something further?" Runcorn demanded, his voice betraying his emotion. "You didn't send for me in this weather to thank me for teaching you a part of your job you'll almost certainly never need again."

A slow stain of color spread up Faraday's cheeks. "Yes I do, but I have more yet to learn. Mrs. Costain is concealing something of which she is deeply ashamed, or if not ashamed, then at least terrified that it might become known. Costain's sister was slaughtered like an animal. This we all know." Faraday shifted his eyes. "And now it looks as if his wife might be an adulteress and have conceived to another man the child she never bore him." His voice choked with emotion, and for a moment he was unable to speak. His strong hands clenched at his sides until the knuckles shone white, and he could not keep them still.

Runcorn felt the wave of misery engulf him also. Had it been Olivia's own need for freedom which had driven her to confront Naomi, or the defense of her brother? Murder is never without pain, but this seemed even more steeped in it than most.

Faraday was staring at him still.

"What is it?" Runcorn demanded.

Faraday's voice was little more than a whisper, all but choking off at the end. "The baby is dead. It looks as if she killed him."

Runcorn was stunned, as if he had walked face-first into a wall and the pain of it dizzied his senses. Naomi Costain with her strange, powerful face, and a late-born, illegitimate child, which she had murdered with her own hands. Why? To hide her adultery? The obvious thought. But perhaps the child had been misshapen, abnormal? He found himself blinking and his throat inexplicably tight and rough. Could that be forgiven, such a helpless child robbed of life? Or snatched from pain? Or was she only saving herself, her humiliation? And then to be faced with blackmail by Olivia? "I can't do anything," he said aloud. "You'll need police authority to follow that." It was not cowardice speaking, even though he was glad he had no jurisdiction here.

"I'll get it for you," Faraday said hoarsely. "Please, Runcorn? These people are my friends, my neighbors. I have no idea how to deal with a crime like this."

Runcorn almost wanted to remind Faraday that it was he who had discovered this element of tragedy while Runcorn had not even guessed at it. He had talked with Naomi and seen nothing of this in her, no unfed hunger that consumed all honor and loyalty, no loss of her only child to whatever brutal end. His professional skills had failed him completely.

And it was Faraday, whose profound judgment he so despised, who had seen the answer. Faraday, who was going to marry Melisande.

He should be grateful, for her sake, that he was not the fool Runcorn had thought him. If he loved her, he was no fool.

He knew this thought should comfort him as he walked away down the hill, wind harder and traces of snow making a flurry of white in the gloom.

*D*uring the night the sense of his own failure deepened. He had come to Anglesey a stranger. He loved the vast silence disturbed only by the wind and the echo of waves on the shore. People here spoke more slowly, and there was a lilt of music in their voices, but he knew now that he only imagined he understood them. He had been as wrong as possible, not only about Olivia, who may have threatened to expose her own family, but also about Naomi, whom he had believed so strong but who had betrayed her husband, then her child, and finally Olivia. The one skill he believed he possessed had left him.

How did Faraday know about Olivia? Had Naomi admitted anything? Runcorn would not leave it like this, so many questions unanswered, so many of his own impressions mistaken.

As soon as he had dressed and had breakfast, he walked across the crisp frost and the pale fingers of new snow whitening the windward sides of the uneven ground. Far in the distance Snowdonia gleamed white.

He was admitted to the vicarage straight away, and Naomi came to the morning room where he had been asked to wait. He rose to his feet as she closed the door behind her and invited him to be seated again.

"Good morning, Mr. Runcorn," she said gravely.

He struggled to remove all emotion from his face, even his voice. He was unnaturally stiff, but he could not help it. Defeat and an overwhelming sense of loneliness almost choked him.

"Good morning, Mrs. Costain." What could he say

to her that was not absurd? Obviously Faraday had not spoken to her yet. She was almost at the end, and she had no idea. Within months she could be hanged.

"What can I do for you? There is nothing further I can tell you." Her face was bland, polite, not exactly at peace, but less scoured with grief than before, as if she were beginning to come to terms with the murder. Was she denying to herself what she had done, or was she merely a superb actress?

"Miss Costain had three suitors that I know of, ma'am: Mr. Faraday some time ago, then Mr. Newbridge, and most recently Mr. Barclay. She declined them all. Did you favor any of those for her?"

"No," she said easily. "I had no desire that she should marry without love. Mere affection would never have been enough for Olivia. She would have been wretched with a good but tepid man like Alan Faraday. It would have made them both unhappy, because he would have been aware of his failure to please her and it would have both confused and hurt him. She was not wise enough to know how to hide it. Melisande Ewart is gentler, much older within herself. She will probably accept the inevitable and if she has tears of despair, she will hide them from him. She is also, I think, kinder than Olivia. She will bring out the best in Alan, and he will never know it was she who did it, nor will she ever say so."

Runcorn was overtaken with a sense of loss, as if he were exiled far from all light and fire and the sound of laughter. He was too numb even to answer her.

"Newbridge is a good man, so far as I know," she went on gravely, almost as if she were speaking as much to herself as to him. "But I cannot say that I like him. My husband chides me now for it. But regardless, I had no wish that Olivia should marry him if she did not wish to. He wants many children, in order to establish his family again. I am not sure Olivia wanted to be that kind of woman. If you are devoted to a man then it is a pleasure and a privilege to work beside him, but if you are not, it is an imprisonment, a lifelong denial of yourself."

In his mind's eye he saw the woman in green who had walked past, her head high, and he almost was glad she had escaped these loveless fates. Then he realized what he was thinking, and who had brought him to that vision, and he was disgusted with himself. What had happened to his basic instincts?

"And as for John Barclay," Naomi went on. "Olivia did not refuse him, it was he who rejected her, suddenly and very bluntly." Now there was pain in her voice, but not the anger Runcorn would have expected. It was like an old wound reopened, not the outrage of a new one. Again he had the certainty that there was something profound about Olivia that this woman was hiding from him, perhaps from everyone.

"Did she know Mr. Barclay before this recent courtship?" he asked, the matter suddenly urgent.

Now the anger was there in her eyes, blazing up for an instant. "No," she said without hesitation. "Why do you ask?"

"It seems . . . brutal, if she did not rebuff him."

"It was," she agreed with a twist of her mouth. "But I do not think John Barclay is a nice man. He did not love Olivia, he wanted her, as a collector wants a rare and beautiful butterfly, to preserve it, not for its happiness. He will be content to put a pin through its body and capture its colors forever in death."

Runcorn remembered Olivia's body on the graveside, stained with blood, and thought for a moment that he was going to be sick.

"I'm sorry," Naomi said very quietly. "That was a bad thing for me to say. I apologize for it. Perhaps my grief is not as well-controlled as I imagined. Please forgive me."

Faraday was wrong, he had to be. There was a deeper answer to find. Perhaps he, too, was trying to protect Melisande from the fact that her brother was a cruel and manipulative man. But Runcorn knew that it could not be done. No matter how much you love, covering evil and allowing the innocent to walk in the shadow of blame is not a path you can take. There is no light at the end of it.

"Thank you, Mrs. Costain," he said gently. "Anger is like a knife, it can be dangerous when out of control, but you need it sometimes, to cut away what must go."

Her eyes widened with a flare of surprise. "Are you still working on the case, Mr. Runcorn? I thought you had given up. I'm so glad I was mistaken." The shadow was still there across her face; the lie she clung to.

"Yes. I'm still working," he said, knowing that that, at least, was true.

❧

$\mathcal{D}$isliking every step of it, Runcorn traced Barclay's actions over the last days before Olivia's death. It was not easy to be discreet, but it was a skill he had learned over his professional life. Barclay had clearly shown a great curiosity about Olivia. He was courting her, in rivalry with Newbridge, and it was natural that he should seek to know all he could about her, following her journeys.

Then it grew clearer as he asked questions, heard descriptions, that it was actually Naomi whose actions he was following, she in whose travels, whose expenditures he showed such an interest, not Olivia.

Runcorn's mind whirled. What had Barclay been seeking? He had come here to Caernarfon asking questions about Naomi, looking for times and dates, patterns of behavior. He had visited a hotel, a church which led him to a hospital, a quiet doctor with a small, expensive practice. Runcorn went to see Dr. Medway, inventing an excuse, and found a handsome man in his fifties, courteous and distinctly uncommunicative.

Was it possible Faraday was right after all? An illegitimate child fitted all these facts and places. In the later stages Runcorn learned that Olivia had come with her sister-in-law.

Why had she come? Had Naomi been desperate, perhaps heavy with child and in need of help? Had she trusted the one person on earth she should not have?

Except how could her husband not have known? Were they really so distant? What ice was in that house, or what storms, in those days?

All this happened some time after Olivia had sought refuge in friendship with the explorer poet, and longed to go with him to Africa, or wherever it was he intended. Had she remained at home because it was impossible for a woman to go to such parts of the world? Had he simply not asked her? Or was it from a duty to look after her sister-in-law in terrible distress, and for the life of the child, if nothing else?

And then Naomi had killed the child anyway.

But how could Runcorn have seen nothing of that in their faces? Or was he looking at the whole thing from the wrong side? Maybe the love story was Olivia's, not Naomi's. The child was Olivia's, and it was Naomi who had protected her, and was still protecting her name, even after she was dead.

What had happened to the child? Was it not a far greater sin to kill a live child than to abort one before it was born? Abortion was dangerous for the mother, but so was birth.

He turned and walked into the wind, back to the doctor's house. He knocked on the door, in spite of the late hour. If he missed the last train and spent the night on this side of the strait, it was immaterial.

"Yes, Mr. Runcorn?" Dr. Medway said curiously.

Runcorn already knew what he meant to do. "I have a story to tell you," he said. "And it is necessary that you listen to what I say. If you are not free to comment, I will understand, but you know the truth of what is being said, and you may decide that I need to know the truth of what happened."

The doctor smiled. "In that case you had better come in."

Runcorn accepted swiftly, and over an excellent supper by the fire, he told Dr. Medway of Olivia's death, what he had deduced, and what was said or hinted at darkly.

"I see," Medway said finally, his voice carrying the weight of tragedy. "You understand I cannot betray confidences, Mr. Runcorn? I will tell you no names, nor will I confirm any."

"Yes," Runcorn agreed.

Medway's face was very pale. "The child died soon after birth. It was one of the most harrowing losses of my career. I fought all I could to save him, but it was beyond my skill, or I believe, anyone's. No one was to blame, least of all the mother."

Runcorn pictured Olivia, weeping over the baby for which she had paid so much to bring into the world. Perhaps Percival had been the man whom she had truly loved. She had given up going with him in order to carry and deliver the child, and yet the baby had died. Or perhaps he had not been worthy of her, had not loved her for more than the swift infatuation of the moment. Runcorn chose to believe the former.

Thank God Naomi had been there, so at least she had not been alone. And she was even now protecting Olivia's memory, even if narrow and vicious men like John Barclay were happy to malign her.

Of course! That was why he had quarreled with her and dramatically ceased to court her! Did he hate her for her pregnancy? She had, in his mind, deceived him, allowed him to believe she was fit for him to marry. Would she ever have told him? Or if he had not found out, might she have accepted his proposal? No. But did Newbridge know that? Or did he arrogantly imagine she was intent upon trapping him?

Had Newbridge known? Was that why he, too, had apparently lost interest in her? There was nothing to suggest he had suspected anything. Runcorn had found no trace of him in his pursuit of Naomi. If he had known, then could it be that Barclay had told him?

Why? He could have let Newbridge marry her, and told him afterwards. That would have been an exquisite revenge.

But upon whom? Newbridge! And it was Olivia who had deceived him. Runcorn had learned enough about the gentry to understand that if that had happened, Barclay himself might have suffered a certain ostracism. They would have closed ranks around Newbridge to protect him, here in Anglesey at least. But word would have spread. Faraday, soon to be Barclay's brother-in-law, would also have believed it a betrayal, and despised Barclay accordingly.

However, if Barclay told Newbridge beforehand, that could be regarded as the act of a friend, a warning in time. What would Melisande think of his warning? Runcorn was uncertain. To him it was an act of cruelty he found repellent, but then he had in his own mind seen so much of Melisande in Olivia, the same loneliness, the dreams that could never be realized, the hunger for something more than daily obedience to the expectations of those who loved them, protected them, and imprisoned them with failure to understand.

Or perhaps it was he who did not really understand. He confused the romantic with the real.

And he was still no closer to proving who had slashed Olivia with a carving knife in hatred for duping him, letting her believe she was all he wanted, when in fact he was nothing she wanted. Was it Barclay? Newbridge? He was terribly afraid that it was Barclay, and the revelation of it would hurt Melisande unbearably. It might even prevent her marriage to Faraday, or anyone else that could make her happy and safe.

What could Runcorn do to prove Barclay's innocence, that would not ruin Olivia's reputation and hurt irreparably the people who had loved her? And even showing Barclay innocent of murder could not conceal that his cruelty was self-serving and repellent.

He would start again with every detail about Barclay. It might be possible to prove that he could not have taken the knife from the kitchen and followed Olivia up to the graveyard, or perhaps that he could not have returned and changed his clothes, disposed of them without anyone knowing! Maybe he could prove no clothes were missing? It would be long and tedious, but for Melisande's sake it could be done.

It was now only three days before Christmas, but here there was no excitement in the air, no shouts of "Merry Christmas," or sounds of laughter. Even the smell of Christmas was blown away in the wind.

It took Runcorn two careful, unhappy days to ascertain that Barclay had learned enough of the story to be sure of the rest, and had certainly spoken alone with Newbridge just before Newbridge had been seen in such a rage as to be white-faced, and almost blind to those around him, two days before Olivia's death.

Runcorn felt gradually sicker with every new piece of information. It looked as if Barclay could have killed Olivia, and was carefully making it appear that Newbridge had.

In the evening he met with Faraday.

Faraday was angry and embarrassed, his face was pink not only from the warmth of the room, but from the high flush of emotion.

"You've been investigating John Barclay," he said as soon as Runcorn had closed the door. "For God's sake, man, if you felt you had to do it, could you not at least have been a little more careful? I told you he had discovered Mrs. Costain's secret, I didn't expect you to tread exactly in his footsteps, and then all but imply he was incriminated in it! He'd never even been to Anglesey at that time! What on earth are you thinking of?"

Runcorn was startled. Had he really been so clumsy that Barclay already knew he was pursued? Apparently. Or was it the suspicions of a guilty man, always looking over his shoulder because he expected pursuit?

The only honest answer now was to tell Faraday what he had learned.

When he finished, Faraday stared at him, all the hectic color drained from his face. "Are you certain of this, Runcorn?" he asked.

"I'm certain of all I've told you," Runcorn replied. "I'm not yet sure what it means."

"It means poor Olivia was killed for it," Faraday said sharply.

Runcorn was still standing, cold and unhappy, yet

again blocked from the fire by Faraday. "Yes, but by Newbridge, or Barclay?"

"Find out," Faraday commanded him. "And for the love of heaven, this time be discreet."

❧

*I*n the morning, Runcorn left early to begin again. The ground was rock hard from the frost and the grass edges were white. Even so, Melisande was waiting for him at the end of the road. He barely recognized her at first; she was so closely wrapped within her cloak that it hid the outline of her body and shielded her face. She seemed to be staring towards the sea, until she heard his boots crunching the ice, then she turned.

"Good morning, Mr. Runcorn." Even in so few words her voice was sharpened with fear.

He felt that twist of emotion inside himself, but fiercer than before.

"Good morning, Mrs. Ewart." It would be absurd to ask her if she was waiting for him. There was no other reason she would be standing here growing steadily colder. He searched her eyes, wide and dark with dread.

She did not waste words. She was trembling with cold. "Alan told me that he had discovered why Mr. Newbridge abandoned Olivia so hastily, and why John also ceased to court her. I believe he told you also?" That was barely a question, but the disappointment was painful, a dull ache beneath the words.

Temptation surged up inside him to tell her that it was he, not Faraday, who had found the truth, but he did not want to tell her until he had proven that it was not Barclay who had killed Olivia, but Newbridge. He drew in his breath to explain, and realized how intensely such an explanation was for his own sake. It was not she whose heart he longed to ease, but his own, because she thought he had let her down. He wished her to think well of him. Vanity, and above all, his own hunger.

That was why Faraday had taken the credit for something he had not done, because he needed Melisande to think him cleverer than he was.

Runcorn took a deep breath and swallowed it down. "Yes," he said simply. "The child was hers. He died almost immediately, so she never needed to tell anyone else. And perhaps the loss was easier to bear if other people did not speak of it."

Melisande's eyes swam with tears. She struggled to speak and failed. Her pity for Olivia was so intense it drowned out even her fear for Barclay. For moments they stood there in the ice and the widening morning light, overshadowed by the same aching grief. The sun sparkled on the frost, as if the rough grass were encrusted with diamonds. In the distance the sea was flat calm, its surface disturbed only by currents and little ruffles of breeze, like the weft of silk.

"I wish I had known," Melisande said at length. "I would at least have told her that it made no difference to me. How terribly alone she must have been."

"Not alone," he said gently. "Naomi was always with her."

She turned to him, hope flaring up in her eyes. "Was she? Please don't tell me something to comfort me if it is not true. Please, always tell me the truth. I need one person who doesn't lie, however kind the reason."

"I won't lie," he promised rashly. He would have promised her anything. "Naomi never let her down."

She smiled slowly, a soft sadness filling her face, more beautiful to him than the radiance of the sun over the ground. "Thank you," she said sincerely. "I must go, before they ask me why my morning walk took so long. Please . . . please don't stop your search. It is too late now to hide anything." And without waiting for his answer, she walked with increasing speed up the hill back towards the great house.

Runcorn began straight away. He loathed Barclay and despised him for what he seemed to have done both to Olivia and to Newbridge, but still, he wanted to prove beyond all further question that he was not legally guilty of murder even if morally he was. That was a different issue and the law had no remedy for it.

Runcorn knew the date of the birth, it was a matter of tracing back to nine months before that. He was already convinced that Costain knew nothing about the child. His eagerness to marry Olivia to first Faraday, then Newbridge, and finally Barclay, meant that either he was unaware of her child and its death, or he was unbelievably insensitive. Runcorn was certain it was the former.

Still, he should ask Naomi again.

She received him in her own room in the vicarage, a quiet space on the ground floor filled with gardening gloves, secateurs, string, outdoor boots and trugs for carrying cut blooms and greenery. She was arranging a bowl of holly with berries the color of blood, small golden onions, and sprigs of leaves and evergreen that he could not name. Some leaves were dark red as wine, and the bowl glowed with purple, green, gold, and red. He admired it, quite honestly. There was a rich warmth to it, as if it proclaimed hope and abundance in a dark season.

He did not waste her time, or his own, with prevarication. "Do you know who was the father of Olivia's child, Mrs. Costain?"

"Yes," she said simply. "But it was no one you know, and I have no desire to tear up his emotions or ruin his reputation, so there is no purpose in your pursuing it. He never knew she was with child, and he is too far away from here to have had any part in her death."

"Percival, I assume," he concluded. "I had not thought it was Mr. Newbridge, but I needed to be certain."

"Newbridge?" she looked startled, almost amused. "Good heavens, no! Whatever made you imagine that?"

"You are perfectly sure?" he persisted.

"Perfectly," she said with feeling. "But if you doubt me, you can prove it for yourself. He was away in England at the time, Wiltshire, I think. Certainly he was miles from here. He was staying with his sister, and buying cattle, or something of the sort. At that time he was more concerned with improving his livestock than gaining a wife."

"What sort of man was Percival?" Another idea was gaining strength in his mind.

She smiled, placing a last golden onion in its place to complete the light and shade of the arrangement.

"I never thought of using onions like that," he said.

"One uses what one has," she replied. "And onions

keep very well. What was he like? He was fun, full of ideas, an imagination which could make you laugh and cry at the same time. He was not particularly handsome, but his face was unique, and he had a smile that lit up his eyes and made you feel as if you could survive anything as long as he liked you."

"And did he like Olivia?" He did not want to hear that he had not. But if it had been true, he had to know.

Naomi looked away. "Oh yes, as much as she loved him, I think. But he was young and poor, a dreamer. It will be years before he can afford to marry, if ever. And he was not suitable for a girl of Olivia's breeding. My brother would look far higher than a penniless wanderer for her. My mother-in-law was a lady," she added. "Very little money, but a heritage back to Norman days." She sighed. "Which is slightly absurd, since if you think about it, we must all have a heritage back to Eve, or we would not be here. I don't give a fig who my ancestors were, only what I am, because that I can do something about."

Runcorn stared at her.

She looked back levelly. "Are you asking me if

Olivia could or would have married him? She would have, but he had more sense than to ask her. Newbridge did, and she refused him. Kindly, I hope."

There it was, as clear as it would ever be. Newbridge had offered her all he had, and she had refused him. And John Barclay had told him that she had been willing to lie with an explorer with neither land nor family, and to bear his illegitimate child. To Newbridge that must have been the ultimate insult, not only to his love but to all his lineage, his values, and his manhood. It remained now only to trace his exact actions on the night of her death, perhaps even to find the knife, or prove from where it was missing, or the clothes he had worn, and probably destroyed.

These were things Faraday had the power to do. Runcorn thanked Naomi and left, out into the day so cold the air stung his skin and the breath of the wind was like ice between the folds of his scarf.

❧

*F*araday conducted the search and found the last pieces, as Runcorn had suggested. The knife was hidden in one of the barns. It took great care, but traces of blood were found, and Trimby agreed that the blade's shape matched the wounds. More incriminating than that, they found the ashes of the clothes Newbridge had worn that night. There were not sufficient remains to identify them, but the suit in question was gone and Newbridge could not explain its absence. He might have considered claiming to have given it to someone, but there was no one to substantiate it. The truth was terribly and agonizingly clear.

By mid-morning Newbridge was arrested and taken to the police cells in Bangor. Faraday told the waiting journalists and the public, briefly and with dignity, that the case was over, and justice would be done. The truth would be told at trial in due course. For now, the solution was plain, and he spoke for Olivia's family and for all the people of Anglesey when he reminded them that tomorrow was Christmas Day. He asked for respite so they might all, for a brief time, remember the season and give thanks for the birth and life of Christ, and the hope of forgiveness and renewal in the world.

Runcorn stood in the crowd and felt the surge of

gratitude that some kind of resolution had been reached, and there was justice and healing ahead. The admiration for Faraday was palpable, a new respect for more than the office. This was for the man himself, and the patience and skill he had shown. They believed in him. They would not forget this, please heaven, the most horrific case Anglesey would ever know.

Not once did Faraday mention Runcorn's name, let alone suggest that he had been the one to find the solution.

Runcorn separated himself from the crowd and walked away towards the wide sweep of the water. The sun, low in the west, made the great span of the bridge look like black fretwork on the sky across the burning colors of the sunset-painted water.

He would leave now. Melisande was as safe as he could make her. Barclay was shallow and manipulative, a man of innate cruelty, but Faraday would protect her from the worst of that. It was the best he could hope for. At least now Faraday would not have to prove himself any more. There must be a certainty that he had succeeded and so Barclay would be held back from ever criticizing him. Runcorn could hardly do anything but give his blessing to the marriage.

The wind stung Runcorn's eyes and he blinked hard. He refused to acknowledge, even to himself, that he was crying. But he was smiling as well. It was he who had solved the case, he who had found justice for Olivia, and some kind of safety for Melisande. She would never know Faraday had not been as inquisitive, or as successful, as he allowed people to suppose.

Runcorn was second fiddle, never first, but he had played the more beautiful tune. He had allowed himself to be guided by his emotions, and that was something he had never done before. This great clean land and water, with its light, its horizon beyond dreaming, had made a better man of him. He did not need anyone else to reassure him of that. He would carry it away with him, a better gift for Christmas than all the wealth, the food, the colors, or the rejoicing.

"Mr. Runcorn."

He turned around slowly. Melisande was standing on the quay behind him, the wind in her hair and the sunset light on her face. He gulped, all his resolve blown away in a single instant.

"Thank you," she said gently. Her cheeks were burning, more than the fire on the water could reflect. "I know it was you who worked out who killed Olivia, and why. And I know my brother well enough to guess at the part he played. I long ago ceased to believe he was a nice person, but I am grateful that you tried to protect me from knowing the extent of his cruelty."

He could still think of nothing to say. He wanted to tell her that he loved her, he would always love her, and no price to his own pride or ambition was too great to pay for her happiness. But that would only embarrass her, and forfeit the last, brief thread of friendship that they had, which he could keep bound to his heart.

"You gave Alan all the pieces, didn't you?" she asked.

He would not answer. It was the last temptation, and he refused to succumb. He smiled at her. "He's going to make a good policeman."

"I hope so," she agreed. "I think it matters to him.

But he is not as good as you are, because there will probably never be another case like this." She took a deep breath and let it out slowly. "And he is not as good a man as you are. Truth means less to him, and he does not seek it for its own sake."

He felt his cheeks burn. He would never in all his life forget this moment. From now on, forever, he would strive to be the man she had said he was to her. He wanted to tell her how great a gift that was, that the fire of it burned inside him, lighting every corner, every wish and thought, but there were no words big enough, gracious enough, articulate enough to do this feeling justice.

"Mr. Runcorn," she said impatiently, her face burning. "Do I have to ask you if you love me? That is so undignified for a woman."

He was stunned. She knew. All his careful concealment, his efforts to behave with dignity had been for nothing.

"Yes," he said awkwardly. "Of course I do. But—"

"But you don't want a wife?"

"Yes! Yes, I do . . . but . . ."

He was paralyzed. This was not possible.

She lowered her eyes and slowly turned away.

He took a step after her, and another, catching her arm gently, but then refusing to let go. "Yes, I do, but I could not marry anyone else. Every time I looked at her, I would wish she were you. I've never loved before, and I cannot again."

She smiled at him. "You don't need to, Mr. Runcorn. Once will be enough. If you would be so good as to ask me, I shall accept."

A Christmas Grace

*D*edicated to all those
who long for a second chance

$\mathcal{E}$MILY RADLEY STOOD IN THE CENTER OF HER magnificent drawing room and considered where she should have the Christmas tree placed so that it would show to the best advantage. The decorations were already planned: the bows, the colored balls, the tinsel, the little glass icicles, and the red and green shiny birds. At the foot would be the brightly wrapped presents for her husband and children.

All through the house there would be candles, wreaths and garlands of holly and ivy. There would be bowls of crystallized fruit and porcelain dishes of nuts, jugs of mulled wine, plates of mince pies, roasted chestnuts, and, of course, great fires in the hearths with apple logs to burn with a sweet smell.

The year of 1895 had not been an easy one, and

she was happy enough to see it come to a close. Because they were staying in London, rather than going to the country, there would be parties, and dinners, including the Duchess of Warwick's; everyone she knew would be at that dinner. And there would be balls where they would dance all night. She had her gown chosen: the palest possible green, embroidered with gold. And, of course, there was the theater. It would not be the same without anything of Oscar Wilde's, but there would be Goldsmith's *She Stoops to Conquer,* and that was fun.

She was still thinking about it when Jack came in. He looked a little tired, but he had the same easy grace of manner as always. He was holding a letter in his hand.

"Post?" she asked in surprise. "At this time in the evening?" Her heart sank. "It's not some government matter, is it? They can't want you now. It's less than three weeks till Christmas."

"It's for you," he replied, holding it out for her. "It was just delivered. I think it's Thomas's handwriting."

Thomas Pitt was Emily's brother-in-law, a policeman. Her sister, Charlotte, had married considerably beneath her. She had not regretted it for a day, even if it had cost her the social and financial comforts she had been accustomed to. On the contrary, it was Emily who envied Charlotte the opportunities she had been given to involve herself in some of his cases. It seemed like far too long since Emily had shared an adventure, the danger, the emotion, the anger, and the pity. Somehow she felt less alive for it.

She tore open the envelope and read the paper inside.

Dear Emily,

I am very sorry to tell you that Charlotte received a letter today from a Roman Catholic priest, Father Tyndale, who lives in a small village in the Connemara region of Western Ireland. He is the pastor to Susannah Ross, your father's younger sister. She is now widowed again, and Father Tyndale says she is very ill. In fact this will certainly be her last Christmas.

I know she parted from the family in less than happy circumstances, but we should not allow her to be alone at such a time. Your mother is in Italy, and unfortunately Charlotte has a bad case of bronchitis, which is why I am writing to ask you if you will go to Ireland to be with Susannah. I realize it is a great sacrifice, but there is no one else.

Father Tyndale says it cannot be for long, and you would be most welcome in Susannah's home. If you write back to him at the enclosed address, he will meet you at the Galway station from whichever train you say. Please make it within a day or two. There is little time to hesitate.

I thank you in advance, and Charlotte sends her love. She will write to you when she is well enough.

Yours with gratitude,

Thomas

Emily looked up and met Jack's eyes. "It's preposterous!" she exclaimed. "He's lost his wits."

Jack blinked. "Really. What does he say?"

Wordlessly she passed the letter to him.

He read it, frowning, and then offered it back to her. "I'm sorry. I know you were looking forward to Christmas at home, but there'll be another one next year."

"I'm not going!" she said incredulously.

He said nothing, just looked at her steadily.

"It's ridiculous," she protested. "I can't go to Connemara, for heaven's sake. Especially not at Christmas. It'll be like the end of the world. In fact it is the end of the world. Jack, it's nothing but freezing bog."

"Actually I believe the west coast of Ireland is quite temperate," he corrected her. "But wet, of course," he added with a smile.

She breathed out a sigh of relief. His smile could still charm her more than she wished him to know. If he did, he might be impossible to manage at all. She turned away to put the letter on the table. "I'll write to Thomas tomorrow and explain to him."

"What will you say?" he asked.

She was surprised. "That it's out of the question, of course. But I'll put it nicely."

"How nicely can you say that you'll let your aunt

die alone at Christmas because you don't fancy the Irish climate?" he asked, his voice surprisingly gentle, considering the words.

Emily froze. She turned back to look at him, and knew that in spite of the smile, he meant exactly what he had said. "Do you really want me to go away to Ireland for the entire Christmas?" she asked. "Susannah's only fifty. She might live for ages. He doesn't even say what's wrong with her."

"One can die at any age," Jack pointed out. "And what I would like has nothing to do with what is right."

"What about the children?" Emily played the trump card. "What will they think if I leave them for Christmas? It is a time when families should be together." She smiled back at him.

"Then write and tell your aunt to die alone because you want to be with your family," he replied. "On second thoughts, you'll have to tell the priest, and he can tell her."

The appalling realization hit her. "You want me to go!" she accused him.

"No, I don't," he denied. "But neither do I want to live with you all the years afterwards when Susannah is dead, and you wish you had done. Guilt can destroy even the dearest things. In fact, especially the dearest." He reached out and touched her cheek gently. "I don't want to lose you."

"You won't!" she said quickly. "You'll never lose me."

"Lots of people lose each other." He shook his head. "Some people even lose themselves."

She looked down at the carpet. "But it's Christmas!"

He did not answer.

The seconds ticked by. The fire crackled in the hearth.

"Do you suppose they have telegrams in Ireland?" she asked finally.

"I've no idea. What can you possibly say in a telegram that would answer this?"

She took a deep breath. "What time my train gets into Galway. And on what day, I suppose."

He leaned forward and kissed her very gently, and

she found she was crying, for all that she would miss over the next weeks, and all that she thought Christmas ought to be.

*B*ut two days later, when the train finally pulled into Galway a little before noon and Emily stepped out onto the platform in the fine rain, she was in an entirely different frame of mind. She was stiff, and extremely tired after a rough crossing of the Irish Sea and a night in a Dublin hotel. If Jack had had the remotest idea what he was asking of her, he wouldn't have been nearly so cavalier about it. This was a sacrifice no one should ask. It was Susannah's choice to have turned her back on her family, married a Roman Catholic no one knew, and decided to live out here in the bog and the rain. She had not come home when Emily's father was dying! Of course, no one had asked her to. In fact, Emily admitted to herself reluctantly, it was quite possible no one had even told her he was ill.

The porter unloaded her luggage and put it on the

platform. She had not asked him to—it was quite unnecessary. This was the end of the line, in every possible sense.

She paid him to take it out to the street, and followed him along the platform, getting wetter every minute. She was in the roadway when she saw a pony and trap, a priest standing very conspicuously talking to the animal. He turned as he heard the porter's trolley on the cobbles. He saw Emily and his face lit with a broad smile. He was a plain man, his features unremarkable, a little lumpy, and yet in that moment he was beautiful.

"Ah,"—he came forward with his hand out—"Mrs. Radley. Surely it is very good of you to come all this way, and at this time of the year. Was your crossing very bad? God put a rough sea between you and me, to make us all the more grateful to arrive safely on the farther shore. A bit like life." He shrugged ruefully, his eyes for a moment filled with sadness. "How are you, then? Tired and cold? And it's a long journey we have yet, but there's no help for it." He looked her up and down with sympathy. "Unless you're not well enough to make it today?"

"Thank you, Father Tyndale, but I'm quite well enough," Emily replied. She was about to ask how long it could be, then changed her mind. He might take it for faintheartedness.

"Ah, I'm delighted," he said quickly. "Now let's get your cases up here into the back, and we'll set off then. We'll make most of the way in daylight, so we will." He turned and picked up one of the cases, and with a mighty heave set it on the back of the cart. The porter was barely quick enough to get the lighter one up by himself.

Emily drew in her breath to say something, then changed her mind. What was there to say? It was midday, and he did not think he would reach Susannah's house before nightfall! What benighted end of the world were they going to?

Father Tyndale helped her up into the cart on the seat beside him, tucked a rug around her, and a waterproof cloth after that, then went briskly around and climbed in the other side. After a word of encouragement the pony set off at a steady walk. Emily had a hideous feeling that the animal knew a lot more about it than she did, and was pacing itself for a long journey.

As they left the town, the rain eased a little and Emily started to look around at the rolling land. There were sudden vistas of hills in the distance to the west as the clouds parted and occasional shreds of blue sky appeared. Shafts of light gleamed on wet grasslands, which seemed to have layers of color, wind-bleached on top but with a depth of sullen reds and scorched greens below. There was a lot of shadow on the lee side of the hills, peat-dark streams, and the occasional ruin of an old stone shelter, now almost black except where the sun glistened on the wet surfaces.

"In a few minutes you'll see the lake," Father Tyndale said suddenly. "Very beautiful, it is, and lots of fish in it, and birds. You'll like it. Quite different from the sea, of course."

"Yes, of course," Emily agreed, huddling closer into her blanket. She felt as if she should say more. He was looking resolutely ahead, concentrating on his driving, although she wondered why. There was

205

nowhere else to go but the winding road ahead, and the pony seemed to know its way perfectly well. If Father Tyndale had tied the reins to the iron hold provided, and fallen asleep, he would no doubt have got home just as safely. Still, the silence required something.

"You said that my aunt is very ill," she began tentatively. "I have no experience in nursing. What will I be able to do for her?"

"Don't let it worry you, Mrs. Radley," Father Tyndale replied with a softness in his voice. "For sure Mrs. O'Bannion will be there to help. Death will come when it will. There's nothing to do to change that, simply a little care in the meantime."

"Is . . . is she in a lot of pain?"

"No, not so much, at least of body. And the doctor comes when he can. It's more a heaviness of the spirit, a remembrance of things past . . ." He gave a long sigh and there was a slight shadow in his face, not a change in the light so much as something from within. "There are regrets, things that need doing before it's too late," he added. "That's so for all of us, it's just that the knowledge that you have little time makes it more pressing, you understand?"

"Yes," Emily said bleakly, thinking back to the ugly parting when Susannah had informed the family that she was going to marry again, not to anyone they approved of, but to an Irishman who lived in Connemara. That in itself was not serious. The offense was that Hugo Ross was Roman Catholic.

Emily had asked at the time why on earth that mattered so much, but her father had been too angry and too hurt over what he saw as his sister's defection to pursue the subject of history and the disloyalties of the past.

Now Emily stared at the bleak landscape. The wind rippled through the long grasses, bending them so the shadows made them look like water. Wild birds flew overhead, she counted at least a dozen different kinds. There were hardly any trees, just wet land glistening in the occasional shafts of sun, a view now and then of the lake that Father Tyndale had spoken of, long reeds growing at the edges like black knifemarks. There was little sound but the pony's hoofs on the road, and the sighing of the wind.

What did Susannah regret? Her marriage? Losing touch with her own family? Coming here as a stranger to this place at the end of the world? It was too late to change now, whatever it was. Susannah's husband and Emily's father were both dead; there was nothing to say to anyone that would matter. Did she want someone from the past here simply so she could feel that one of them cared? Or would she say that she loved them, and she was sorry?

They must have been traveling for at least an hour. It felt like more. Emily was cold and stiff, and a good deal of her was also wet.

They passed the first crossroads she had seen, and she was disappointed when they did not take either turning. She asked Father Tyndale about it.

"Moycullen," he replied with the ghost of a smile. "The left goes to Spiddal, and the sea, but it's the long way around. This is much faster. In about another hour we'll be at Oughterard, and we'll stop there for a bite to eat. You'll be ready, no doubt."

Another hour! However long was this journey?

She swallowed. "Yes, thank you. That would be very nice. Then where?"

"Oh, it's a little westwards to Maam Cross, then south around the coast through Roundstone, and a few more miles and we're there," he replied.

Emily could think of nothing to say.

Oughterard proved to be warmly welcoming and the food was delicious, eaten in a dining room with an enormous peat fire. It gave off not only more heat than she would have imagined, but an earthy, smoky aroma she found extremely pleasing. She was offered a glass of something mildly alcoholic, which looked like river water but tasted acceptable enough, and she left feeling as if so long as she did not count the time or the miles, she might survive the rest of the way.

They passed Maam Cross and the weather cleared as the afternoon faded. There was a distinct gold in the air when Father Tyndale pointed out the Maumturk Mountains in the northeast.

"We never met Susannah's husband," Emily said suddenly. "What was he like?"

Father Tyndale smiled. "Oh, now that was a

shame," he replied with feeling. "A fine man, he was. Quiet, you know, for an Irishman. But when he told a story you listened, and when he laughed you laughed with him. Loved the land, and painted it like no one else. Gave it a light so you could smell the air of it just by looking. But you may be knowing that yourself?"

"No," Emily said with amazement. "I . . . I didn't even know he was an artist." She felt ashamed. "We thought he had some kind of family money. Not a lot, but enough to live on."

Father Tyndale laughed. It was a rich, happy sound in the empty land where she could hear only bird cries, wind, and the pony's feet on the road. "That's true enough, but we judge a man by his soul, not his pocket," he answered her. "Hugo painted for the love of it."

"What did he look like?" she asked. Then she felt self-conscious for thinking of something so trivial, and wanted Father Tyndale to understand the reason. "Just so I can picture him. When you think of someone, you get an idea in your head. I want it to be right."

"He was a big man," Father Tyndale replied thoughtfully. "He had brown hair that curled, and blue eyes. He was happy, that's what I remember he looked like. And he had beautiful hands, as if he could touch anything without hurting it."

With no warning at all, Emily found herself almost on the edge of tears that she would never meet Hugo Ross. She must be very tired. She had been traveling for two days, and she had no idea what sort of a place she was going to, or how Susannah would be changed by time and illness, not to mention years of estrangement from the family. This whole journey was ridiculous. She shouldn't have allowed Jack to talk her into coming.

It was over four hours now since they had left Galway. "How much longer will it be?" she asked the priest.

"Not more than another two hours," he replied cheerfully. "That's the Twelve Fins over there," he pointed to a row of hills now almost straight to the north. "And the Lake of Ballynahinch ahead. We'll turn off before then, down towards the shore, then past Roundstone, and we're there."

They stopped at another hotel, and ate more excellent food. Afterwards it was even more difficult going out into the dusk and a damp wind from the west.

Then the sky cleared and as they crested a slight rise the view opened up in front of them, the sun spilled across the water in a blaze of scarlet and gold, black headlands seeming to jut up out of liquid fire. From the look of it, the road before them could have been inlaid with bronze. Emily could smell the salt in the air and, looking up a moment, her eye caught the pale underside of birds circling, riding the wind in the last light.

Father Tyndale smiled and said nothing, but she knew he had heard her sharp intake of breath.

"Tell me something about the village," she said when the sun had almost disappeared and she knew the pony must be finding its way largely by habit, knowing it was almost home.

It was several moments before he answered, and when he did she heard a note of sadness in his voice, as if he were being called to account for some mistake he had made.

212

"It's smaller than it was," he said. "Too many of our young people go away now." He stopped, seeming lost for further words.

Emily felt embarrassed. This was a land in which neither she nor her countrymen had any business, yet they had been here for centuries. She was made welcome because they were hospitable by nature. But what did they really feel? What had it been like for Susannah coming here? Little wonder she was desperate enough to ask a Catholic priest to beg anyone of her family to be with her for her last days.

She cleared her throat. "Actually I was rather thinking of the houses, the streets, the people you know . . . that sort of thing."

"You'll meet them, for sure," he answered. "Mrs. Ross is well liked. They'll call, even if only briefly, not to tire her, poor soul. She used to walk miles along the shore, or over towards the Roundstone Bog, especially in the spring. She went with Hugo when he took his paints. Just sat and read a book, or went looking for the wildflowers. But the sea was the best for her. Never grew tired of looking at it. She

213

was collecting some papers about the Martin family, but I don't know if she kept up with that after she fell ill."

"Who are the Martins?" Emily asked.

His face cleared. "Oh, the Martins are part of the Rosses, or the other way around," he said with pride. "Once it was the Flahertys and the Conneeleys that ruled the area. Fought each other to a standstill, so they did. But there are still Flahertys in the village, for all that, and Conneeleys too, of course. And others you'll meet. But for history, Padraic Yorke is the one. He knows everything there is to know, and tells it with the music of the land in his voice, and the laughter and tears of the people."

"I must meet him, if I can."

"He'll be happy to tell you where everything happened, and the names of the flowers and the birds. Not that they're so many at this time of year."

She imagined she would have no time for such things, but she thanked him anyway.

They arrived a little after six in the evening, and it was already pitch-dark, with a haze of rain obscuring the stars to the east. But clear in the west there was a low moon, sufficient to see the outline of the village. They drove through, and on to Susannah's house beyond—closer to the shore.

Father Tyndale alighted and knocked on the front door. It was several minutes before it opened and Susannah was silhouetted against a blaze of candlelight. She must have had at least a dozen lit. She came out onto the step, peering beyond Father Tyndale as if to make sure there was someone else with him.

Emily walked over the gravel and up the wide entrance paving into the light.

"Emily . . ." Susannah said softly. "You look wonderful, but you must be very tired. Thank you so much for coming."

Emily stepped forward. "Aunt Susannah." It seemed absurd to say very much more. She was tired, as must be clear, but looking at Susannah's gaunt face and her body so obviously fragile, even under a woolen dress and shawl, it would be childish even to think of herself. And to ask how Susannah was would seem to trivialize what they both knew to be the truth.

"It was an excellent journey," she lied. "And Father Tyndale has been most kind to me."

"You must be cold and hungry." Susannah stepped back into the light. "And wet," she added.

Emily was shocked. She remembered Susannah as interesting more than pretty, but with good features and a truly beautiful skin, like her own. The woman she saw now was haggard, the bones of her face prominent, her eyes sunken in shadowed sockets.

"A little," Emily said, trying to force her voice to sound normal. "But it will soon mend. A night's sleep will make all the difference." She felt an urgent temptation to talk too much in order to fill the yawning silence.

Susannah looked at Father Tyndale and Emily suddenly became aware that she must be finding it hard to stand here at the door in the cold.

Father Tyndale set the cases down just inside. "Would you like me to take them upstairs?" he asked.

Emily knew it would be next to impossible for her to carry the larger one, so she accepted.

Five minutes later Father Tyndale was gone and

Emily and Susannah stood alone in the hall. Now it was awkward. There was a barrier of ten years' silence between them. It was duty that brought Emily, and she could not pretend affection. Had she cared, they would have corresponded during that time. Susannah must feel the same.

"Supper is ready," Susannah said with a faint smile. "I imagine you would like to retire early."

"Thank you. Yes." Emily followed her across the chilly hallway into a wood-paneled dining room whose warmth embraced her the moment she was through the door. A peat fire in the huge stone hearth did not dance with flame, like the fires she was used to at home, but its sweet, earthy aroma filled the air. There were candles burning in all the holders, and a polished wooden table was set for two. There was no sign of any servant. Perhaps none resided there. Emily had a sudden, sinking fear that in spite of what Father Tyndale had said, she might have more duties than she had expected, and for which she was ill-equipped.

"May I help?" she said tentatively. Decency required it.

217

Susannah gave her a glance with unexpected humor. "I didn't ask you here to be a servant, Emily. Mrs. O'Bannion does all the heavy work, and I can still cook, adequately at least. I pick the times of day when I feel best." She stood in the doorway leading to the kitchen. "I wanted someone here who was of my own family, you or Charlotte." The light vanished from her face. "There are things to see to before I die." She turned and went out, leaving the door open behind her, perhaps so she could return with both hands full.

Emily was relieved that Susannah had gone before any reply to that last remark was necessary. When she came back with a tureen of stew, and then a dish of mashed potatoes, it was easy to let the previous conversation slip.

The stew was excellent, and Emily was happy enough to enjoy it, and then the apple pie that followed. They spoke of trivialities. Emily realized that she hardly knew Susannah. Being aware of the facts of someone's life is quite different from understanding even their opinions, let alone their dreams. Susannah was her father's sister, and yet they were strangers sitting across a table, alone with each other, at the edge of the world. Outside the wind sighed in the eaves and rain splattered the glass.

"Tell me about the village," Emily said, unable to let the silence extend. "It was too dark to see much on my way through."

Susannah smiled, but there was a sharp sadness in her eyes. "I don't know that there's anything different about them, except that they're my people. Their griefs matter to me." She looked down at the table with its gleaming surface, close-grained and polished like silk. "Perhaps you'll come to know them, and then I won't need to explain. Hugo loved them, in the quiet way you do when something is part of your life." She took a deep breath and looked up, forcing herself to smile. "Would you like anything more to eat?"

"No, thank you," Emily said quickly. "I have eaten excellently. Either you or Mrs. O'Bannion is an excellent cook."

"I am with pastry, not much else," Susannah replied. She smiled, but she looked desperately tired. "Thank you for coming, Emily. I'm sure you would rather have spent Christmas at home. Please don't feel it necessary to deny that. I am perfectly aware of how much I am asking of you. Still, I hope you will be comfortable here, and warm enough. There is a fire in your bedroom, and peat in the box to replenish it. It's better not to let it go out. They can be hard to start again." She rose to her feet slowly, as if trying to make sure she did not sway or stumble. "Now, if you will excuse me, I think I will go upstairs. Please leave everything as it is. Mrs. O'Bannion will see to it when she comes in the morning."

❖

*E*mily slept so well she barely moved in the bed, but when she woke to hear the wind gusting around the eaves she was momentarily confused as to where she was. She sat up and saw the embers of the fire before she remembered with a jolt that there was no maid to help. She had better restoke it quickly, before it died completely.

Surprisingly, when she was out of bed the air was not as chill as she had expected. When the new peat was on the fire, she opened the curtains and stared at the sight that met her eyes. The panorama was breathtaking. The sky was a turmoil of clouds, rolling in like a wild reflection of the sea below, white spume topping the waves, gray water heaving. Far to the right was a long headland of dark, jagged rocks. Below was a sandy shore with the tide high and threatening. To the left the land was softer, stretching away in alternate sand and rock until it disappeared in a belt of rain and the outlines melted into one another. It was fierce, elemental, but there was a beauty about it that no static landscape could match.

She washed in the water that had been left in an ewer beside the fire, and was quite pleasantly warm, and dressed in a morning gown of plain, dark green. Then she went downstairs to see if Susannah was awake, and if she might like any assistance.

In the kitchen she found a handsome woman in her late thirties with shining brown hair and dark-lashed eyes of a curious blue-green color. She smiled as soon as she realized Emily was there.

"Good morning to you," she said cheerfully. "You'll be Mrs. Radley. Welcome to Connemara."

"Thank you." Emily walked into the warm, spacious kitchen, her feet suddenly noisy on the stone floor. "Mrs. O'Bannion?"

The woman smiled broadly. "I am. And that's Bridie you can hear barging about in the scullery. Never known such a girl for making a noise. What'd you like for breakfast, now? How about scrambled eggs on toast, an' a nice pot of tea?"

"Perfect, thank you. How is Mrs. Ross?"

Maggie O'Bannion's face shadowed. "She'll not be down yet for a while, the poor soul. Sometimes mornings are good for her, but more often they're not."

"Is there anything I can do to help?" Emily asked, feeling foolish and yet compelled to offer.

"Enjoy your breakfast," Maggie replied. "If you want to take a breath of air, I'd do it soon. The wind's rising fit to tear the sky to pieces, and it's best you're well inside the house when it gets bad."

Emily looked at the window. "Thank you. I'll take your advice, but it doesn't look unpleasant."

Maggie shivered, her lips pressed together. "There's a keening in the wind. I can hear it." She turned away and began to prepare breakfast for Emily.

Susannah came down at about ten. She was pale-faced, and there was more gray in her hair than Emily had appreciated in the warmth of the previous evening's candlelight. However, she seemed rested and her smile was quick when she saw Emily in the drawing room writing letters.

"Did you sleep well? I hope you were comfortable? Did Maggie get you breakfast?"

Emily stood up. "Excellent to all of the questions," she replied. "And Mrs. O'Bannion is charming, and I have eaten very well, thank you. You are quite right, I like her already."

Susannah glanced at the notepaper. "May I suggest you take them to the post before lunch? I think the wind is rising." She gave a quick look towards the window. "We might be in for a bad storm. They can happen this time of the year. Sometimes they are very dreadful."

Emily did not reply. It seemed an odd remark to make. Everybody had storms in the winter. It was part of life. As far as she had heard, they did not have the snow in Connemara that they did in England.

She returned to her letters and at eleven o'clock she joined Susannah and Maggie for a mug of cocoa. With the wind whining outside and occasional gusts of rain on the glass, sitting at the kitchen table with biscuits and a hot cup in her hands seemed almost like revisiting the comforts of childhood.

A twig clattered against the window and Maggie turned quickly to stare at it. Susannah's thin hands clenched on the porcelain of her cup. She drew in her breath sharply.

Maggie looked away, meeting Emily's eyes and forcing herself to smile. "We'll be quite warm inside," she said unnecessarily. "And there's enough peat cut to last into January."

Emily wanted to make some light remark to relieve the tension with laughter, but she could not think of anything. She realized that she did not know either of these women well enough to understand why they were afraid. What did a little wind matter?

But in the middle of the afternoon, the sky darkened with heavy clouds to the west and the wind was considerably fiercer. Emily did not realize just how hard it was until she went outside to clip a handful of red willow twigs to add to the bowl of holly and ivy in the hall. It was not as cold as she had expected, but the force of the gale whipped her skirt as if it had been a sail, carrying her backwards off balance. It was a moment before she steadied herself and leaned into it.

"Be careful, ma'am," a man's voice said, so close she spun around, startled, as if he had threatened her.

He was almost ten feet away, a large man with blunt features and dark, troubled eyes. He smiled at her tentatively, no lightness in his expression.

"I'm sorry," Emily apologized for her overreaction. "I hadn't expected the wind to be so hard."

"Sure, it's going to get worse," the man said gently, raising his voice only just enough to be heard. He looked up at the sky, narrowing his eyes.

"Are you looking for Mrs. Ross?" Emily asked him.

He spread his hands in a gesture of apology. "An' I have no manners at all. I'm thinking because I know you're Mrs. Ross's niece, that you must know me too.

I'm Fergal O'Bannion. I've come to walk Maggie home." Again he looked at the sky, but this time westwards, towards the sea.

"Do you live far away?" She was disappointed. She liked Maggie and had hoped she lived close by and would be able to come to Susannah even in the worst of the winter. Otherwise Susannah would be very much alone, especially as her illness became worse.

"Over there." Fergal pointed to what appeared to be little more than half a mile away.

"Oh." Emily could think of no answer that made sense, so she merely smiled. "I'm just going to cut a few twigs. Please go in. I'm sure Mrs. O'Bannion is just about ready."

He thanked her and went inside, and Emily went to look for bright, unblemished stems. She was puzzled. What could Fergal possibly be afraid of that he came to walk Maggie home for less than a mile? There was no imaginable danger. It must be something else—a village feud, perhaps?

She found the twigs and returned to the house five minutes later. Maggie was in the hallway putting her shawl on and Fergal was waiting by the door.

"Thank you," Susannah said with a quick smile at Maggie.

Emily laid the twigs on the hall table.

"I'll be back in the morning," Maggie told them. "I'll bring bread, and a few eggs."

"If the weather holds," Fergal qualified.

She shot him a sharp glance, and then bit her lip and turned to face Susannah. "Of course it'll hold, at least enough for that. I won't let you down," she promised Susannah.

"Maggie—" Fergal began.

" 'Course I won't," Maggie repeated, then smiled warningly at her husband. "Come on. Let's be going, then. What are you waiting for?" She opened the front door and strode out into the wind. It caught her skirts, billowing them out and making her lose her balance very slightly. Fergal went after her, catching up in a couple of strides and putting his arm around her to steady her a moment before Maggie leaned into him.

Emily closed the front door. "Shall I get us a cup

of tea?" she offered. She had missed her chance to take her letters to the post today. They would have to go tomorrow.

Fifteen minutes later they were sitting by the fire, tea tray on the low table between them.

Emily swallowed a mouthful of shortbread. "Why is Fergal so worried about the weather? It's a bit blustery, but that's all. I'll walk with Maggie, if it'll make her feel better."

"It isn't—" Susannah began, then stopped, looking down at her plate. "Storms can be bad here."

"Enough to blow a sturdy woman off her feet in half a mile of roadway?" Emily said incredulously.

Susannah drew in her breath, then let it out without answering. Emily considered what it was she had been going to say, and why she had changed her mind. But Susannah evaded the subject all evening, and went to bed early.

"Good night," she said to Emily, standing in the doorway with a faint smile. Her face was lined and bleak, the hollows around her eyes almost blue in the shadows, as if she were at the end of a very long road and had little strength left. There was no real reason why, but Emily had the impression that she was afraid.

"If you need me for anything, please call," Emily offered quietly. "Even if it's just to fetch something for you. I'm not a guest, I'm family."

There were sudden tears in Susannah's eyes. "Thank you," she replied, turning away.

*E*mily slept well again, tired by the newness of her surroundings and the distress of realizing how very ill Susannah was. Father Tyndale had said that she was not going to live much longer, but that conveyed little of the real pain of dying. At only fifty she was far too young to waste away like this. She must have so much more yet to do, and to enjoy.

Emily got up too early to make breakfast for Susannah. She had no idea how long to wait. She made herself a cup of tea in the kitchen, listening to the wind buffeting the house, occasionally rising to a shrill whine around the edges of the roof.

She decided to explore. There did not seem to be

any part of the house that was specifically private; no doors were locked. She wandered from the dining room to the library, where there were several hundred books. She looked at titles and picked randomly off the shelves. It did not take her long to realize that at least half of them had been Hugo Ross's. His name was written on the flyleaves. They were on subjects Emily suspected Susannah might never have read without his influence: archaeology, exploration, animals of the sea, tides and currents, several histories of Ireland. There were also volumes on philosophy, and many of the great novels not only of England but also of Russia and France.

She began to regret that she would never meet the man who had collected these, and so clearly enjoyed them.

She looked on the mantelshelf, and the small semicircular table against the wall. There were cut-crystal candlesticks that might have been Susannah's, and a meerschaum pipe that could only have been Hugo's. It was left as if he had just put it down, not gone years ago.

There were other things, including a silver-framed photograph of a family group outside a low cottage, the Connemara hills behind them.

Emily went next into Hugo's study. There were haunting seascapes on the walls and there was still pipe tobacco in the humidor, an incomplete list of colors on a slip of paper, as if a reminder for buying paints. Had Susannah deliberately left these things because she wanted to pretend that he would come back? Perhaps she had loved him enough that it was not death she was afraid of, but something quite different, something against which there was also no protection.

If Jack had died, would Emily have done the same—left memories of him in the house, as if his life were so woven into hers that it could not be torn out? She did not want to answer that. If it were, how could she bear losing him? If it were not, then what fullness of love had she missed?

She went back to the kitchen, made breakfast of boiled eggs and fingers of toast, and took Susannah's upstairs for her. It was a fine day and the wind seemed to be easing. She decided to take her letters to the post office now. "I won't be more than an hour," she promised. "Can I bring you anything?"

Susannah thanked her but declined, and Emily set out along the road by the shore, which led a mile and a half or so to the village shop. The sky was almost clear and there was a strange, invigorating smell that she had not experienced before, a mixture of salt and aromatic plants of some kind. It was both bitter and pleasing. To her left the land seemed desolate all the way to the hills on the skyline, and yet there were always wind patterns in the grass and layers of color beneath the surface.

To her right the sea had a deep swell, the smooth backs of the waves heavy and hard, sending white-spumed tongues up the sand. There were headlands to either side, but directly out from the shore for as far as she could see there was only the restless water.

Gulls wheeled in the air above her, their cries blending with the sighing of the wind in the grass and the constant sound of the waves. She walked a little faster, and found herself smiling for no apparent reason. If this was what the local people thought of as a storm, it was nothing!

She reached the low, straggling houses of the village, mostly stone-built and looking as if they had grown out of the land itself. She crossed the wiry turf to the roadway and continued along it until she came to the small shop. Inside there were two other people waiting to be served and a small, plump woman behind the counter weighing out sugar and putting it into a blue bag. Behind her the shelves were stacked with all kinds of goods—groceries, hardware, and occasional household linens.

They all stopped talking and turned to look at Emily.

"Good morning," she said cheerfully. "I'm Emily Radley, niece of Mrs. Ross. I've come to spend Christmas with her."

"Ah, niece, is it?" a tall, gaunt woman said with a smile, pushing gray-blonde hair back into its pins with one hand. "My neighbor's granddaughter said you'd come."

Emily was lost.

"Bridie Molloy," the woman explained. "I'm Kathleen."

"How do you do?" Emily replied, uncertain how to address her.

"I'm Mary O'Donnell," the woman behind the counter said. "What can I be doing to help you?"

Emily hesitated. She knew it was unacceptable to push ahead of others. Then she realized they were curious to see what she would ask for. She smiled. "I have only letters to post," she said. "Just to let my family know that I arrived safely, and have met with great kindness. Even the weather is very mild. I fancy it will be much colder at home."

The women looked at each other, then back at Emily.

"Nice enough now, but it's coming," Kathleen said grimly.

Mary O'Donnell agreed with her, and the third woman, younger, with tawny-red hair, bit her lip and nodded her head. "It'll be a hard one," she said with a shiver. "I can hear it in the wind."

"Same time o' the year," Kathleen said quietly. "Exact."

"The wind has died down," Emily told them.

Again they looked at each other.

"It's the quiet before it hits," Mary O'Donnell said softly. "You'll see. The real one's out there waiting." She pointed towards the west and the trackless enormity of the ocean. "I'll have your letters, then. We'd best get them on their way, while we can."

Emily was a trifle taken aback, but she thanked her, paid the postage, and wished them good day. Outside again in the bright air, she started along the path back, and almost immediately saw ahead of her the slender figure of a man with his head turned towards the sea, walking slowly and every now and then stopping. Without hurrying she caught up with him.

At a distance, because of the ease with which he moved, she had thought him young, but now that she could see his face she realized he was probably sixty. His hair flying in the wind was faded and his keen face deeply lined. When he looked at her his eyes were a bright gray.

"You must be Susannah's niece. Don't be surprised," he observed with amusement. "It's a small village. An incomer is news. And we are all fond of Susannah. She wouldn't have been without friends for Christmas, but that isn't the same as family."

Emily felt defensive, as if she and Charlotte had been to blame for Susannah's situation. "She was the one who moved away," she replied, then instantly thought how childish that sounded. "Unfortunately, after my father died, we didn't keep in touch as we should have."

He smiled back at her. "It happens. Women follow the men they love, and distances can be hard to cross."

They were standing on the shore, the wind tugging at their hair and clothes, rough but mild, no cruelty in it. She thought the waves were a little steeper than when she had set out, but perhaps she was merely closer to them here on the sand.

"I'm glad she was happy here," she said impulsively. "Did you know her husband?"

"Of course," he replied. "We all know each other here, and have done for generations—the Martins, the Rosses, the Conneeleys, the Flahertys. The Rosses and Martins are all one, of course. The Conneeleys and the Flahertys also, but in an entirely different way. But perhaps you know that?"

"No, not at all?" she lifted her voice to make it a question.

He did not need a second invitation. "Years ago, last century, the Flahertys murdered all of the Conneeleys, except Una Conneeley. She escaped alive, with the child she was carrying. When he was born and grew up he starved himself to force her to tell him the truth of his birth." He glanced at her to make sure she was listening.

"Go on," Emily prompted. She was in no hurry to be back inside the house again. She watched the seabirds careening up the corridors of the wind. The smell of salt was strong in the air, and the surf pounding now white on the shore gave her a sense of exhilaration, almost of freedom.

"Well, she told him, of course," he continued, his eyes bright. "And when he was fully grown he came back here and found the Flaherty tyrant of the day living on an island in a lake near Bunowen." His face was vivid as if he recalled it himself. "Conneeley measured the distance from the shore to the island,

and then set two stones apart on the hillside, that exact space, and practiced until he could make the jump."

"Yes?" she urged.

He was delighted to go on. "Flaherty's daughter nearly drowned in the lake and young Conneeley rescued her. They fell in love. He jumped the water to the island and stabbed Flaherty's eyes out."

Emily winced.

He grinned. "And when the blind man then offered to shake his hand, the girl gave her lover a horse's leg bone to offer instead of his hand, which shows she knew her father very well. Flaherty crushed it to powder with his grip. Conneeley killed him on the spot, and he and Flaherty's daughter lived happily ever after—starting the whole new clan, which now peoples the neighborhood."

"Really?" She had no idea if he was even remotely serious; then she saw the fire of emotion in his face and knew that, for all his lightness of telling, he was speaking of passions that were woven into the very meaning of his life. "I see," she added, so that he would know she understood its validity.

"Padraic Yorke," he said, holding out his thin, strong hand.

"Emily Radley," she replied, taking it warmly.

"Oh, I know," he nodded. "Indirectly you are part of our history here, because you are Susannah's niece, and Susannah was Hugo Ross's wife." His voice dropped. "It hasn't been the same since he died."

She should have felt this was slightly imprisoning, but actually she was happy to be part of this enormous, wind-torn land, just for a season, and of its people who knew each other with such fierce intimacy.

Padraic Yorke started walking again, and she kept pace with him. He pointed out the various plants and grasses, naming them all, and telling her what would flower here in the spring, and what in the summer. He told her where the birds would nest, when their chicks would hatch and when they would fly. She listened not so much to the information, which she would never remember, but to the love of it in his voice.

It was a different world from London, but she

began to see that it had a unique beauty, and perhaps if you loved a man deeply enough, and he loved you, then it could be a good land. Perhaps in Susannah's place she would have come here too. Jack had asked nothing of her, no sacrifice at all, except the forfeit of a little of the social position gained from her first husband. She still had the money she had inherited from him in trust for their son.

Jack had asked for no change in her, no sacrifice, not even an accommodation of awkward relatives. She realized with a chill of dismay that she did not even know his parents, or any of the friends he had had before they met. It was always her family they turned to. The belonging was all hers.

For the first time in their years together, she recognized a loss, and she was not certain how deep it was. With her acknowledgement of it entered a fear she had not known before. There were things she needed to learn, bitter or sweet. The ignorance was no longer acceptable.

*W*hen Emily arrived back at the house and went into the drawing room, she found to her surprise that Susannah had visitors. A rather portly older woman, with a handsome face and hair as rich as polished mahogany, was sitting in one of the armchairs, and standing beside her was a man at least twenty years younger, but with a very similar cast of features, only in him they were even more becoming, and his eyes were a finer hazel brown.

Susannah was sitting opposite them, dressed in blue and with her hair coiled up elegantly. She looked very pale, but she appeared attentive and cheerful. Emily could only imagine what the effort must cost her. She introduced the visitors as Mrs. Flaherty and her son Brendan, explaining to them that Emily was her niece.

"Did you have a pleasant walk?" she asked.

"Yes, thank you," Emily replied, sitting in one of the other chairs. "I had not expected to find the shore so very beautiful. It is quite different from anything I know, much . . ." she searched for the right word.

"Wilder," Brendan Flaherty offered for her. "Like

241

a beautiful animal, not savage intentionally, just doesn't know its own strength, and if you anger it, it will destroy you, because that is its nature."

"You must excuse Brendan," Mrs. Flaherty apologized. "He's overfanciful. He doesn't mean to alarm you."

The color rushed up Brendan's cheeks, but Emily was certain it was embarrassment for his mother's intervention, not for his own words.

"I find it a perfect description." Emily smiled to take the correction out of her words. "I think it was the power of it I found beautiful, and in a way the delicacy. There were still some tiny wildflowers there, even at this time of the year."

"Glad you saw them today," Mrs. Flaherty said. "The storm will finish them. No idea how much sand it will put on top of everything. And weed, of course."

Emily could think of no adequate reply. The look of bleakness in Mrs. Flaherty's face made it impossible to be light about it.

"I met Mrs. O'Donnell at the shop," she said instead, "and posted my letters. And then on the way back I walked a little way with a most interesting man, a Mr. Yorke, who told me some stories about the village, and the area in general."

Brendan smiled. "He would. He's our local historian, sort of keeper of the collective spirit of the place. And something of a poet."

Mrs. Flaherty forced a smile as well. "Takes a bit of liberty," she added. "A good bit of myth thrown in with his history."

"True enough at heart, if not in every detail," Brendan said to Emily.

"You're too generous." His mother's voice was sharp. "Some of what is passed around as history is just malicious. Idle tongues with nothing better to do."

"There was nothing unpleasant," Emily said quickly, although that was a slight stretch of the truth. "Just old tales."

"That's a surprise," Mrs. Flaherty responded disbelievingly. She glanced at Brendan, then back to Emily. "I'm afraid we are a small village. We all know each other rather too well." She rose to her feet stiffly. "But I hope you'll enjoy yourself here. You're most welcome. We're all glad that Susannah has family to spend Christmas with her." She made herself smile, and it lightened her face until one could see an echo of the young woman she had once been, fresh, full of hope, and almost beautiful.

"I'm sure I shall, Mrs. Flaherty, but thank you for your good wishes."

Brendan bade her good-bye as well, holding her gaze for a moment longer as if he would say something else, but when his mother looked at him urgently, he changed his mind.

Emily had a sharp image of Mrs. Flaherty taking Brendan's arm, gripping it, not as if she needed his support but as if she dared not let him go.

When the door was closed and they were back inside, Emily looked more closely at Susannah.

"It's a good day," Susannah assured her. "I slept well. Did you really like the shore?"

"Yes, I did." Emily was pleased to be honest. She had a sudden conviction that Hugo had loved it, and it mattered to Susannah that Emily could see its beauty also. "And Mr. Yorke didn't say anything except a little history of the Flahertys long ago," she added.

Susannah lifted a hand in dismissal. "Oh, don't take any notice of Mrs. Flaherty. Her husband was a colorful character, but no real harm in him. At least that's what I choose to think, but I'm glad I wasn't married to him all the same. She adored him, but I think her memory must be a little kinder than the facts bear out. He was too handsome for his own good—or for hers."

"I can believe it," Emily agreed with a smile, thinking of Brendan walking away down the path with his easy stride.

Susannah understood her instantly. "Oh, yes, Brendan too. Naturally he took advantage of it, and she spoiled him, in his father's memory, I think."

"Did she remarry?" Emily asked.

Susannah's eyebrows shot up. "Colleen Flaherty? Good heavens, no! As far as she's concerned, no one could fill Seamus's shoes. Not that I think anyone tried! Too busy guarding Brendan from what she saw as his father's weaknesses. Mostly women, the drink, and an overdose of imagination, so I gather. She's terrified Brendan'll go the same way. I don't think she's doing him a kindness, but it wouldn't help to say so."

"And will he go the same way?" Emily asked.

Susannah looked at her, for a moment her eyes frank, almost probing, then she turned away. "Maybe, but I hope not. From what Hugo used to say, Seamus Flaherty was a nightmare to live with. People with that kind of charm can jerk you up and down like a puppet on the end of a string. Sooner or later the string will break. Are you ready for lunch? You must be hungry after your walk."

"Yes, I am. I'll make lunch, if you like?"

"Maggie was here and it's all done," Susannah replied.

"Really?" Emily gestured towards the window. "In spite of the storm?" She smiled.

"It'll come, Emily." Susannah shuddered, her whole body closing in on itself as if she had wrapped her arms around it. "Maybe tonight."

*B*y dusk the wind was very definitely rising again, and with a different sound from before. The keening was higher, a more dangerous edge to it. Darkness came very early and Emily noticed as she put things away after dinner that there were cold places in the house. In spite of all the windows being closed, somehow the air from outside found its way in. There seemed to be no lull between the gusts, as though nothing could rest anymore.

The curtains were drawn closed, but Susannah kept looking towards the windows. There was no rain to hear, just the wind and occasionally the sudden hard bang as a twig hit the glass.

They were both happy to go to bed early.

"Perhaps by morning it will have blown itself out," Emily said hopefully.

Susannah turned a white face towards her, eyes filled with fear. "No, it won't," she said quietly, the wind almost drowning her words. "Not yet. Maybe not ever."

Emily's common sense wanted to tell her that that was stupid, but she knew it would not help. Whatever Susannah was talking about, it was something far more than the wind. Perhaps it was whatever she was really afraid of, and the reason she had wanted Emily here.

Emily thought as she undressed that in London Jack would be at the theater, possible enjoying the interval, laughing with their friends at the play, swapping gossip. Or would he not have gone without her? It wouldn't be the same, would it?

Surprisingly, she went to sleep fairly quickly, but she woke with a jolt. She had no idea what time it was, except that she was in total darkness. She could see nothing whatever. The wind had risen to a high, constant scream.

Then it came—a flare of lightning so vivid that it lit the room even through the drawn curtains. The thunder was all but instantaneous, crashing around and around, as if it came from all directions.

For a moment she lay motionless. The lightning blazed again, a brief, spectral glare, almost shadow-less, then it was gone and there was only the roaring of thunder and shrill scream of the wind.

She threw the covers off and, picking up a shawl

from the chair, went to the window. She pulled the curtains back but the darkness was impenetrable. The noise was demonic, louder without the muffling of the curtains. This was ridiculous; she would have seen as much if she had stayed in bed with the covers over her head, like a child.

Then the lightning struck again, and showed her a world in torment. The few trees in the garden were thrashing wildly, broken twigs flying. The sky was filled with roiling clouds so low they closed in as if to settle on the earth. But it was the sea that held her eyes. In the glare it seethed white with spume, heaving as if trying to break its bounds and rise to consume the land. The howl of it could be heard even above the wind.

Then the darkness returned as if she had been blinded. She could not see even the glass inches from her face. She was cold. There was nothing to do, nothing to achieve, and yet she stood on the spot as if she were fixed to it.

The lightning flared again, at almost the same moment as the thunder, sheets of colorless light across the sky, then forks like stab wounds from heaven to the sea. And there, quite clearly out in the bay, was a ship struggling from the north, battered and overwhelmed, trying to make its way around the headland to Galway. It was going to fail. Emily knew that as surely as if it had already happened. The sea was going to devour it.

She felt almost obscene, standing here in the safety of the house, watching while people were destroyed in front of her. But neither could she simply turn around and go back to bed, even if what she had seen were a dream and would all have vanished in the morning. They would be dying, choking in the water while she lay there warm and safe.

It was probably pointless to waken Susannah, as if Emily were a child who could not cope with a nightmare alone, and yet she did not hesitate. She tied the shawl more tightly around her and went along the corridor with a candle in her hand. She knocked on Susannah's bedroom door, prepared to go in if she were not answered.

She knocked again, harder, more urgently. She heard Susannah's voice and opened the door.

Susannah sat up slowly, her face pale, her long

hair tousled. In the yellow light of the flame she looked almost young again, almost well.

"Did the storm disturb you?" she asked quietly. "You don't need to worry; the house has withstood many like this before."

"It's not for me," Emily closed the bedroom door behind her, a tacit signal she did not mean to leave. "There's a ship out in the bay, in terrible trouble. I suppose there's nothing we can do, but I have to be sure." She sounded ridiculous. Of course there was nothing. She simply did not want to watch its sinking alone.

The horror in Susannah's eyes was worse than anything Emily could have imagined.

"Susannah! Is there somebody you know on it?" she went forward quickly and grasped Susannah's hands on the counterpane. They were stiff and cold.

"No," Susannah replied hoarsely. "I don't think so. But that hardly makes it different, does it? Don't we all know each other, when it matters?"

There was no answer. They stood side by side at the window staring into the darkness, then as the lightning came again, a searing flash, it left an imprint on the eyes of a ship floundering in cavernous waves, hurled one way and then another, struggling to keep bow to the wind. As soon as they were tossed sideways they would be rolled over, pummeled to pieces and sucked downwards forever. The sailors must know that, just as Emily did. The two women were watching something inevitable, and yet Emily found her body rigid with the effort of hope that somehow it would not be so.

She stood closer to Susannah, touching her. Susannah took her hand, gripping it. The ship was still afloat, battling south towards the point. Once it was out of sight, would anyone ever know what had happened to them?

As if reading Emily's thoughts, Susannah said, "They're probably bound for Galway, but they might take shelter in Cashel, just beyond the headland. It's a big bay, complicated. There's plenty of calm water, whichever way the wind's coming."

"Is it often like this?" Emily asked, appalled at the thought. Susannah did not answer.

"Is it?"

"Once before . . ." Susannah began, then drew in her breath in a gasp of pain so fierce that Emily all but felt it herself as Susannah's fingers clenched around hers, bruising the bones.

Emily stared out into the pitch-darkness, and then the lightning burned again, and the ship was gone. She saw it in a moment of hideous clarity, just the mast above the seething water.

Susannah turned back to the room. "I must go and tell Fergal O'Bannion. He'll get the rest of the men of the village out. Someone . . . may be washed ashore. We'll need to . . ."

"I'll go." Emily put her hand on Susannah's arm, holding her back. "I know where he lives."

"You'll never see your way . . ." Susannah began.

"I'll take a lantern. Anyway, does it really matter if I get the right house? If I wake someone else, they'll get Fergal. Can we do anything more than give them a decent burial?"

Susannah's voice was a whisper forced between her lips. "Someone could be alive. It has happened before . . ."

"I'll go and get Fergal O'Bannion," Emily said. "Please keep warm. I don't suppose you can go back to sleep, but rest."

Susannah nodded. "Hurry."

Emily went back to her room and dressed as quickly as she could, then took a lantern from the hall and went out of the front door. Suddenly she was in the middle of a maelstrom. The wind shrieked and howled like a chorus of mad things. In the lightning she could see trees breaking as if they were plywood. Then the darkness was absolute again, until she raised the lantern, shining a weak yellow shaft in front of her.

She went forward, picking her way on the unfamiliar path, having to lean all her weight against the gate to force it open. On the road she stumbled and felt a moment of terror that she would fall and smash the lantern, perhaps cut herself. Then she would be utterly lost.

"Stupid!" she said aloud, although she could not hear her own words in the bedlam of the elements. "Don't be so feeble!" she snapped at herself. She was on dry land. All she had to do was keep her feet, and walk. There were people out there being swallowed by the sea.

She increased her pace, holding the lantern as high as she could until her arm ached and she was weaving around in the road as the wind knocked her off her path, then relented suddenly and left her pushing against nothing.

She was gasping for breath as she finally staggered to the doorway of the first house she came to. She really didn't care whether it was Fergal O'Bannion's or not. She banged many times, and no one answered. She backed away and found several pebbles from the garden and threw them up at the largest window. If she broke it she would apologize, even pay for it. But she would have smashed every window in the house if it gave her even a chance of helping any of those men out there in the bay.

She flung them hard and heard them clatter, the last one cracked ominously.

A few moments later the door opened and she saw Fergal's startled face and rumpled hair. He recognized Emily immediately. "Is Mrs. Ross worse?" he asked hoarsely.

"No. No, there's a ship gone down in the bay," Emily gasped. "She said you'd know what to do, in case there were any survivors."

A sudden fear came into his face and he stood motionless in the doorway.

"Do you?" her voice cracked in panic.

He looked as if she had struck him. "Yes. I'll get Maggie to get the others. I'll set out for the shore, in case . . ." He did not finish the sentence.

"Can anyone really survive this?" she asked him.

He did not answer, but retreated into the house, leaving the door wide for her to follow. A few moments later he came down the stairs again fully dressed, Maggie behind him.

"I'll fetch everyone I can," she said, after briefly acknowledging Emily. "You go to the shore. I'll get blankets and whiskey and we'll bring them. Go!"

White-faced, he picked up a lantern and stepped out into the night.

Emily looked at Maggie.

"Come with me," Maggie said without hesitation. "We'll get who else we can." She lit another lantern, pulled her shawl around her, and went out also.

Together they struggled along the road, although it would not be as bad here as on the shore. Maggie pointed to one house and told Emily the name of the people in it, while she went to one farther along. One by one, shouting and banging, occasionally throwing more stones, they raised nearly a dozen men to go down along the beach, and as many women to get whiskey and blankets, and cans of stew off the stove and chunks of bread.

"Could be a long night," Maggie said drily, her face bleak, eyes filled with fear and pity. In twos and threes they made their way across the hummocks of grass and sand. Emily was confused by how many houses they had missed out. "Would they not come?" she asked, having to shout above the clamor. "Surely anyone would help when people are drowning. Do you want me to go back and try?"

"No." Maggie reached out and took her arm, as if to force her forward, into the wind. They were closer to the water now and could hear the deep roar of it like a great beast.

"But—" Emily began.

"They're empty," Maggie shouted back. "Gone."

"All of them?" That was impossible. She was speaking of almost half the village. Then Emily remembered Father Tyndale's apology for the sparseness of the place now, and a great hollowness opened up as if at her feet. The village was dying. That was what he had meant.

Another flare of lightning burned across the sky and she saw the enormity of the sea far closer than she had imagined. The power and savagery of it was terrifying, but it was also beautiful. She felt a kind of bereavement when the flare died and again she could see nothing but the bobbing yellow lanterns, the fold of a skirt, a leg of trouser, and a swaying movement of sand and grass below. Several of the men had great lengths of rope, she wondered what for.

They were strung out along the beach, some closer to the white rage of the water than she could bear to look at. What could they do? The strongest boat ever built could not put to sea in this. They would be smashed, overturned, and dragged under before they were fifty yards out. That would help no one.

She looked at Maggie.

Maggie's face was set towards the sea, but even in the wavering gleam of the lantern Emily could see the fear in her, the wide eyes, the tight muscles of her jaw, the quick breathing.

She looked away, along the shore, and saw in the next flash the large figure of Father Tyndale, the farthest man along the line.

"I'll take the Father some bread and whiskey," Emily offered. "Or does he not . . . ?"

Maggie forced a smile. "Oh, he wouldn't mind in the least," she assured her. "He gets as much cold in his bones as anyone else."

With a brief smile Emily set out, leaning into the wind, pushed and pulled by it until she felt bruised, her feet dragging in the fine sand, the noise deafening her. She judged where she was by the slope of the shore, and every now and then climbed a little higher as the wind carried the spray and she was drenched. The thunder was swallowed up by the noise of the waves, but every lightning flare lit up the whole shore with a ghastly, spectral clarity.

She reached Father Tyndale, shouting to him just

as another huge wave roared in and she was completely inaudible. She held out the whiskey and the packet of bread. He smiled at her and accepted it, gulping down the spirits and shuddering as the fire of it hit his throat. He undid the parcel of bread and ate it hungrily, ignoring the sea spray and wind-driven rain that must have soaked it. Even in the smothering darkness in between the lightning flares, he never seemed to have moved his gaze from the sea.

Emily looked back the way she had come, seeing the string of lanterns, each steady as if they were gripped hard. No one appeared to move. She had no idea what time it was, or how long since she had woken and seen the ship.

Did this happen every winter? Was that why they had spoken of the storm with such dread, nights waiting for the sea to regurgitate its dead? Perhaps people from the surrounding villages, whom they knew?

The wind had not abated at all, but now there were gaps between the lightning and the thunder that followed it. Very slowly the storm was passing.

Then, after three flashes of sheet lightning, two of the lanterns were raised high in the air and swung in some kind of a signal. Father Tyndale gripped Emily's arm and pulled her along as he started to run, floundering in the sand. She scrambled after him, hanging on to her lantern.

By the time they reached the spot where the signal had been given, four men were already roped together and the leading one was fighting his way against the waves deeper into the sea, battered, pummeled, but each flare of lightning showed him farther out.

It seemed an endless wait, but in fact it was probably little more then ten minutes before the others started heaving on the rope and backing farther up the beach onto the weed-laced shore. The women huddled together, lanterns making a pool of light on the sodden men as one by one they were hauled ashore, exhausted, stumbling to their knees before gasping, and turning back to help those still behind them.

The last man, Brendan Flaherty, was carrying a body in his arms. Others reached forward to help

him, and he staggered up the sand to lay it gently beyond the sea's reach. Father Tyndale clasped his
shoulder and shouted something, lost in the wind
and roar of the water, then bent to the body.

Emily looked at the villagers' faces as they stood
in a half-circle, the yellow flares of the lanterns
under-lighting their features, hair wet and wind-
whipped, eyes dark. There was pity in their knowledge of death and loss, but more than anything else
she was touched again by the drenching sense of
fear.

She looked down at the body. It was that of a
young man, in his late twenties. His skin was ashen
white, a little blue around the eye sockets and lips.
His hair looked black in this lantern light, and it
clung to his head, straggling across his brow. He was
quite tall, probably slender under the seaman's
jacket and rough trousers. Above all, he was handsome. It was a dreamer's face, a man with a world inside his head.

Emily wanted to ask if he was dead, against her
will imagining how it had happened, but she dreaded
the answer. She looked one by one at the ring of faces

around her. They were motionless, gripped by pity, and more than that, by horror.

"Do you know him?" Emily asked, a sudden lull in the wind making it seem as if she were shouting at them.

"No," they answered. "No . . ."

And yet she was certain that they were looking at something they had half expected to see. There was no surprise in them at all, no puzzlement, just a dreadful certainty.

"Is he dead?" she asked Father Tyndale.

"No," Father Tyndale answered. "Here, Fergal, help me get him up on my shoulder, and I'll carry him to Susannah's. We'll need to get him warm and dry. Maggie, will you stay with him? And Mrs. Radley, no doubt?"

"Yes, of course," Emily agreed. "We're by far the closest, and we have plenty of room."

❧

*W*hen they reached the house Susannah must have been up and looking out of the window, because she opened the door before anyone knocked. The young man was carried upstairs, awkwardly, booted feet scraping and numb hands knocking against the banisters. He was laid on the floor and the women asked to leave. Susannah had already put out a nightshirt, presumably one of Hugo's she had kept. Emily wondered if she had kept all his clothes.

There were no sheets on the bed, only blankets. "Shall I—" Emily began.

"Blankets are warmer," Susannah cut across her. "Sheets later, when the blood's flowing again." She looked down at the young man's face and there was sadness in her own, and fear, as if something long-dreaded had happened at last.

Then they excused themselves and went to get bowls of hot soup for the men, and all the dry woolens and socks they could find. The men would all have to go back again. There could be more people washed up, dead or alive.

The rest of the night Emily spent taking turns with Maggie O'Bannion to watch the young man, rub his hands and feet, change the oven-warmed stones wrapped in cloths in the bed, and looking for any signs of returning consciousness. No one had any idea how much water he had swallowed, and there were dark bruises and abrasions on his chest, legs, and shoulders, as if he had been driven up against the wreckage again and again.

"I can't manage two of you to nurse," Maggie said tartly when Susannah tried to argue about staying to help. "Nor can Mrs. Radley. She's come to visit you, not to watch you waste yourself away to no purpose."

Susannah obeyed with a bleak smile, her eyes meeting Emily's before she turned away.

"Maybe I shouldn't have spoke harshly to her." Maggie looked guilty. "But she's—"

"I know," Emily responded. "You did the right thing."

Maggie smiled briefly and bent to wrap some hot stones in flannel. But Emily had seen the tension in her, the tight shoulders and the quick averting of her eyes.

Later, towards six o'clock in the morning, the young man still had not stirred, but he was definitely warmer and his pulse quite strong. It was not dawn yet and Emily set out to take more whiskey and hot meals down to the men waiting on the shore, watching for the sea to yield more bodies.

She found them easily by the yellow light of their lanterns. The waves were crashing like huge avalanches of water, breaking on the sand and roaring higher and higher as the tide swept in. They hissed out long white tongues of foam right into the grass, as if trying to tear out its roots.

Emily went first to Father Tyndale. In the yellow lantern light he looked exhausted, his large frame somehow hunch-shouldered, his face bleak.

"Ah, thank you, Mrs. Radley." He accepted the hot drink, but took of it sparingly to leave plenty for the others. "It's a hard night." He did not look at her as he spoke but out over the ocean. "Has he woken yet?"

"No, Father. But he looks better."

"Ah."

She searched his expression, but the wavering light was deceptive and she could read nothing. He handed the flask back, and she took it to Brendan Flaherty, then Fergal O'Bannion, and on around the rest of them. Finally she walked back towards the house, so tired it was hard to keep upright against the wind. She thought of Jack at home in bed in London. How much was he missing her? Had he even the remotest idea what he had asked of her, he would not have done it—would he?

She slept for perhaps an hour. It seemed almost impossible to climb out of the depths of unconsciousness when Maggie shook her and spoke her name. At first Emily could not even remember where she was.

"He's awake," Maggie said quietly. "I'm going to get him something to eat. Perhaps you'd sit with him. He seems a bit distressed."

"Of course." Emily realized she still had most of her clothes on, and she was stiff as if she had walked miles. Then she remembered the storm. The wind was howling and keening in the eaves, but less violently than before. "Did he say anything? Did you tell him he was the only one?" she asked.

"Not yet. I'm not sure how he'll take it." Maggie looked guilty, and Emily knew she was afraid to do it. She shivered and reached for her shawl. In all that had happened last night, she had not thought to add peat to the fire, and it had gone out. The air was chill.

She went to the room where the young man was, knocked, and went in without waiting for an answer. He was lying propped against the pillows, his face still ashen, eyes dark and hollow. She walked over and stood beside him.

"Maggie's gone to get you something to eat," she said. "My name is Emily. What is yours?"

He thought for several moments, blinking solemnly. "Daniel," he said at last.

"Daniel who?"

He shook his head and winced as though it hurt. "I don't know. All I can remember is the water all around me. And men calling out, fighting, to . . . to stay alive. Where are they?"

"I don't know," she said honestly. "I'm sorry, but you were the only one we found. We stayed on the beach all night, but no one else was washed up."

"They all drowned?" he said slowly.

"I'm afraid it seems so."

"All of them." There was deep pain in his face and

his voice was very quiet. "I can't remember how many there were. Five or six, I think." He looked at her. "I can't even think of the ship's name."

"I expect it'll come back to you. Give yorself a little time. Do you hurt anywhere?"

He smiled with a grim humor. "Everywhere, as if I'd taken the beating of my life. But it'll pass." He closed his eyes, and when he opened them again they were full of tears. "I'm alive." He reached out his hands, strong and slender, and clasped them over the softness of the quilt, digging into its warmth.

Maggie came in with a dish of porridge and milk. "Let me help you with this," she offered. "I daresay it's long enough since you had anything inside you." She sat down and held the bowl in her hands, offering him the spoon. Emily saw that in spite of the fact that she was smiling, her knuckles were white.

Daniel looked at her and clasped the spoon. Slowly he filled it and raised it to his mouth. He swallowed, then took some more.

Maggie continued to watch him but her eyes were concentrated on something far away, as if she had no need to focus anymore to know what she would see.

She still gripped the dish tightly, and Emily watched her chest rise and fall and the pulse beat in her throat.

*E*mily went back to bed briefly, this time falling asleep immediately. She woke to find Susannah beside her with a tray of tea and two slices of toast. She set it down on the small table and drew the curtains wide. The wind was moaning and rattling, but there were large patches of blue in the sky.

"I sent Maggie home for a little sleep," Susannah said with a smile as she poured the tea, a cup for each of them. "The toast is for you," she added. "Daniel has eaten some more, and gone back to sleep again, but when I looked in on him he was disturbed. I'm sure he must be having nightmares."

"I imagine he will for years." Emily sipped her tea and picked up a slice of the crisp hot-buttered toast. "Now I see why everyone so dreaded the storm."

Susannah looked up quickly, then smiled and said nothing.

"Do they come like this often?" Emily went on.

Susannah turned away. "No, not often at all. Do you feel well enough to go to the store and get some more food? There are a few things we will need, with an extra person here."

"Of course," Emily agreed. "But he won't stay long, will he?"

"I don't know. Do you mind?"

"Of course not."

But later, as she was walking along the sea front towards the village, Emily wondered why Susannah had thought the young man would stay. Surely as soon as he had rested sufficiently, he would want to be on his way to Galway, to contact his family, and the people who owned his ship. His memory would return with a little more rest, and he would be eager to leave.

She came over the slight rise towards the shore and looked out at the troubled sea, wracks of white spume spread across it, the waves, uncrested now in the falling wind, but still mountainous, roaring far up the shore and into the grass with frightening speed, gouging out the sand, consuming it into itself.

271

It was the shadowless gray of molten lead, and it looked as solid.

At the shop she found Mary O'Donnell and the woman who had introduced herself as Kathleen. They stopped talking the moment Emily walked in.

"How are you, then?" Kathleen asked with a smile, as if now that Emily had endured the storm she was part of the village.

Mary gave her a quick, almost guarded look, then as if it had been only a trick of the light, she turned to Emily also. "You must be tired, after last night. How's the young sailor, poor soul?"

"Exhausted," Emily replied. "But he had some breakfast, and I expect by tomorrow he'll be recovering well. At least physically, of course. He'll be a long time before he forgets the fear, and the grief."

"So he's not badly hurt, then?" Kathleen asked.

"Bruised, so far as I know," Emily told her.

"And who is he?" Mary said softly.

There was a sudden silence in the shop. Mr. Yorke was in the doorway, but he stood motionless. He looked at Kathleen, then at Mary. Neither of them looked at him.

"Daniel," Emily replied. "He seems to have forgotten the rest of his name, just for the moment."

The jar of pickles in Mary O'Donnell's hands slipped and fell to the floor, bursting open in splintered glass. No one moved.

Mr. Yorke came in the door and walked over to it. "Can I help you?" he offered.

Mary came to life. "Oh! How stupid. I'm so sorry." She bent to help Mr. Yorke, bumping into him in her fluster. "What a mess!"

Emily waited; there was nothing she could do to help. When the mess was all swept and mopped up, the pickles and broken glass were put in the bin, and there was no more to mark the accident than a wet patch on the floor and a smell of vinegar in the air. Mary filled Emily's list for her and put it all in her bag. No one mentioned the young man from the sea again. Emily thanked them and went out into the wind. She looked back once, and saw them standing together, staring after her, faces white.

She walked back along the edge of the shore. The tide was receding and there was a strip of hard, wet sand, here and there strewn with weed torn from the bottom of the ocean and thrown there by the waves. She saw pieces of wood, broken, jagged-ended, and found herself cold inside. She did not know if they were from the ship that had gone down, but they were from something man-made that had been broken and drowned. She knew there were no more bodies. Either they had been carried out to sea and lost forever, or they were cast up on some other shore, perhaps the rocks out by the point. She could not bear to think of them battered there, torn apart and exposed.

In spite of the wild, clean air, the sunlight slanting through the clouds, she felt a sense of desolation settle over her, like a chill in the bones.

She did not hear the steps behind her. The sand was soft, and the sound of the waves consumed everything else.

"Good morning, Mrs. Radley."

She stopped and twisted round, clasping the bag closer to her. Father Tyndale was only a couple of yards away, hatless, the wind blowing his hair and making his dark jacket flap like the wings of a wounded crow.

"Good morning, Father," she said with a sense of relief that surprised her. Who had she been expecting? "You . . . you haven't found anyone else, have you?"

"No, I'm afraid not." His face was sad, as if he too were bruised.

"Do you think they could have survived? Perhaps the ship didn't go down? Maybe Daniel was washed overboard?" she suggested.

"Perhaps." There was no belief in his voice. "Can I carry your shopping for you?" He reached out for it and since it was heavy, she was happy enough to pass it to him.

"How is Susannah this morning?" he asked. There was more than concern in his face—there was fear. "And Maggie O'Bannion—is she all right?"

"Yes, of course she is. We're all tired, and grieved for the loss of life, but no one is otherwise worse."

He did not answer; in fact he did not even acknowledge that he had heard her.

She was about to repeat it more vehemently, then she realized that he was asking with profound anxiety, the undercurrent of which she had felt increasingly since the wind first started rising. He was not asking about health or tiredness, he was looking for something of the heart that battled against fear.

"Do you know the young man who was washed ashore, Father Tyndale?" she asked.

He stopped abruptly.

"His name is Daniel," she added. "He doesn't seem to remember anything more. Do you know him?"

He stood staring at her, buffeted by the wind, his face a mask of unhappiness. "No, Mrs. Radley, I have no idea who he is, or why he has come here." He did not look at her.

"He didn't come here, Father," she corrected him. "The storm brought him. Who is he?"

"I've told you, I have no idea," he repeated.

It was an odd choice of words, a total denial, not merely the ordinary claim of ignorance she had expected. Something was wrong in the village. It was dying in more than numbers. There was a fear in the air that had nothing to do with the storm. That had been and gone now, but the darkness remained.

"Perhaps I should ask you what Daniel means to

these people, Father," Emily said suddenly. "I'm the stranger here. Everyone seems to know something that I don't."

"Daniel, is it?" he mused, and a lull in the wind made his voice seem loud.

"So he says. You sound surprised. Do you know him as something else?" She heard the harshness of her words, the edge of her own fear showing through.

"I don't know him at all, Mrs. Radley," he repeated, but he did not look at her, and the misery in his genial face deepened.

She put her hand on his arm, holding on to him hard, obliging him either to stop, or very deliberately to shake her off, and he was too well mannered to do that. He stopped in front of her.

"What is it, Father Tyndale?" she asked. "It's the storm and Daniel, and something else. Everybody's afraid, as if they knew there was going to be a ship go down. What's wrong with the village? What is it that Susannah really wants me here for? And don't say it's family at Christmas. Susannah was estranged from the family. Her love was Hugo Ross, and perhaps this place and these people. This is where she was happiest in her life. She wants me here for something else. What is it?"

His face filled with pity. "I know, my dear, but she is asking more than you can do, more than anyone can."

She tightened her fingers on his arm. "What, Father? I can't even try if I don't know what it is."

He gave a deep sigh. "Seven years ago there was another storm, like this one. Another ship was lost out in the bay; it too was trying to beat its way around to Galway. That night too, there was just one survivor, a young man called Connor Riordan. He was washed ashore half dead, and we took him in and nursed him. It was this time of the year, a couple of weeks before Christmas." He blinked hard, as if the wind were in his eyes, except that he had his back to it.

"Yes?" Emily prompted. "What happened to him?"

"The weather was very bad," Father Tyndale went on, speaking now as if to himself as much as to her. "He was a good-looking young man, not unlike this one. Black hair, dark eyes, something of the dreamer in him. Very quick, he was, interested in everything. And he could sing—oh, he could sing. Sad songs, all on the half note, the half beat. Gave it a kind of haunting sound. He made friends. Everyone liked him—to begin with."

Emily felt a chill, but she did not interrupt him.

"He asked a lot of questions," Father Tyndale went on, his voice lower. "Deep questions, that made you think of morality and belief, and just who and what you really were. That's not always a comfortable thing to do." He looked up at the sky and the shredded clouds streaming across it. "He disturbed both dreams and demons. Made people face dark things they weren't ready for."

"And then he left?" she asked, trying to read the tragedy in his face. "Why? Surely that wasn't a bad thing? He went back home, then probably out in another ship."

"No," Father Tyndale said so quietly the wind all but swallowed his words. "No, he never left."

She crushed on the fear rising inside her. "What do you mean? He's still here?"

"In a manner of speaking."

"Manner . . . what kind of manner?" Now that she had asked, she did not want to know. But it was too late.

"Over there." He lifted his hand. "Out towards the point, his body's buried. We'll never forget him. We've tried, and we can't."

"His family didn't . . . didn't come and take his body?"

"No one knew he was here," Father Tyndale said simply. "He came from the sea one night when every other soul in his ship was lost. It was winter, and the wind and rain were hard. No one from outside the village came here during those weeks, and we knew nothing of him except his name."

The cold was enlarging inside her, ugly and painful. "How did he die, Father?"

"He drowned," he replied, and there was a look on his face as if he were admitting to something so terrible he could not force himself to say it aloud.

There was only one thought in Emily's mind, but she too would not say it. Connor Riordan had been murdered. The village knew it, and the secret had been poisoning them all these years.

"Who?" she said softly.

He could not have heard her voice above the wind in the grass. He read her lips, and her mind. It was the one thing anyone would ask.

"I don't know," he said helplessly. "I'm the spiritual father of these people. I'm supposed to love them and keep them, comfort their griefs and heal their wounds, and absolve their sins. And I don't know!" His voice dropped until it was hoarse, painful to hear. "I've asked myself every night since then, how can I have been in the presence of such passion and such darkness, and not know it?"

Emily ached to be able to answer him. She knew the subtle and terrible twists of murder, and how often nothing is what it seems to be. Long ago her own eldest sister had been a victim, and yet when the truth was known, she had felt more pity than rage for the one so tormented that they had killed again and again, driven by an inner pain no one else could touch.

"We don't," she said gently, at last letting go of Father Tyndale's arm. "I knew someone quite well, once, who killed many times. And when in the end everything was plain, I understood."

"But these are my people!" he protested, his voice trembling. "I hear their confessions. I, above all, know their loves and hates, their fears and their dreams. How can I listen to them, and yet have no idea who has done this? Whatever it was, they could have come to me, they should have known they could!" He spread his hands. "I didn't save Connor's life, and infinitely worse than that, I didn't save the soul of whoever killed him. Or those who are even now protecting him. The whole village is dying because of it, and I am powerless. I don't have the faith or the strength to help."

She could think of nothing to say that was not trite and would sound as if she had no understanding of his pain.

He looked down at the sand shifting and blowing about their feet. "And now this new young man has come, like a revisiting of death, as if it were all going to happen again. And I am still useless."

Emily hurt for him, for all of them. Now she understood what it was that Susannah wanted resolved before she died. Did she think Emily could do it because of the times she and Charlotte had involved themselves in Pitt's cases? They had found facts, but she had no idea how to detect from the beginning, understand what mattered and what didn't, and put everything in its right place to tell a story. Always a tragic story.

Hugo Ross had been alive when Connor Riordan had been here. What had he known? Was Susannah afraid that he had been involved somehow, shielding someone from the law because they were his own people? Or was she afraid that they would blame Hugo, once she was gone and could no longer protect his memory?

Emily wanted to help, with a fierceness that consumed and amazed her, but she had no idea how.

Father Tyndale saw it in her face. He shook his head. "You can't, my dear. I told you that. Don't blame yourself. I have known these people all of their lives, and I don't know. You've come here just days ago from a foreign land—how could you?"

But that was no comfort to Emily as she unpacked the shopping on the kitchen table for Maggie to put away.

She went into the drawing room, to find Daniel up

and dressed in clothes that were far too big for him, but at least were of the right length. They must have been Hugo Ross's, and one look at Susannah's face confirmed it to her.

"Thank you for your care, Mrs. Radley," Daniel said with a smile that gave him a sudden warmth and that kind of acute but gentle intelligence that comes with humor. "I feel fine, except for a good many aches and some bruises a prizefighter would be proud of." He shrugged. "But I still can't remember much, except choking and freezing, and thinking I was going to die."

"What did the other men call you?" Emily asked curiously.

He hesitated, racking his memory. "Daniel, I suppose. That's all I can remember."

"And them?" she pressed.

"There was a . . . a Joe, I think." He frowned. "There was a big man with a lot of tattoos. I think his name was Wat, or something like that. Are they all gone? Are you sure?"

"We don't know," Susannah answered him. "We

waited all night, but no one else was washed up here. I'm sorry." Her voice was gentle but her eyes searched his face. What was she looking for, traces of a lie? A memory of something else? Or did she see in him the ghost of Connor Riordan and the tragedy he awakened?

"What day is it?" Daniel asked suddenly, looking from Susannah to Emily, and back again.

"Saturday," Emily replied.

"There must be a church here. I saw a priest. I'd like to go to Mass tomorrow. I need to thank God for my own deliverance and, more than that, I must pray for the souls of my friends. Perhaps God will grant me my memory back. No man should die so alone that his name is not said by those who survived."

"Yes, of course," Susannah said immediately. "I'll take you. It isn't far."

Emily clenched inside. "Are you sure you are well enough?" She wanted to find any way, any excuse for her not to. It was natural that Daniel should wish to go and say Mass for his comrades—what decent man would not? He had almost certainly never heard of Connor Riordan, whose death had nothing to do with this storm, or this loss. But the village could see ghosts in his face, and one person at least would feel guilt.

"Yes, of course," Susannah said a trifle sharply. "We'll all feel better tomorrow."

But in the morning Susannah was so weak that when she came into the kitchen she had to clutch at the back of a chair to keep from losing her balance and falling.

Emily leaped to her feet and caught her, steadying her with both arms and easing her to sit.

"I'm all right!" Susannah said weakly. "I just need a little breakfast. Have you seen Daniel this morning?"

"Not yet, but I heard him up. Susannah, please go back to bed. You aren't well enough to walk to church. The wind is still strong."

"I told you," Susannah said sharply, "I'll feel far better when I've had a cup of tea and something to eat—"

"Susannah," Emily cut across her, commanding her attention, "you can't go to church like this. It will embarrass everyone, mostly you. We should be there to thank God for Daniel's life, and to pay our respects to those who were lost, whoever they were."

"Daniel can't go alone . . ." Susannah started.

"I'll go with him. The church can't be difficult to find."

"You're not Catholic," Susannah pointed out. There was a very slight smile in her eyes. "I know you don't even approve, never mind believe."

"Do *you*?" Emily asked. "Or was it for Hugo?"

Susannah smiled ruefully. "To begin with it was for Hugo. But afterwards, it was for myself." Her voice dropped. "Especially after Hugo died. I believed it because he had. It reminded me of all that he was."

Emily felt an overwhelming sorrow for her. And she realized with a stab of ugly surprise that she knew Jack's politics in detail. She had helped him in all kinds of projects and battles and she was proud of what he had achieved. But she had no idea what his religious beliefs were. They both went to church on

287

most Sundays, but so did everyone else. They had never discussed why.

"This would be a good time for me to look," she said aloud. "Ignorance is not a reason for disbelieving anything."

"But you don't know—"

"Why you want to go?" Emily finished for her. "Yes I do. Father Tyndale told me."

Susannah looked confused. "Told you what? About the church?"

"No, about Connor Riordan—seven years ago."

"Oh! He told you . . ."

"Isn't that why you wanted me here?" Emily persisted. "To help you look for the truth?"

"I didn't know there was going to be a storm this bad," Susannah said quietly, her face ashen. "And no one could have known Daniel would come."

"Of course not. But you still needed to know who killed Connor and be sure in your own heart that Hugo was not protecting someone he cared for out of loyalty, or pity."

Susannah was so pale it seemed as if there could be no blood under her skin. Emily felt pierced by guilt, but to retreat now would leave the matter torn open, yet still unresolved, worse than if she had not touched it.

"I'll take Daniel to church," she repeated. "I'll watch, and tell you what happens. Don't worry about luncheon. There's cold meat, and a few vegetables will take no time at all."

She walked along the road beside Daniel, who was dressed in one of Hugo's better suits. It was too large for him, but he made no comment on it except to smile at himself, and touch the texture of the cloth with appreciation.

They spoke little. Daniel was still weak and bruised, and it took him both effort and self-discipline to move with the appearance of ease, and to keep up a reasonable pace against the wind.

Emily thought of her family at home, and wondered with a touch of self-mockery what Jack would think if he could see her walking briskly along a rough road in a village she did not know, accompanying a young man washed up by the sea. And to crown it all, she was taking him to a Catholic church. It could hardly be what he had intended when he had coerced her into leaving her children at Christmas!

Then as the wind buffeted her and blew her skirts, almost knocking her off balance, she thought of Susannah and her marriage to Hugo Ross, and wondered if her father had ever met Hugo, or if he had shut Susannah out without knowing what she had chosen instead of a conventional marriage he would have approved of, and she would have hated. She had done that once, obediently, in her youth. The death of her first husband had freed her. She had married Hugo for love. Losing him took the heart from her life. She walked on alone towards that horizon beyond which they would be together again.

Emily and Daniel reached the low stone church and went inside. It was only half full, as if it had been built for a far larger congregtion. She saw a startled look on Father Tyndale's face, and that was possibly what caused several other people to turn and stare as she and Daniel found seats towards the back. She recognized the women from the shop, sitting with men and children who must be their families. She also saw Fergal and Maggie O'Bannion, and

Mrs. Flaherty with Brendan beside her, head bent. She knew him only from his thick, curling hair. She thought the straggling gray head belonged to Padraic Yorke.

Beside her Daniel said nothing but kneeled slowly in silent prayer. She wondered if any memory at all had come back to him of the shipmates he had lost, and she ached for his confusion and what must be a consuming loneliness.

She found the service alien, and seemed always to be a step behind everyone else, and yet reluctantly she had to admit there was a beauty in it, and a strange half familiarity, as if once she might have known it. Watching Father Tyndale solemnly, almost mystically, blessing the bread and the wine, she saw him in a different light, far more than a decent man doing what he could for his neighbors. For that short space he was the shepherd of his people, and she saw the pain in his face with a dreadful clarity.

But she was here to observe for Susannah. While the service was continuing she could watch only from behind. Fergal and Maggie O'Bannion sat very close to each other, he constantly adjusting his weight so

that his arm touched hers, she leaning away from
him whenever she could, as though she felt crowded.
Did they feel as apart as that suggested?

Mrs. Flaherty had a hand quite openly on Brendan's arm, and once Emily saw him deliberately
shake it off, only for his mother to replace it a few
moments later. Emily glanced sideways at Daniel,
and saw that he had noticed also. Was that chance?
Looking at his solemn face, with its huge, hollow
eyes and sensitive mouth, all humor gone from it
now, he seemed to be studying the people as much as
she was.

After the service it was the same. She saw Fergal
and Maggie standing side by side talking to Father
Tyndale, looking as if they were physically so close
only by accident. Both of them seemed uncomfortable. Something here disturbed them rather than offered them the sweetness of God's redemption of
man. She looked at Daniel, and the thought came to
her that exactly the same perceptions were in his
mind.

Brendan Flaherty was talking to a young woman,

and his mother was hovering nearby, making movements as if she would interrupt. A middle-aged woman intruded. Mrs. Flaherty flashed back at her with something that was clearly sharp, from the expressions of all of them. The girl blushed. The woman who spoke took a step backwards, and Brendan himself was hurt and turned away, leaving his mother standing defensively, but with no one to shield.

Fergal O'Bannion said something to him, mockery in his face, and put his hand over Maggie's. She froze, distress clear in her eyes. She said something to Fergal and closed her other hand over his. Watching them, Emily was certain it was restraint, not affection.

Brendan said something lightly, his voice too soft for Emily to hear anything of it. Maggie smiled and lowered her eyes. Fergal altered the way he was standing so that somehow in the moving of weight he had become vaguely belligerent.

Brendan looked at Maggie, and Emily thought she saw a tenderness in his expression that brought a shiver of awareness to her of a hunger far deeper than friendship. Then she looked again, and there was nothing more than a pleasant courtesy, and she was not sure she had seen anything at all.

She turned to Daniel to see if he had noticed it, but he was watching Padraic Yorke.

"It seems to have caught them hard," Daniel said to her quietly.

She did not understand.

"The ship," he explained. "Do you suppose they knew some of the men? Or their families, maybe?"

"I don't think we know who they were," she answered. "Not that it matters. Anyone's death is a loss just the same. You don't have to have known them to feel it."

"There's a weight in the air," he said slowly. "As if a spark of lightning would set it afire. It's good people, they are." His voice was so soft she barely heard it. "To grieve so much for those they never knew. I guess that there's a common humanity in the best of us, and there's nothing like death to draw the living together." He bit his lip. "But I still wish I could mourn my fellows by name."

Emily said nothing. It was not the loss of the others from the ship that haunted the village; it was the murder of Connor Riordan, and the certainty that it was one of them who was responsible.

"Of course," she said after a moment's hesitation. The dead from the ship were his only connection with who he was, all that he had been and had loved. Without them he might never know again that part of himself. All they had endured together, the laughter, the triumph, and the pain, could be lost. "I'm sorry," she added with profound feeling.

He smiled suddenly, and it changed every aspect of his face. Suddenly she could see in him the boy he had been a few years ago.

"But I'm alive, and it's poor thanks to the Good Lord who saved me if I'm not grateful for that, don't you think?" Then without waiting for her answer he walked towards the nearest small huddle of people and introduced himself, telling how much he appreciated their hospitality, and the courage of the men who had spent all night in the gale to bring him in alive.

She watched as he went to every person or group, saying the same thing, searching their faces, listening to their words. It occurred to Emily that it was almost as if he were trying desperately to find some echo of familiarity among them, someone who knew seamen, knew disaster, and understood him.

As they were drifting away and only half a dozen were left, she stood on the rough pathway between the gravestones and was only yards from where Father Tyndale was saying good-bye to an old gentleman with white hair, like down on the weed heads. Father Tyndale's eyes seemed to look beyond the man's face to where Daniel was talking to Brendan Flaherty, and she saw in him horror, as if this were what had happened before, in the days leading up to Connor Riordan's death.

❦

*E*mily and Daniel walked home slowly along the road. Daniel seemed tired, and she knew from the way he kept adjusting Hugo's coat on his shoulders that his body still ached from the bruises. Perhaps he was lucky that the wreckage hurled about by the sea had not injured him more. He seemed lost in thought, as if the underlying pain of the village had added to his own.

It could not go on like this. Someone must find the truth of Connor Riordan's death. Whatever it was, it had to be better than the corroding doubt. Daniel's presence had made the fear sharper than before, as if he had unknowingly woken it from sleeping.

He spoke suddenly, startling her. "You're not Catholic, are you." It was a statement.

"No," she said with surprise. "Sorry. Was I so out of place?"

He grinned. He had beautiful teeth, very white and a little uneven. "Not at all. It's good to see it through the eyes of a stranger once in a while. We take it all for granted too easily. Was your aunt a Catholic before she came here and married?"

"No."

"That's what I thought. It's a big thing she did. She must have loved him very much. I'd lay money— if I had any—that Connemara is not like where she came from."

"You'd win," she conceded, smiling back at him.

"More than double, I expect," he said ruefully. "And your family wouldn't be pleased."

"No. My father—he's dead now—he was very upset."

He looked at her, and she had the uncomfortable feeling that he knew she was evading the truth, making her part in it look kinder than it had been.

"You're Church of the English," he concluded.

"Yes."

"It's a big thing, so I've heard, this difference between us. I don't know enough about the Church of the English to understand that. Is it so very different, then?"

"It's a matter of loyalty," she replied, repeating what her father had said. "The first is to our country."

"I see." He looked puzzled.

"No you don't!" She was not managing to say what she meant. "It's your loyalty to Rome that's the problem."

"Rome, is it? I thought it was to God . . . or Ireland?"

He was laughing at her, but she found it impossible to resent. Put like that, it was absurd. The whole estrangement was foolish, not about loyalties at all. Obedience and conformity were closer to the truth of it.

"You've not visited her here before?" he observed.

It would be pointless to deny it. She was obviously a stranger.

"She's ill now." That was obvious too. She had made it sound as if that was the only reason she had come, and would not have were Susannah well. But then that also was true. In fact she would not even have now if Jack had not coerced her. It was his opinion of her that had made the difference. She cared what he thought of her more than she had realized. But that was none of Daniel's business either.

"And you've come to look after her?" he said.

"No. I've come to be with her over Christmas."

"It's a good time to forgive," he said with a slight nod.

"I'm not forgiving her," Emily snapped.

He winced.

"I'm not forgiving her because there's nothing to forgive," she said angrily. "She's a right to marry anyone she chooses."

"But your father had someone else in mind for her? Someone from the Church of the English? Perhaps with money?" He looked at Emily's fine woolen cape with its neat fur collar, then at her polished leather boots, suffering a little on the rough road.

"No, he didn't. Our family is comfortable, not more than that. My first husband had money, and a title. He died."

"I'm sorry." His compassion was instant.

"Thank you. But I love my second husband very much." She sounded defensive and she heard it in her own voice.

"Has he money and a title as well?" Daniel asked.

"No he hasn't!" She said it as if it had been faintly insulting to ask. "He has neither, nor any prospects. I married him because I love him. He is a Member of Parliament and he does some very fine work."

"And is your father very happy, then? Oh . . . I forgot. You said he was dead too. Did he mind you marrying a man with no title or prospects?" He was keeping exact step with her on the rough road. "Did you dare his anger, like your aunt Susannah? I see now why you are here with her. You have a natural sympathy. Not exactly a black sheep of the family, but at least one of a different color?"

She wanted to laugh, and be furious, and she was embarrassed because she had taken a wild risk in marrying Jack Radley. He had had no money at all, and she had had a great deal, but even more than that, he flirted outrageously, and made his way by being such an entertaining guest at other people's house parties that he hardly ever had to pay towards the roof over his head. But he was fun, he was kind, and when things were hard and dangerous, he was brave. The best qualities within himself he had discovered after they were married.

But she had accepted him without having to dare her father's wrath, or lose a penny of her own money inherited as a widow. Would she have had the courage to marry Jack even if it had not been so easy? She hoped so, but she had not had to prove it. Compared with Susannah she was shallow, and yet she had passed judgment so easily.

"It's very good of you to be here, over Christmas especially," Daniel interrupted her thoughts. "Your husband will miss you."

"I hope so," she said with an intensity of feeling that surprised her. Would Jack be missing her? He had been very quick to insist that she go. She tried to recall the last few weeks before that letter from Thomas had arrived. How close had she and Jack been, beyond the courtesy of habit? He was always agreeable. But then he was to everyone. And as she had just reminded herself, it was she who had the money. Or more correctly, it was her son Edward— George's son, not Jack's. Ashworth Hall, and all that went with it, was her inheritance only through him.

Was Jack missing her? Or might he perhaps be enjoying himself accepting the sympathy, and the hospitality, of half the women in London who found him nearly as attractive as Emily did?

She became unpleasantly aware that Daniel was watching her, studying her face as if he could read her emotions in it. She had given herself away with "I hope so."

"He will be looking after my children," she said a

little abruptly. Then she wished she had said "our children." "Mine" sounded proprietorial, defensive. But to go back and correct it would make her sound even more vulnerable.

"Very good of you," he repeated. "Has Susannah children? She does not speak of them, and there are no pictures."

"No, she doesn't."

"So there is only you?"

"Not at all!" That sounded awful, as if she had abandoned Susannah all those years. "My mother is traveling in Europe and my sister is unwell."

"She is an invalid?"

"Not at all. She is very healthy indeed, she simply has a touch of bronchitis."

"So she will miss the Christmas parties too."

"She does not go to parties very much. She is married to a policeman—of high rank." She did not know why she added that last bit. Pitt had been quite lowly when Charlotte had married him. She too had married for love, not caring much what anyone else thought. And looking back, Emily missed the days when she and Charlotte had played a part in some of

Pitt's most difficult cases. Since he had been in Special Branch, such help had been rarely possible. Balls, theater, dinners were all fun, but lacking in depth after a while, a superficial world, full of wit and glamour, but no passion.

"I've hurt you," Daniel said with contrition. "I'm sorry. You have been so kind to me I wished to know you better. I think I asked insensitive questions. Please forgive me."

"Not at all," Emily lied, needing immediately to deny that he had struck any truths. She had no unhappiness, and he mustn't think she had. She looked at him to make sure he understood. He was smiling, but she could not read what lay behind his eyes. She was left thinking that he had understood her far better than she wished.

With a sudden and very painful clarity she remembered what Father Tyndale had said about Connor Riordan asking questions, exposing the vulnerable so it could no longer be lied about or ignored. Whose dreams had he stripped so unbearably? Had he even known he was doing it? Was it now happening again, beginning with her?

Should she pursue it? Dare she? The alternative might be worse: cowardice that would allow the village to die. She would have to bend her mind very seriously to detecting, not merely skirt around the edges, beginning fears and doubts, and completing nothing. She could awaken even uglier things than were stirring. Once begun, it would be morally impossible to stop before all the truth was laid bare. Was she ready for that? Was she even competent to do such a thing, let alone deal with the results?

She would very much rather not tell Susannah—she had more than enough distress to deal with—and yet Emily could not succeed without her help. She realized as she said that to herself that she had already made up her mind. Failure might be a tragedy, but not to attempt it was defeat.

❧

*E*mily did not get the opportunity to speak to Susannah alone until afternoon teatime when Daniel had gone back to sleep, still aching from his deep bruises and finding himself overcome by tiredness, and perhaps as much by grief. She had given little thought to the loneliness he must be feeling, the loss to which he could put no names or faces, only a consuming void.

Emily and Susannah sat by the fire with tea and scones, butter, jam, and cream. Emily missed the bright flames of a coal or log fire, but she was growing used to the earthy smell of peat.

She told Susannah of the morning at church, and then of her walk back with Daniel, the questions he had asked and how his probing had disturbed her thoughts, making her realize what Father Tyndale had meant of Connor Riordan.

Susannah sat still for a long time without replying, her face bleak and troubled.

"Is that not what you wanted me here for really?" Emily asked gently, leaning forward a little. She disliked being quite so blunt, but she had no idea how long they had in which to pursue this.

"Actually I wrote to Charlotte," Susannah said apologetically. "But that was before Thomas told me that you actually helped him quite a lot as well, in the beginning. I'm sorry. That's ungracious, but we have no time left for polite evasions."

"No," Emily agreed. "I need your help. Are you wishing to give it? If not, let us agree that we do nothing."

Susannah winced. "Do nothing. That sounds so . . . weak, so dishonest."

"Or discreet?" Emily suggested.

"In this case that is a euphemism for cowardly," Susannah told her.

"What are you afraid of? That it will have been someone you like?"

"Of course."

"Isn't knowing it's one person better than suspecting everybody?"

Susannah was very pale, even in the glow of the candlelight. "Unless it is someone I care for especially."

"Like Father Tyndale?"

"It couldn't be him," Susannah said instantly.

"Or someone Hugo cared for?" Emily added. "Or protected?"

Susannah smiled. "You think I am afraid it was him, to protect the village from Connor's probing eyes."

"Aren't you?" Emily hated saying it, but once the question was asked, evasion was as powerful as an answer.

"You didn't know Hugo," Susannah said softly, and her voice was filled with tenderness. It was as if the years since his death vanished away and he had only just gone out of the door for a walk, not forever. "It's not my fear you are speaking about, my dear, it is your own."

Emily was incredulous. "My own? It doesn't matter to me who killed Connor Riordan, except as it affects you."

"Not your fear of that," Susannah corrected. "Your doubts about Jack, wondering if he loves you, if he's missing you as much as you hope. Perhaps a little realization that you don't know him as well as he knows you."

Emily was stunned. Those thoughts had barely even risen to a conscious level of her mind, and yet here was Susannah speaking them aloud, and the denial that rose to her lips would be pointless. "What makes you think that?" she said huskily.

Susannah's expression was very gentle. "The way you speak of him. You love him, but there is so much of which you know nothing. He is a young man, barely forty, and yet you have not met his parents, and if he has brothers and sisters, you say nothing of them, and it seems, neither does he. You share what he does now, in Parliament and in society, but what do you know or share of who he was before you met, and what has made him who he is?"

Suddenly Emily had the feeling that she was on the edge of a precipice, and losing her balance. This was the night of the Duchess's dinner. Was Jack there? Who was he sitting beside? Did he miss her?

Susannah touched her softly, just with the tips of her fingers. "It is probably of little importance. It does not mean it is anything ugly, but the fact that you do not know suggests that it frightens you. I don't believe it is that you don't care. If you love him, all that he is matters to you."

"He never speaks of it," Emily said quietly. "So I do not ask. I made my family serve for both of us."

She looked up at Susannah. "You love Hugo's people, don't you? This village, this wild country, the shore, even the sea."

"Yes," Susannah answered. "At first I found it hard, and strange, but I became used to it, and then as its beauty wove itself into my life, I began to love it. Now I wouldn't like to live anywhere else. And not just because Hugo lived and died here, but for itself. The people have been good to me. They have allowed me to become one of them and belong. I don't want to leave them with this unresolved, whatever the answer is. I don't want to go with it unfinished."

"Then help me, and I will do anything I can to find the answer," Emily promised.

❖

*E*mily started to think about it seriously that evening, but she was too tired after so much missed sleep with the storm, and it was the following morning before she felt her mind was clear enough to be sensible.

She went for a brisk walk, this time not towards

the village but in the opposite direction, along the shore and around where the rock pools were, and the wind rustling in the grass.

After seven years the questions of means and opportunity to kill Connor Riordan would be difficult, or even impossible to answer. The only clues would lie in motive. Whose secrets could Connor Riordan have known that were dangerous enough, and painful enough for him to be killed? Had he known anyone in the village before he was washed up that night?

When Maggie O'Bannion came to clear out the fires, and do some of the other heavy jobs, such as the bed linen, Emily decided to help her, partly because she felt uncomfortable doing nothing, but actually more to give her the chance to speak naturally with Maggie as they worked together.

"Oh, no, Mrs. Radley, I can do it myself for sure," Maggie protested at first, but when Emily insisted she was happy enough. Emily did not tell her how long it was since she had done any housework of her own, although Maggie might have guessed from her clumsiness to begin with.

"Daniel seems to be recovering," Emily remarked as they put the towels into the big copper boiler in the laundry room, and added the soap. "Although it's taking time."

" 'Course it is, poor boy," Maggie agreed, smiling when she saw Emily's surprise that it was bought soap, not homemade.

Emily blushed. "I can remember making it," she said, although Maggie had made no remark.

"Mr. Ross always did things very nicely," Maggie replied. "Went to Galway once a fortnight at least, and got the best things for her, right up until he died."

"He wasn't ill?" Emily asked.

"No. All of a sudden, it was. Heart attack, out there on the hillside. Died where he'd have wanted to. And a better man you'll never meet."

"His family is from around here?" Now Emily was sweeping the floor with the broom, a job she could hardly mishandle. Maggie was busy mixing ingredients to make more furniture polish. It smelled of lavender, and something else, sharper and extremely pleasant.

"Oh, yes," Maggie said enthusiastically. "A cousin of Humanity Dick Martin, he was."

"Humanity Dick?" Emily was amused, but had no idea who she was talking about. A local hero, presumably.

"King of Connemara, they called him," Maggie said with a smile, her shoulders a little straighter. "Spent his whole life saving animals from cruelty. Over in London, most of the time."

"Are they worse to animals in London than here?" Emily tried to keep the offense out of her voice.

"Not at all. He was a Member of Parliament, and that's where they change the laws."

"Oh, yes, of course." She made a mental note to ask Jack if he had heard of Humanity Dick. But now she must bring the conversation back to the thing she needed to know. "Daniel still hasn't any memory yet." She felt as if she were being ungraciously obvious, but she could think of no subtler way of approaching it. "Do you suppose the ship was making for Galway? Where would it have come from?"

"You're thinking we should see what we can do to help him," Maggie said thoughtfully. "Thing is, it could have been anywhere: Sligo, Donegal, or even farther than that."

"Does his accent tell you nothing?" Emily asked. "I don't know in Ireland, but at home I might have an idea. I would at least know Lancashire from Northumberland."

"And would that help you, then?" Maggie said with interest. "I heard England was a very big place, with millions of people."

Emily sighed. "Yes, of course you're right. It wouldn't help much. But Ireland has far fewer, hasn't it?" That was only a polite question. She knew the answer.

"Yes, but it's different being a seaman. They pick up expressions from all over the place, and accents too, sometimes. I'm not good at it. I can hear he's not from this bit of coast, but it doesn't even have to be north that he's from, does it? It could be anywhere. Cork, or Killarny, or even Dublin."

Emily bent and brushed up the dirt into a dustpan, not that there was much. It was a gesture rather than a real task. "No, you are right. He could be from anywhere. Were most of the people in the village born here?"

"Just about all. Mr. Yorke comes from Galway, I think, but I daresay his family are from one of the villages closer. His roots are deep. If you want to know the history, he's the man to ask. It's not just the tales he can tell you, but the meanings behind them." She smiled a little ruefully. "All the old feuds between the Flahertys and the Conneeleys, the good works of the Rosses and the Martins—and the bad too—and the love stories and the fights going back to the days of the Kings of Ireland in the time before history."

"Really? Then I must see if he will tell me." Emily accepted the idea, although it was not the ancient past she was seeking. Again she tried to bring the conversation back to the present. "The Flahertys seem interesting. What was Seamus Flaherty like? I gather Brendan takes after him a lot?"

Maggie avoided her eyes and started to watch what she was doing with great care. "Oh, I suppose so," she said casually, but there was a tension in her voice. "In a superficial sort of way. He certainly looks like him. Same eyes, same way of walking, as if he owned the world, but was happy for you to have a share in it."

Emily smiled. "Did you like him?" she asked.

Maggie was silent, her back stiff, her hands moving more slowly.

"Seamus, I mean," Emily clarified.

"Oh, well enough, I suppose." Maggie started to move briskly again. "As long as you didn't take him too seriously, he was fine enough."

"Seriously?"

"Well, you couldn't trust him," Maggie elaborated. "Charm the birds out of the sky, he could, and make you laugh till you couldn't get your breath. But half of what he said was nonsense. Got the moon in his eyes, that one. And drank most men under the table."

"An eye for the women?" Emily asked bluntly.

Maggie blushed. "Oh, for sure. That was one thing you could rely on. That, and a fistfight."

Emily did not need to ask if Mrs. Flaherty had loved him; she had seen it in her face. Behind the overprotection of her son, the slight distance she placed between herself and others, there was a deep vulnerability. Now its explanation was easy to see.

But Emily also heard in Maggie's voice a tenderness, a self-consciousness that betrayed her too, not for the father, but for the son. Was that also a defense of one of their own, a man too easily misunderstood by an English stranger? Or was it more than that?

She bent her attention to helping complete the household tasks. Maggie did the ironing, quite a skilled work when the two flatirons had to be heated alternately on the stove, and used at a narrow range of temperatures, not so hot so it scorched the linen, nor too cool to press out the creases.

Emily peeled and sliced vegetables and set them in cold water until Maggie was ready to make the stew.

*I*n the afternoon Emily walked along the shore to the shop. They needed more tea, sugar, and a few other things. The air was fresh and crisp, but with no sting of ice in it, as there would have been in London. It was still westerly off the ocean, and the salt and kelp were in every breath. The sky was clouded far out to sea, but overhead it was clear blue with only a few thunderclouds towering in bright drifts, moving slowly, dazzling white.

The shore itself was uneven, sand obliterating some of the old grass and flower-strewn stretches, dunes moved from one place to another as if she had mistaken where they had been. Here and there were tangles of weed, some kelp torn up from the deep beds and left dark and untidy on the sand. She could not help seeing the jagged ends of wood poking out of them, splinters of the ship that had gone down, as if the sea could not digest it but had cast it back. It was a kind of monument to human daring, and grief.

It was when she stopped to stare at one of the larger pieces, pale, raw ends of wood jutting up through the black tangle of weed, that she became aware of Padraic Yorke standing a little behind her. She turned and looked into his eyes, and saw a reflection of the same overwhelming sadness that she felt, and of the fear that the power and beauty of the sea gives rise to when one lives through all its moods.

"Do you get wrecks like this every winter?" she asked.

"Not only winter," he replied. "But the storms are very rarely as bad as this one was." His face looked pinched, hollow around the eyes, and she wondered if he too was thinking of that other storm, seven years ago, and the young man who had been washed up then, and had never left.

"Daniel still can't remember anything," she said impulsively. "Do you think anyone here could help?"

"How?" He was puzzled. "No one knows him, if that's what you mean? He isn't related to anyone in the village, or any of the other villages around." He smiled bleakly. "Everyone is related to everyone else, or knows who is. It's a wild country. Its people belong. They have to. He isn't from anywhere in the west of Connemara, Mrs. Radley."

It seemed a preposterous thing to say, an assumption he could not have reason to make. And yet she believed him. "You know the land well enough to say that?"

His face lit. "Yes, I do. I know the land, and all the people who live here, and their history." He gazed around him, narrowing his eyes a little as he looked across the high tussock grasses where the wind knifed through them, tugging, swaying, and rippling all the way to the hills against the horizon. The colors changed, moving with every shadow. One moment paler, the next undershot with darkness, then a faint patina of gold.

Perhaps he saw some momentary wonder in her face, or possibly he had been going to speak anyway. "Before you leave, you must go to the bog," he told her. "At first it'll seem desolate to you, but the longer you look, the more you will see that every yard of it shows you some flower, some leaf, a beauty that'll haunt you always after that."

She smiled in spite of herself. "I'd like to. Thank you. But tell me about the people. I can't understand the land without knowing some of the people it shaped."

They had left the splintered wood and tangles of weed, but she was happy to walk slowly. She had all afternoon, and she wanted to learn what he had to say.

"Is Brendan Flaherty really so wild?" she said with a slight smile. "Of course I only saw the charming side of him, when he and his mother visited Susannah."

Mr. Yorke gave a shrug, lifting one shoulder more than the other, making the gesture oddly humorous. "He used to be, but there's no harm in him. He pushed the rules to the limit, and beyond, when he was younger. No scrape in the village he wasn't involved in, one way or another. And no pretty girl he didn't flirt with. How far any of that went I don't know, and I didn't ask. I suppose he was over the edge, at times. But that's what happens when you're young."

"But not real trouble?" Emily found herself defensive, remembering sharply the flash of hurt she had seen in Brendan's eyes.

"Of course not," Mr. Yorke said ruefully. "His mother would always see to that. She spoiled him

321

from the beginning. And after his father died, nothing was too good for him."

"How do you mean?" She needed to understand, not to assume. Could Connor have challenged Brendan in some way, and having always been given anything he wanted, Brendan could not bear losing? Had there been a fight, a flare of temper, blows, and suddenly Connor was dead? Mrs. Flaherty would have covered for Brendan, excused him, lied for him, as she had always done. Perhaps believing it was an accident, Hugo Ross would have too.

Was it necessary? Or did they fear that Brendan was going to show that element beyond indiscipline, the true selfishness that destroys? Was it fear that Emily had seen in Colleen Flaherty's face when she watched her son, or only an anxiety that others would believe of him what they had witnessed in his father?

Was it true? And had Connor Riordan come into the village, with vision not clouded by history and excuses, and seen Brendan more clearly than the others? Or was Mrs. Flaherty's fear only her own experience with the husband she was so in love with, crowding out the truth that Brendan was another man, a different one. She could not cling on to her husband, or put right what may have been wrong, revisit the old failings.

Was that what Emily had seen in Brendan's eyes? A fear that he was turning into his father, with his father's weaknesses? Or a fear that his mother would neither see him for himself, or allow him to be free of Seamus's ghost, and still love him?

Was she still protecting him because he needed it, or because *she* did? Did she feed his weaknesses so he would still need her, rather than curbing them?

Had Connor seen that, and probed the wound? Sometimes legends matter more than reality, dreams more than truth. Would Daniel see it too?

"Thank you, Mr. Yorke," Emily said suddenly. "You are right. I may very well come to see a beauty in the bog that I had not thought possible."

She went on quickly now, aware that she was cold. She was glad to reach the shop and go inside where it was agreeably warm.

"Good day to you, Mrs. Radley," Mary O'Donnell said with a smile. "A bit chill it is, for sure. Now what can I get for you? I have some nice heather honey, which I saved for poor Mrs. Ross. Very fond of it, she is. And it'll do her good." She bent down and picked a jar from below the counter. "And a dozen fresh eggs," she went on. "What with that poor creature washed up by the sea, an' all, you'll be cooking more than usual. How is he, then?"

"Bruised," Emily replied. "I think he was a bit more seriously injured than he said at first. But he'll recover."

"And stopping here in the meantime, no doubt." Mary pulled her lips tight.

"Where would he go?" Emily asked.

"Some mother's missing him," Mary responded. "God comfort the poor creature."

Emily put the shopping into her basket and paid for it. "The shop is quiet this afternoon," she observed, allowing a slight look of concern into her expression.

Mary's gaze moved away, as if caught by something else, except there was nothing, no movement except the wind.

"It'll get busy later, I daresay," she said with a smile.

Emily knew she would learn nothing if she did not ask. "I met Mr. Yorke along the beach. He was telling me something of the history of the village."

"Oh, he would," Mary agreed, relieved to have something general to talk about. "Knows more than anyone about the place."

"And the people," Emily added.

The light vanished from Mary's eyes. "That too, I suppose. By the way, Mrs. Radley, I have half a loaf of bread here for Mrs. Flaherty. If you're going that way, would you mind dropping it in for her?" She produced a bag, carefully wrapped. It was not quite an invitation to conclude the conversation, but the suggestion was there.

Emily seized it. "Of course. I would be happy to."

Immediately Mary gave her directions to the Flaherty house.

"You can't miss it," she said warmly. "It's the only

one along that road with stone gateposts and two trees in the front. And would you mind taking a pound of butter at the same time?"

❧

*M*rs. Flaherty looked startled to see Emily on the doorstep.

Emily held out the loaf and the butter, explaining how she came to have them.

Mrs. Flaherty took them and invited Emily, who had remained standing on the doorstep, in to have a cup of tea. Emily accepted immediately.

The kitchen was warm from the big stove against the wall, and the polished copper pans gave it a comfortable feeling, along with strings of onions hanging from the ceiling beams, the bunches of herbs and the blue and white china on the old wooden dresser.

"What a lovely room," Emily said spontaneously.

"Thank you." Mrs. Flaherty smiled. She pushed the kettle over onto the hob and started taking down cups and saucers. She had gone to the larder to fetch milk when a movement outside the window caught Emily's eye. She was staring into the garden, watching Brendan Flaherty deep in conversation with someone just beyond her sight when Mrs. Flaherty returned. She glanced outside and saw Brendan, and her face filled with a kind of exasperated pride as she looked at him. He was holding up a carved wooden frame, such as might have fitted around a painting.

"His father made that," Mrs. Flaherty said quietly. "Seamus had wonderful hands, and he loved the wood. Knew the grain of it, which way it wanted to go, as if it spoke to him."

"Has Brendan the same gift?" Emily asked, watching as Brendan's hand caressed the piece he held.

A shadow crossed Mrs. Flaherty's face. "Oh, he's like his father inasmuch as one man can be like another." Her voice was low and hollow with a kind of regret, and in that moment Emily had a sudden awareness of Mrs. Flaherty's loneliness, and how different it was from Susannah's. It was incomplete, there were doubts in it, things unresolved.

Then Brendan moved and Emily saw that it was

Daniel he was talking to. Daniel laughed and held out his hand. Brendan gave him the wooden frame. Daniel's eyes met his, and he said something. Brendan put his hand on Daniel's shoulder.

Mrs. Flaherty dropped the cups and saucers the short distance onto the table with a clatter and strode to the back kitchen door. She threw it open and went outside.

Brendan turned, startled. His hand dropped from Daniel's shoulder. He looked embarrassed. Daniel simply stared at Mrs. Flaherty as if she were incomprehensible.

She snatched the carved frame out of his hands. "That isn't Brendan's to give," she said hoarsely. "None of his father's work is. I don't know what you want here, young man, but you aren't getting it."

"Mother—" Brendan began.

She turned on him. "You don't give away your father's work until you can equal it!" she told him fiercely, her voice shaking.

"Mother—" Brendan began again.

Daniel cut across him. "He wasn't giving me anything, Mrs. Flaherty. He only showed it to me. He's proud of his father, as you would want him to be."

Mrs. Flaherty's cheeks were flaming now. She was confused, wrong-footed without knowing how it had happened, and still angry.

"Perhaps I had better walk Daniel home, and not trouble you just now," Emily interrupted. "I'll accept your invitation for tea another time." She could see the hot embarrassment in Brendan's face as he glared at his mother, and the next moment looked away, searching for words without finding them.

"Thank you," Daniel accepted, looking at Emily, then taking a step towards her. He swiveled slightly and smiled at Brendan, with gentleness and a quick flash of amusement in it. Then touching Emily lightly on the arm, he guided her along the path to the gate, and the road.

As Emily latched the gate behind them, she saw Brendan and Mrs. Flaherty arguing fiercely. Once Mrs. Flaherty jabbed her finger towards the road, without looking or seeing Emily staring at her. Brendan was shouting back, but she could not hear the words, only his shaking head made it clear he was denying something.

Daniel was looking at her. "Poor Brendan," he said sadly. "Competing with the ghosts?"

"Ghosts?" she asked as they began to walk back along the road towards the shore. "His father. Who else?"

"I don't know," he replied with a quick smile. "Whoever it was that he liked, and his mother is so afraid of."

He was right. It had been fear she had seen in Mrs. Flaherty's eyes. Why? Was it an unsuitable friendship? Was she jealous, afraid of losing some part of him—his time, his attention, his need? Might someone else take from her the role of his protector?

Or was she afraid of something that Brendan might do? Did it concern Connor Riordan's death? Was that why the sight of his friendship with Daniel had woken such fear in her? History repeating itself?

Later in the afternoon, Emily made the opportunity to speak to Susannah alone, and tried to find the words to ask her.

"Daniel seems to have made something of a friendship with Brendan Flaherty," she remarked casually.
They were standing in the drawing room looking out
of the long window at the storm-battered garden.

"Oh, really?" Susannah said with some surprise.

Emily seized on it. "Mrs. Flaherty was very upset.
She disapproved so violently she practically ordered Daniel to leave, and it embarrassed Brendan
acutely."

Susannah looked confused. "Are you sure?"

"Yes. Does that have anything to do with Connor
Riordan?"

"How could it?"

"Were they friends too?"

"Are you asking me if Brendan killed him?" Susannah said in surprise. "I have no idea. I can't think
why he would."

Emily refused to give up. "We don't know why
anyone would, but it is inescapable that somebody
did. Why is Mrs. Flaherty so protective of Brendan?
You know them. Was his father really so wild, and is
Brendan the same? He seems very likable to me, and
more gentle than Mrs. Flaherty."

Susannah smiled. "Seamus Flaherty was a drinker, a brawler, and a womanizer. Mrs. Flaherty is afraid Brendan will be the same. He looks like his father, but I don't know that it's much more than that."

"He isn't married, though," Emily pointed out. "Does he have girls in the different villages? Or one after another?"

Susannah was amused. "Not more than most young men, so far as I know. But if he did, that might get him killed, but not Connor Riordan."

Emily abandoned the pursuit, and went for a walk in the fading sun, watching it die over the sea in the long winter twilight. She heard the crunch of footsteps on the gravel and Daniel came up the shore towards her. The wind had stung some color into his cheeks and his dark hair was tangled. He climbed up the slithering shingle to where she stood, and waited beside her for several moments before speaking. The fading light sharpened his features, making the hollow of his cheeks more pronounced, the lines of his mouth and the lean curve of his throat. He was almost beautiful.

Emily was achieving nothing. She had tried subtlety and observation. Time was closing in. Perhaps in a few days Daniel would go, or even worse, Susannah's health would fail and Emily would not learn what had happened to Connor Riordan in time. The village remained steeped in its poison.

"Did Brendan Flaherty make a sexual advance towards you?" she said impulsively, and was shocked at her own directness.

Daniel's mouth dropped open and he stared at her in amazement. Then he started to laugh. It was a joyous sound, bubbling up inside him in total spontaneity.

Emily felt her face burning, but she refused to look away. "Did he?" she insisted.

Daniel controlled himself and the laughter died away. "No, he most certainly didn't. He's more patient with his mother than many a man might be, but there's nothing of that sort about him."

"I wasn't thinking of his mother," Emily said tartly. "She's terrified he's going to be a womanizer like his father, and a drunkard. And yet she admired him. She wants Brendan to be just like him, and yet she doesn't. There's no way he could succeed for her."

"Ah! So wrong, and yet so right," Daniel said appreciatively. "Ask Mrs. O'Bannion. Though I doubt she'll tell you. Come on, let's go back to the house. You'll catch your death standing here. That wind off the sea has knife blades in it." He offered her his hand to balance as she stepped down over the rough shingle into the sand.

When they got home, Susannah was in the kitchen. She looked pale—drained of all strength.

"What is it?" Emily said quickly, going towards her and putting her arm around her to support her weight.

"I'm all right," Susannah said impatiently, although it was obviously not true. "I was just putting things out ready for breakfast."

"Maggie'll do that in the morning," Emily told her.

"No," Susannah said with a little catch in her voice. "Fergal came by to say she won't be coming anymore. I'm sorry. It will mean more work for you, until I can find someone else."

Emily was appalled, but she tried to mask it. "Don't worry," she said with all the strength of conviction she could assume. "We'll manage very well. I used to know something about cooking. I'm sure I can manage again. We'll be fine. Now please go to bed."

Susannah gave her a weak smile, barely touching the corner of her lips, and together they made a slow and painful way up the stairs.

❖

*E*mily woke in the night with a sense of unease. The wind was rising again and she thought she could hear something banging. She got up, wrapping her shawl around her, and tiptoed out onto the landing. She could still hear the rattle, but now it seemed to be more the wind in the chimneys, and even if there was a slate loose, there was nothing she could do about it.

As she was turning she saw the light under Susannah's door. She hesitated a moment, wondering whether to intrude or not, then there was a flicker of movement, shadows across the light, and she knew Susannah was up. She went to the door and knocked. There was no answer. The tension tightened inside her, fear for Susannah overwhelming her. She turned the handle and went in.

Susannah was standing by the bed, her face completely colorless, her hair straggling and damp. There were dark shadows around her eyes as if she were bruised, and her nightgown clung damply to her skeletal body.

Emily did not need to ask if she was feverish, or even if she had been sick. The bed linen was tangled, trailing on the floor to one side, and Susannah was shaking.

Emily took off her shawl and wrapped it around Susannah's shoulders, then guided her to the bedroom chair. "Sit here for a few minutes," she said gently. "I'll go and put my clothes on, then I'll heat some water, get clean towels, and remake the bed. I know where the linen cupboard is. Just wait for me."

Susannah nodded, too spent to argue.

Emily had very little idea what she was doing, except to try to make Susannah as comfortable as she could. She had no experience in nursing the sick. Even her own children had always had a nanny for the occasional colds or stomach upsets. Susannah was dying, Emily knew she could do nothing to prevent it, and she realized how intensely that mattered to her. Care no longer had anything to do with duty, or even with earning Jack's good opinion.

When she was dressed she went downstairs, lighting the candles on the way, and banked up the fire to heat the water. If she were as ill as Susannah, she imagined she would long to be in a clean and uncrumpled bed, and perhaps not alone. Not spoken to, but just to know that if she opened her eyes, someone would be there.

It did not take her more than half an hour to strip the bed and remake it with clean linen, but in doing so she noticed that there was only one more set of sheets. She would have to launder tomorrow, without Maggie.

When the bed was ready, she carried up a bowl of warm water, and helped Susannah to strip off her soiled nightgown. She was horrified at how gaunt her body was, her flesh sunken until her skin seemed to hang empty on her arms and across her stomach. The mercy of clothes had hidden it before, and Susannah was not so ill as to be unaware of the change in herself.

Emily struggled to hide her fear at the wasting of disease, the change from a beautiful woman to one who was a ghost of her old self. She washed her gently, patting her dry because she was afraid the rub of the towel would bruise her, or even tear the fragile skin.

Afterwards she helped her into a clean nightgown, and half carried her to the bed.

"Thank you," Susannah said with a faint smile. "I'll be all right now." She lay back on the pillows, too exhausted to attempt concealing it.

"Of course you will," Emily agreed, and sat in the armchair near the bed. "But I have no intention of leaving you."

Susannah closed her eyes and seemed to drift into a light sleep.

Emily stayed there all night. Susannah stirred several times, and at about four in the morning, when the wind was higher, for some time she felt as if she might be sick again, but eventually the nausea passed away and she lay back. Emily went down to the kitchen and made her a cup of weak tea, and brought it up, offering it to her only after it had considerably cooled.

By daylight Emily was stiff and her eyes ached with tiredness, but there had been no more episodes, and Susannah seemed to be asleep and breathing without difficulty.

Emily went down to the kitchen to make herself tea and toast to see if she could revive her strength enough to begin the laundry.

She was halfway through the tasks when Daniel came in. "You look bad," he said with sufficient sympathy to rob the words of insult. "Did the wind keep you up?"

"No. Susannah was ill. I'm afraid you're going to have to get your own breakfast, and maybe luncheon as well. With Maggie not coming I've too much to do to be cooking for you."

"I'll help you," he said quickly. "Toast will be fine. Maybe I'll fry an egg or two. Can I do one for you as well?"

"No, I'll do the eggs. You fetch the peat in and

stoke the fires," Emily replied. "I've got sheets to wash, and in this weather it won't be easy to get them dry."

He looked up. "There's an airing rail," he pointed out. "We'd best keep the kitchen warm and use that. Rough dry will have to do, if that's all we have time for."

"Thank you," she accepted.

"Is she bad?" he asked.

"Yes." She had not the will or the strength to keep it from him.

"Maggie shouldn't have gone," he shook his head. "That's my fault."

"Is it? Why?" She asked not because she doubted him, but she needed the reason explained.

He looked a little uncomfortable. "Because I upset her. I was asking questions."

"About what?"

"People," he replied. "The village. She told me about Connor Riordan, some years ago. It was a powerful memory for her."

"Was it?" Emily ignored the kettle, merely pushing it to the side off the hob. "Why? Did she know him well?"

His dark eyes were puzzled. "What are you trying to do, Mrs. Radley? Find out who killed him? Why do you want to know, after all this time?"

"Because his death is eating the heart out of the village," she replied. "It was someone here who killed him, and everybody knows that."

"Did Susannah ask you to? Is that why you came? You haven't come before, have you, in all the years she's been here? And yet I think you care for her."

"I . . ." Emily began, intending to say that she had always cared for Susannah, but it was not true and the lie died on her tongue. Again she thought, is this how Conner Riordan was, seeing too much, saying too much? And with that thought the icelike grip in the pit of her stomach tightened. Was it all going to happen again? Would Daniel also be murdered, and the village die a little more? She realized that not only was he right in that she cared for Susannah, she cared about him also.

"I'm sorry," he apologized ruefully. "You've been

up all night trying to help Susannah, watching her suffer and knowing there's nothing you can do except be there, and wait, and I'm not helping. I'll get the peat in and see to the fires, and I'll start the laundry. That can't be too hard. But first we'll eat."

She smiled back at him, the warmth opening inside her like a slow blossom. She would find out what happened to Connor Riordan, and she would make absolutely certain it did not happen again, however difficult that was, and whatever it cost her.

She and Daniel had just finished the heavy laundry when Father Tyndale arrived. They had the sheets put through the mangle until they were twisted as dry as possible, then she hung them on the airing rail in the kitchen, winched up to where the warm air from the stove would reach them. Father Tyndale looked tired in spite of the rosy color in his face from the buffeting of the wind. He seemed almost bruised by it, and his eyes watered in the warmth of the room.

"I'll take you up to see Susannah," Emily said, immensely relieved to see him. His mere presence lifted the responsibility from her. As long as he was here, she was not alone. "She had a bad night, so don't be surprised to see her looking ill. I'll bring you both tea as soon as I make it."

"Thank you." He looked at her closely, and she knew he saw her own weariness, and perhaps something of the fear in her, however he made no remark on it, simply following her up the stairs.

"Father Tyndale?" Susannah said quickly, pulling herself up in the bed and lifting her hand to tidy her hair into some semblance of the beauty it had once had. Emily fetched the comb and did it for her. She even wondered whether to bring some of her own rouge to put a little color in Susannah's white cheeks, but decided it would look artificial, and deceive no one. She finished the hair instead, smiling back in approval before turning to invite Father Tyndale to come in.

She went back downstairs. This was a conversation that should have complete privacy. She returned with tea and a little thinly sliced bread and butter, hoping that with company Susannah would be able to eat.

It was over an hour later when Father Tyndale

came into the kitchen carrying the tray with him. Daniel was occupied with jobs outside, and Emily was busy with getting vegetables ready for lunch, and then dinner. Before she came here it had been years since she'd done such tasks herself.

Father Tyndale sat in one of the hard-backed chairs, looking tired and too big for it.

"Brendan Flaherty has left the village," he said quietly. "No one knows where he's gone, except maybe his mother, and she won't say."

Emily was stunned. Her instant thought was that the quarrel between Brendan and his mother was much worse than she had assumed at the time. Then she wondered if it was whatever Daniel had said to him. What was Brendan running away from? The past, or the future? Or both?

"I was there at Mrs. Flaherty's house yesterday," she said hesitantly. "Daniel was there, but out in the garden, talking to Brendan. Mrs. Flaherty saw them and was very angry. She went out and told Daniel to leave, pretty abruptly."

Father Tyndale looked troubled, searching for words he knew already that he would not find.

She wanted to tell him about her suspicion that Brendan might have had some relationship with Connor Riordan that Mrs. Flaherty disapproved of violently, but she did not know how to frame it without offending him. "She was very upset," she said again. "As if she were afraid of him." She took a deep breath. "Was it Connor she was seeing in her mind? Why else would she be so fierce with Daniel? He's only been here a couple of days."

"She's afraid of many things," he replied. "Sometimes history repeats itself, especially if you fear that it will."

"Was Brendan close to Connor?" She was being evasive, saying nothing much, but always at the forefront of her mind was this man's calling as a priest.

"You didn't know Connor," he said softly. "He was a stranger here, and yet he seemed to know everything about us. It might have been something of himself he was looking for, but it was disturbing nonetheless." He smiled at her, and changed the subject to Susannah's illness, and all that they might do to make things easier for her.

When he had gone Emily was annoyed with her-self for having been so ineffectual. She stood in the kitchen, staring out of the window. The wind was harsher, the sky gray and bleak. She was afraid Su-sannah would die soon, before anything was re-solved. She hugged her shawl around herself, cold inside, amazed to realize how much it mattered to her. Daniel was right, she cared about Susannah, not for the aunt of her childhood with whom her father had been so angry, but for the woman now who loved the village that had welcomed her, and who were the people of the man with whom she had shared so much happiness.

Who could help heal the wound in them? She needed someone who was an observer, not personally involved with the loves and hates of the village. And as soon as she had framed the question to herself, she knew the answer. Padraic Yorke.

After making sure that Susannah was well enough to leave for a short time, Emily put on a heavy cloak and walked in the wind to Padraic Yorke's house. She knocked on the door and received no answer. She was cold and impatient. She needed his help, and yet she was unhappy away from the house for any longer than was necessary. She shivered and wrapped the cloak more closely around her. She knocked again, and again there was no answer.

She looked at the house, very neat, traditional. There was a tidy garden with herbs. Like everywhere else, most of them were cut back or had withdrawn into the earth for winter. This would gain her nothing. She was growing colder by the moment, and Mr. Yorke was clearly not in.

She turned and walked down by the shore. She did not want to be in the open wind off the water, but the turbulence of the sea was like a living thing, and the vitality of it drew her, as she felt it might have drawn Padraic Yorke also.

She walked along the edge of the sand. The waves broke with a sustained roar, varying in pitch only slightly. Beyond the last dark mound of kelp she saw the lone, slender figure of Padraic Yorke.

He did not look around until she was almost up to him, then he turned. He did not speak, as though the broken wood in the kelp and the water spoke for themselves.

"Brendan Flaherty's gone from the village," Emily said after a moment or two. "Susannah is very ill. I don't think she's going to live a great deal longer."

"I'm sorry," he replied simply.

"Where would he go, and why now?" she asked.

Mr. Yorke's face was bleak. "Do you mean so close to Christmas?"

"No, I mean with Daniel here." She told him of the scene that she and Mrs. Flaherty had witnessed through the kitchen window.

"The Flahertys have a long history in the village," he said thoughtfully. "Seamus was one of the more colorful parts. Wild in his youth, didn't marry until he was over forty, and even then near broke Colleen's heart more than once. But she adored him, forgave him with more excuses than he could think of himself."

"And for Brendan too?" she asked.

He shot a quick glance at her. "Yes. And a poor gift it was to him."

"Do you know where he will have gone, or why?"

"No." He was silent for several moments. The waves continued pounding the shore and the gulls wheeled above, their cries snatched away by the wind. "But I could guess," he continued suddenly. "Colleen Flaherty loved her husband, and she wants her son to be like him, and yet she also wants to keep a better control of him, so he can't hurt her the way Seamus did."

Emily had a sudden vision of a frightened and lonely woman deluding herself that she had a second chance to capture something she had missed in the beginning. No wonder Brendan was angry, and yet unwilling to retaliate. Why had he finally broken away?

"Thank you for telling me," she said with profound gratitude, and a sense of humility. "You have helped me to realize why Susannah loves the people here. It is remarkable that they accepted her so well. None of you has much cause to make the English welcome." She felt a sense of shame as she said it, and that was an entirely new experience for her. All her life she had thought of being English as a blessing, like being clever or beautiful, a grace that should be honored, but never questioned.

Mr. Yorke smiled, but there was embarrassment

in his eyes. "Yes," he said quietly. "They are good people; quick to fight, long to hold a grudge, but brave to a fault, never beaten by misfortune, and generous. They have a faith in life."

Emily thanked him again and started walking back towards the path to Susannah's house. As she reached the road, she saw Father Tyndale in the distance walking the other way, his head bowed as he turned into the wind, struggling against it. She doubted he would agree with Mr. Yorke that the people of the village had a faith in life. The murder of Connor Riordan had set a slow poison in them, and they were dying. She must find the truth, even if it destroyed one of them, or more, because not knowing was killing them all.

*S*usannah had another bad night and Emily sat up with her through nearly all of it. The hour or so of sleep she snatched was spent still propped upright in the big chair near the bed. She ached to help, but there was little she could do except sit with her, occasionally hold her in her arms, when she was drenched with sweat, wash and dry her, help her into a clean nightgown. Several times she brought her warm tea, to try to keep some fluid in her body.

Daniel came in quietly and stoked the fire. He took the soiled and crumpled sheets and nightgown away, saying nothing, but his face was pale and racked with pity.

A little before dawn Susannah was sleeping at last, and Daniel said he would watch with her. Emily was too grateful to argue. She crept to her bed and when at last she was warm, she slept.

It was broad daylight when she woke and after a moment's bewilderment she remembered how ill Susannah had been, and that she had left Daniel alone to look after her. She threw the covers back, scrambled out of bed, and dressed hastily. First she went along the corridor to Susannah's room. She found her sleeping quietly, almost peacefully, and Daniel in the chair looking pale, hollows around his eyes, the dark shadow of stubble on his chin.

He looked up at her and held his finger to his lips in a gesture of silence, then he smiled.

"I'll go and get breakfast," she whispered. "Then we'll do the laundry. I can't do it without your help. I've no idea how to get that wretched boiler working."

"I'll be there," he promised.

But when Emily went down the stairs she found the lamps all lit in the kitchen and a smell of baking filling the air. Maggie O'Bannion was at the sink washing dishes after her making and rolling of pastry.

She turned at the sound of Emily's step. "How's Mrs. Ross?" she asked anxiously.

Emily was too relieved to see her to show her anger. "Very ill," she said truthfully. "That was the second really bad night. I'm very glad indeed that Mr. O'Bannion relented. We don't know how to manage without you."

Maggie blinked and looked away. "I've made an apple pie for dinner," she said as if Emily had asked. "And there's a good piece of beef in the oven. I'll save some of it to make beef tea for Mrs. Ross. Sometimes if she's ill she can hold that down but not much else. Is she awake, do you know?"

"No, she's not. She didn't get much sleep last night." Emily saw that Maggie felt quilty, and she was glad of it. "I'll get to the washing," she went on. "Daniel helped me yesterday, but there are more sheets this morning." She glanced up at the crumpled linen on the airing rack close to the ceiling. "We aren't as efficient as you are," she added more gently.

Maggie said nothing, but her hands moved more quickly in the sink, and she banged the dishes together roughly.

Emily put the flatirons on the hob to heat, then wound the airing rack down and took two of the sheets off it. Automatically Maggie turned from the sink to help her fold them neatly. She did not meet Emily's eyes and there was a tension in her shoulders of a deep unhappiness.

Emily wondered if Daniel had left yesterday afternoon, perhaps when Father Tyndale was here, and gone to tell Maggie how much she was missed. And was Maggie's tension this morning caused because she and Fergal had quarreled about it? What had Daniel said to her that she had defied her husband?

353

When the sheets were folded ready to iron, Emily began on the pillowcases, then stopped briefly for a cup of tea and a slice of toast. She was wondering if she should go up to see if Susannah was awake when Daniel came into the kitchen.

"Good morning, Mrs. O'Bannion," he said cheerfully. "I'm more grateful to see you back than you can imagine. We weren't managing so well without you."

Maggie shot him a sharp glance, and neither of them looked at Emily.

"Susannah's awake," Daniel went on. "Can I take some breakfast up to her, if there's something like bread and butter, or at least a fresh cup of tea?"

"You have something yourself," Emily told him. "I'll take it up to Susannah, and you can do something with those sheets. We'll need them again soon enough. Maggie, if you could speak softly to the boiler and get it going again, we need to do last night's sheets for when we need them. Please?"

"Yes, Mrs. Radley, of course," Maggie agreed a trifle stiffly, and, avoiding Daniel, she began to cut thin bread and butter for Susannah, carefully spreading the softened butter on the cut end of the loaf, and then slicing it so razor-thin it barely held together. Then she buttered and halved a second slice and a third, arranging them daintily on a blue-and-white plate.

Emily thanked her and took the tray. She was extraordinarily pleased when Susannah sat up, a faint touch of color in her cheeks, and ate all of it. Emily decided she must remember how it was done and make it herself another time.

An hour later Susannah was dozing and Emily went downstairs again to catch up on some of the household chores she was behind with, and which took her so much longer than it had Maggie.

She stopped at the kitchen door when she heard voices, and then laughter, a man and a woman. It was a rich sound, a welling-up of a kind of happiness.

"Really?" Maggie said with disbelief.

"I swear," Daniel replied. "Trouble is, I can't remember how long ago it was, or why I was there."

"It sounds marvelous," Maggie said wistfully. "I sometimes dream about going to places like that, but I don't suppose I ever will."

"You could, if you wanted to," Daniel assured her.

Emily stood motionless, not making a sound. She could see Maggie's face as she looked at Daniel. She was smiling, but there was a wistfulness in her eyes that betrayed her dreams, and that she believed them beyond her reach.

"Not everything you want can be had for the asking," she said to him. "It's wise to know what to grasp for, and what will only hurt you."

"It's not wise," Daniel replied gently. "It's owning defeat before you've even tried. How do you know what you can reach, if you don't stretch out?"

"You talk like a dreamer," she said sadly. "One with his feet way off the ground, and no responsibilities."

"Is that what it is that holds your feet hard to the earth, then? Or is it Fergal's feet you mean?" he questioned in return.

Maggie hesitated.

In the doorway Emily froze. Had Daniel been telling her stories of travel and adventure, disturbing her contentment with hunger that could never be fed?

"Maybe you could go to Europe?" Daniel suggested. "Find a charm that would feed your heart forever afterwards. There are magic places, Maggie. Places where wonderful things happened, great battles, ideas to set the world alight, love stories to break your heart, and then mend it again all in a new shape. There's music, and laughter till you can hardly breathe from the ache of it! There's food you couldn't imagine, and tales to carry with you to fill the winter nights for every year to come. Wouldn't you like that?"

Emily came in quickly, intending to interrupt them, then she saw Maggie's face and changed her mind. There was a vulnerability in it that was startling, but she was not looking at Daniel, rather into some thoughts of her own.

Emily was suddenly chilled. She remembered how gentle Daniel had been with her when they were walking back from church, how soft his questions were, how natural. And yet they had dug more deeply than she wished, exposing weaknesses she had not acknowledged to herself. Now he was doing the same thing to Maggie, uncovering the loneliness in her, the disappointment. Emily had seen Fergal O'Bannion, a good man but without wings of the mind. He was possessive of her. Was that because he had seen her laugh with Connor Riordan, listen to him, join in his tales and his dreams? And now she was listening to Daniel, and so Fergal had commanded Maggie not to be in this house, and she had disobeyed him? To help Susannah, or to listen to Daniel?

Emily recalled odd remarks, very slight, only glancing, but were they the ugly tips of fact? Had Maggie escaped the enclosing bounds of her life for a brief passion with Connor, and Fergal knew it? Was that why Connor had been killed? The oldest of reasons?

Did Maggie know that? Or at least fear it?

And yet Mrs. Flaherty feared it was Brendan who had killed Connor, and Brendan had disappeared.

"Wouldn't you like to, Maggie?" Daniel repeated, his voice gentle.

Emily stepped forward and saw him. He was smiling and as he folded the sheet over, his slender hand lingered for a moment over Maggie's.

Emily felt the heat burn up inside her and drew in her breath to speak.

"I have things to fill my winter nights, and dreams in plenty already," Maggie replied. "There's nothing I want you to add to them, Daniel. I like your tales of places you've been, and I hope by telling them perhaps you've recalled a thing or two of who you are. That's all. Do you understand me?"

"Yes, I understand you," he said quietly. "Perhaps I expected too much help in my own fancies. A dose of reality can do wonders." He smiled at his own error, gently self-mocking, and Emily saw Maggie ease a little, smiling back. The moment of embarrassment passed.

Daniel moved away, and as he left the kitchen he brushed by Emily, and realized that she must have overheard the conversation. He could not know how long she had been there, but at the very least she had seen Maggie rebuff him. He pulled a slightly rueful face as he caught her eye, and she was at that moment absolutely certain that he knew exactly what she was trying to do to solve the murder of Connor Riordan, and why she was driven to try.

Even so, it made no difference. Emily went on into the kitchen as if she had merely passed him in the passage.

"How is she?" Maggie asked, a faint flush on her cheeks all that there was left from her conversation with Daniel.

"Definitely improving," Emily said cheerfully. "I'm sure she is less anxious now that you are back. I'm grateful to you for returning." She tried to soften her voice to rob the words of offense, but she had no hesitation in speaking them. "Did Daniel come to you yesterday and tell you how ill Susannah was?"

"Yes," Maggie answered. "I'm so sorry. If I'd known, I wouldn't have stayed away even for a day."

There was such unhappiness in her face Emily did not doubt her. "It's difficult to know how much to obey one's husband, against the voice of one's own conscience," Emily responded with more honesty than she had expected. What would she do to please Jack, against her own judgment? How often had he asked her? She realized that the journey to Connemara was probably the first time. Except that it was not against her conscience so much as in response to his. It should have been she who wanted to come, and he who tried to dissuade her.

But what if she had wanted to come, and he had been against it, what would she have done? Made obedience an excuse? Or love? She did love Jack, she hated quarreling with him. But they quarreled very seldom. Why was that? Could it be a lack of passion, or even of conviction? What did she care about enough to do, even if it cost her something? And if there were nothing, what did that say of her? Something too terrible to own.

"Fergal is not a harsh man, Mrs. Radley," Maggie was saying, stopping her work to try to explain. It mattered to her that Emily did not judge him coldly. "He didn't know Mrs. Ross was so bad, and he took Daniel wrong. It all goes back to the other wreck. I daresay you don't know much about that. Fergal got a wrong idea in his head, and it could be I was to blame for it."

Emily could not turn away from such a perfect chance. "You mean Daniel reminds Fergal of Connor Riordan, and he thought history was playing itself out all over again?" she asked.

Maggie lowered her eyes. "Well, something like that."

Emily deliberately sat down at the kitchen table. "What was Connor like, really? Please be honest with me, Maggie. Is history repeating itself in Daniel?"

Maggie put the linen down and bit her own lip as she weighed her answer. "Connor was funny and wise, like Daniel," she answered. "He made us all laugh. We liked his tales of where he'd been, strange lands he'd visited . . ."

"Like Daniel just now?" Emily interrupted.

"Yes, I suppose so. And like Daniel, he was interested in everyone. He kept on asking questions, and we answered because it seemed only kindness that made him say such things. You know how it is when you talk to someone, and they like you, want to know about you, what you like, what your dreams are? You get to thinking. It's rare enough someone wants to know about you instead of it being all about themselves."

Emily admitted ruefully that that was true.

"Connor was interested in everyone," Maggie went on. "I liked him. He was different. He told us new stories, not the same old ones. He made me think, look at everything a bit differently. But I wasn't the only one to feel at times as if he could look into my mind too easily, and too deep. There are things sometimes best not known."

"Things about love, and jealousy, and debts?" Emily asked.

Maggie's voice dropped. "I suppose so. And dreams that shouldn't be told."

"We'd die without dreams," Emily replied. "But you're right, some of them shouldn't be told to others."

"I love Fergal," Maggie said quickly, and on that instant Emily knew that it was at least in part a lie.

"But Connor had a fire of the mind," Emily finished for her. "And Fergal was a bore by comparison, and he came to know it." She was afraid now that she was too close to the truth, and that if she tore off the last covering it would destroy Maggie's world.

"Fergal is a good man," Maggie repeated stubbornly, as if saying it could make it true. "Sure, I liked Connor's tales, but that's all. I didn't love him. You're wrong in that, Mrs. Radley. Like, that's all, because he made me think, and made me laugh. He taught us all how to see a wider world than this village and its loves and hates."

"But he saw your loneliness, and he made Fergal see it too." Emily could not let it go. The pictures were all becoming clearer.

Maggie blinked away tears. "It can hurt very deep to have to face a truth you've been hiding from. It's my fault too. I told Fergal what he wanted to hear, and then felt cheated when he believed me and looked no further. I suppose I let him think I was in love with Connor, and he with me. God forgive me for that."

So Maggie had allowed Fergal to think she was in love with Connor. Was she afraid that it was actually Fergal who had killed him, and inadvertently she had been responsible for it? And now she would protect him, because of her own guilt?

Had she loved someone else? If not Connor, then who?

How much of any of it had Susannah seen, or guessed? And was she telling the truth when she had claimed to be so certain Hugo Ross had known nothing of the passions and weaknesses of these people whose lives for good and ill were so woven with his own?

*F*ather Tyndale came to see Susannah again in the afternoon and stayed for over an hour. Emily walked most of the way home with him. The wind was gusty, and cold with the chill of the sea, but in spite of its violence she found that the salt and the smell of the weeds had a kind of bitter cleanness that pleased her.

"I think she hasn't long now," Father Tyndale said gravely, forcing his voice to carry above the wind.

"I know," Emily agreed. "I hope it isn't before Christmas." Then she did not know why she had said that. It was not Christmas that was the issue, it was learning the truth about Connor Riordan, and whatever it proved to be, letting Susannah believe there was some resolution in it, a healing for the people she loved.

"Tell me more about Hugo, Father," she asked.

He smiled as they walked down through the rough grass, still mounded with the debris of the storm, then into a clear stretch of the beach. It was a longer way to his house, but to take it felt right to both of them.

"How hard it is to say anything of him that gives any idea of what he was really like," Father Tyndale answered thoughtfully. "He was a big man, not just physically, with a big man's gentleness, but he was broad of spirit. He loved this land and its people. But then his family have been here as long as even the legends tell. He made his money in business, but his pleasure was painting, and he might have been good enough to keep himself that way, if he'd tried. Heaven knows, Susannah never asked for wealth. She was happy just to be with him."

"And his faith?" she inquired.

"You know," he said with slight surprise, "I never asked him. I took it for granted from the way he was that he knew there was a greater power than all of mankind, and that it was a good power. Some people talk a lot about what they believe, and the laws they keep, the prayers they say. Hugo never did. He came to church most Sundays, but whatever guilts or griefs he had, he sorted them with God himself."

"Is that all right with you?" she questioned.

"He loved his fellow men, without judgment," he answered. "And he loved the earth in all its seasons. To me, that meant he loved God. Yes, that's all right with me."

"You didn't mind him marrying an English-woman?" she said, almost joking, but not quite.

He laughed. "Yes, I did. Not that it made a ha'penny's difference. His family weren't happy either. They'd have liked him to find a nice young Catholic girl, and have lots of children. But he loved Susannah, and he never asked anyone else what they thought."

"But she became Catholic," Emily pointed out.

"Oh, yes, but not because he ever asked her to. She did it for his sake, and in time she came to believe."

She changed the subject. "What did Hugo think of Connor Riordan?" She had to ask, but she realized she was afraid of the answer. Surely the man Father Tyndale had known would have seen the damage

Connor was doing, the secrets he seemed to understand too easily, the fears and hungers he awoke?

They were walking along the shore, around the wreckage. Father Tyndale did not answer her.

"Where has Brendan Flaherty gone, Father?" she asked. "And why? Was his father alive when Connor was killed?"

"Seamus? No, he was dead by then. But even the dead have secrets. Some of his were uglier than Colleen guessed at."

"But Brendan knows?"

"Yes. And Hugo knew. I think that was why he tried to take Connor back to Galway, but that winter the weather was bad. We had hard and heavy rain, with an edge of sleet on it. And Connor was too frail to go all that way. Five hours in an open cart would have all but killed him. He wasn't as strong as Daniel. Swallowed more of the sea, I think, and half drowned in it for longer too. It's a hard thing to come close to death. I'm not sure that his lungs ever got over it."

"Did he come from Galway?"

"Connor? I don't know if it was where he was

born, or simply where his ship put out from. He spoke like a Galway man."

"And Hugo wanted to take him back there?"

"Yes. But he knew he couldn't, not until he was stronger, and the weather turned."

"Then it was too late?"

"Yes." His face crumpled in grief. "God forgive us."

They were the first ones to walk along the sand since the ebb. There were no footsteps ahead of them, just the bare, hard stretch between the waves and the tide line.

"Was Hugo afraid even then that something would happen, Father?"

He did not answer.

"Were you?" she insisted.

"God knows, I should have been," he said heavily. "These are my people. I've known many of them all their lives. I hear their confessions, I speak to them every day, I see their loves and their quarrels, their illnesses, their hopes, and their disappointments. How could all this have happened, and I did not see it? God forgive me, I still don't." He continued a few paces in silence, then went on as if he had forgotten she was there. "I can't even help them now. They are frightened, one of them is carrying a burden of guilt that is eating his soul, and yet none of them comes to me for intercession with God, for a chance to lay down the weight that is crushing the life out of them, and find absolution. Why not? How have I failed so completely?"

Emily had no answer. Everyone had shame for something, at some time in their lives. What could it have been that Connor Riordan had seen, or guessed? Did it threaten one of the people here whose frailty he knew, and could protect? Even Susannah?

She did not want to hear. She wished she had never embarked on detecting. She was not equipped to succeed, or to deal with the inevitable tragedies that it would bring. She should have had the courage, and the humility, to tell Susannah that in the beginning. What arrogance of hers to imagine she could come in here, a stranger, and solve the grief of seven years!

She looked at Father Tyndale's bent shoulders and his sad face, and wished she could give him some comfort, some hand to grasp in the faith that should have buoyed him up. He believed he had failed his people; his lack of trust in God, or understanding His ways, had caused their failure too.

She had nothing to say that would help.

*I*t was late afternoon, close to dusk, when Emily made her decision. She would need help not only from Father Tyndale, but from Maggie O'Bannion, and possibly from Fergal as well. There was no point in telling Susannah until she was sure the plan would work. She would much rather have waited until her aunt was a little better, but that might not happen. The weather could close in and make it impossible.

Or worse than any of that, whoever had killed Connor might see in Daniel the past occurring again, and kill him too.

She walked through the darkening evening, bright only in the west over the sea, which heaved gray like metal, scarlet from the sun pouring over it as if it were spilled blood. She knocked on Maggie's door.

Maggie answered, and when she saw Emily, the blood drained from her face.

"No," Emily said quickly. "She's not worse. In fact, I think she's quite a bit better. I want to take the chance to go to Galway. I'll have to be there two nights, at the least. Will you stay in the house with Susannah, please? I can't leave her alone. At night she's too ill. And I can't expect Daniel to care for her. Anyway, she should have a woman, someone she knows, and trusts. Please?"

Fergal had come to the door behind her. His face was dark with memory, and guilt. "No," he said before Maggie could speak. "Whatever you want to go to Galway for, Mrs. Radley, it'll have to wait. Poor Mrs. Ross could pass any day. Isn't that what you came for? To be with her?" There was challenge in the line of his jaw and the hard brilliance of his eyes.

"I'm not going for myself, Mr. O'Bannion," Emily said, trying to keep the anger out of her voice. "It is for Susannah—"

"She has all she needs here," he cut her off.

"No, she doesn't. She—"

"Maggie's not staying in that house with Daniel, and that's an end of it," he told her. "Good night, Mrs. Radley."

Maggie was still standing in the doorway and although he reached for the door to close it, she did not move. "Why are you going to Galway?" she asked Emily. "Is it to find out something about Connor Riordan?"

"Yes. Hugo Ross went, and I need to know why." Emily had not wanted to say that, but now it was forced out of her. "And maybe someone there will know Daniel." She turned to Fergal. "If Daniel stays with Father Tyndale until I come back, and you go to Susannah's as well, will you allow Maggie to stay there then?"

"Yes, he will," Maggie said before Fergal could answer.

"Maggie—" he protested.

"Yes, you will," she repeated, glancing at him only briefly. "It is the right thing to do, and we all know that."

He sighed, and Emily saw him look at Maggie

with a tenderness that transformed his face, and a loneliness that would have torn her heart if she had seen it.

"You'd best go tomorrow," he told Emily. "The weather's going to get worse again in a day or two. It won't be a storm like the big one, but it'll be too bad for you to drive a pony across the moors, even Father Tyndale's Jenny. We'll come tomorrow morning. You'll be wanting to set out by nine."

"Thank you," she said warmly. "I'm grateful."

Then she went to Father Tyndale again and told him her plan, asking to borrow Jenny and the trap, and if Daniel could stay with him until she returned. He agreed with her, warned her of the weather, told her he could not leave the village when Susannah was so ill.

"I know," she said immediately. "But what is the alternative? To say to her that I've given up?"

He sighed. "I'll find one of the men from the village to go with you. Rob Molloy, perhaps, or Michael Flanagan."

"No . . . thank you," she said quickly. "Someone

from this village killed Connor. I'm safer alone, and if no one knows that I've gone. Please?"

Father Tyndale's mouth pulled tight and his eyes were black and hurt, but he did not argue. He promised to have the pony and trap ready for her at nine in the morning. She said she would prefer to walk to his house than have him collect her.

She followed the road back to Susannah's. It was now completely dark and she was glad of the lantern she had brought. The wind was hard and heavy, and colder.

❦

*S*he set out in the morning after having gone briefly to say good-bye to Susannah. She had explained everything the previous evening, both where she was going and why, and that Daniel would be staying with Father Tyndale until she returned. She needed to give no reasons for that.

"I'll come back as soon as I can," she said, watching Susannah's face to see in it the hope or the fear that she might not put into words. "Are you sure you want me to go?" she added impulsively. "I can change my mind, if you wish?"

Susannah looked pale, her face even more haggard, but there was no indecision in her. She smiled. "Please go. I'm not afraid of dying, only of leaving this unsolved. The village has been good to me, they've allowed me to belong as if I were really one of them. They're Hugo's people, and I loved him more than I can ever explain. I'm quite ready to die, and to go wherever he is. That is really the only place I want to be. But I want to leave them something for all the love they've given me, and even more for the way he loved them. I want to see them begin to heal. Go, Emily, and whatever you find, bring it back. See that it is known, whether I'm here or not. And never feel guilty. You've given me the greatest gift you had, and I'm grateful to you."

Emily leaned forward and kissed her white cheek, then walked out of the room, tears running swift and easy down her face.

It was a long and bitterly cold journey, but Jenny seemed to know it even without Emily's guidance, or

Father Tyndale's instructions. The landscape had a desolate beauty, which now in a strange way comforted her. Even in the occasional drifting rain there was a depth that changed with the light, as if there were layer beneath layer in the grass. The stones shone bright where a shaft of sun caught them, and the mountains and the distance were full of shifting, ever-changing shadows.

When at last she reached Galway, with a little inquiry she found a hotel with stabling for the pony, and after a good meal and a change into dry clothes and boots, she set out to retrace Hugo's steps of seven years ago.

During the long drive she had given much thought to where Hugo would have begun looking for Connor's family. Father Tyndale had said Hugo possessed a quiet but deep faith, and that he went to church most Sundays. Surely he would begin by asking the churches in Galway if they knew of Connor Riordan's family? Whether they attended or not, the local priest would at least know of them?

It was easy to find a church; any passerby could direct her. It took a little longer to reach the one where the Riordan family was known, and it was after dark when she finally sat in the parlor of the rectory opposite Father Malahide and looked at his thin, gentle face in the candlelight. The room was filled with the earthy odor of peat, and the richness of tobacco smoke.

"How can I help you, Mrs. Radley?" he said curiously. He did not ask what an Englishwoman was doing in Galway, having driven alone, in the middle of winter, all the way from the coast.

Briefly Emily told him about the storm and Daniel being the only survivor from the wreck. As her story progressed she saw in his face that he knew about Connor, with both pity and grief.

"Now Mrs. Ross is very ill indeed," she went on. "I think she will not live much longer. There are things I need to resolve before then. Daniel's arrival has stirred old ghosts that need to be laid to rest, whatever the truth may be."

"I cannot tell you what Hugo Ross said to me, Mrs. Radley," Father Malahide told her gently. "He came to see if he could find Connor's family. The young man was too weak to come himself and all his shipmates were dead. Like your present young man, he seemed to be alone in the world, and to remember very little. I'm afraid many men are lost off the coast of Ireland, especially Connemara. The winter is very bad, and the weather sweeps in off the Atlantic with nothing to break it."

"Did Hugo find any family for him?"

"Yes. His mother lived here in Galway. She worked in a foundling home run by the Church. She cared for the children who had no one else. She was not a nun, of course, but she had been there most of her adult life. I'm afraid there is nothing else I can tell you, Mrs. Radley. All else was in confidence. I'm sure you understand that. I'm sorry to say it, but Connor's mother is dead now. Not that I imagine she could have helped you."

"No," Emily agreed gravely. "I don't know if I will learn the truth of what happened to him, and it would be of little comfort to her to know. But someone else at the foundling home may be able to tell me what Hugo Ross was asking and perhaps what he was told."

"Of course." Father Malahide gave her the address and how to find the place, counseling her to go in the middle of the morning, when they would be best able to spare time to speak with her.

She thanked him, and walked as briskly as she could through the dark streets back to the inn where she was lodging.

In the morning she followed Father Malahide's directions and had no difficulty in finding the foundling home. It was a large, gray stone building with many additional outhouses, looking as if they had been adapted to be further accommodation.

Emily walked up to the front door and lifted the knocker. It was several minutes before it was answered by a slender little girl with a freckled face. Emily told her what she wished, and she was admitted to wait in a small, rather chilly anteroom with carefully stitched samplers on the wall, warning the would-be sinner that God sees all. Opposite it was a very large crucifix with a Christlike figure in agony. It made Emily self-conscious and uncomfortable. She felt suddenly alien, and wondered at her wisdom in having come here at all.

She was conducted to see the matron in charge,

a tired woman with a pale face, deeply lined, and the most beautiful brown hair in thick coils on her head.

Emily sat in her office and heard the busy tap of feet up and down the corridor and voices calling out cheerfully, hurrying people along, bidding a child be good, be quick, tie up her bootlaces, tuck his shirt in, stop chattering.

"I came to Connemara to stay with my aunt, Susannah Ross, who is very ill and will not live much longer," she began frankly. "Seven years ago her husband, Hugo Ross, came here looking for Mrs. Riordan, because her son, Connor, was the only survivor of a shipwreck just off the coast where Mr. Ross lived."

"I remember him," the matron said, nodding her head. "He never returned, nor did the young man he spoke of. I'm afraid Mrs. Riordan is dead now, God rest her soul."

"Yes, I know. So is Mr. Ross. And I'm afraid Connor was killed too," Emily replied.

"Oh dear." The matron's face showed genuine grief, "I'm so sorry. Perhaps it's as well his poor mother never knew. She was so happy when Mr. Ross told her Connor was saved from the wreck. So many men are drowned. The sea's a hard mistress, but you make a living where you can. The land can be hard too. So what is it I can do to help Mrs. Ross now, poor creature?"

Emily had turned over and over in her mind what she would ask, and she was still uncertain, but now there was no more time for debate. She looked at this woman's tired eyes and the gnarled hands on her lap in front of her. She must have seen more than her share of grief. What kind of woman leaves her child to a foundling home to raise? Emily thought of her own children at home, and suddenly she missed them so intensely it was as if they had been torn from her. She could smell their skin, hear their voices, see the bright trust in their eyes. There was only one answer, a desperate woman, driven beyond the end of her strength, a hunted woman or a dying one.

"Connor Riordan was murdered," she said bluntly and saw the matron wince as if she were familiar with that pain as well. "We never found out who killed him, but I believe I know why. I have a deep fear that the same thing is going to happen again, this time to Daniel, if we do not prevent it. I think Hugo Ross may have learned something here that later told him who was responsible, and because he loved his people, he chose not to repeat it. He died shortly after Connor's death himself. He did not know that the poison of that guilt and fear was going to cause the village itself to die slowly. But his widow knows, and she wants above all things, before she dies, to put that right, perhaps for the village, but more, I think, for Hugo himself."

"A good woman." The matron nodded her head and made the sign of the cross with profound solemnity. "I cannot tell you much myself, but I recall that he spoke for some time to Mrs. Riordan, and that he asked quite a bit about Mrs. Yorke. That seemed to distress him. I asked him if I could do anything to help him, and he said not. Mrs. Riordan seemed upset as well, but when I spoke to her, she seemed to know little, but would not tell me why."

"Mrs. Yorke?" Emily said confused.

"Well, we called her Mrs.," the matron answered

with a slight gesture of her hand, as if dismissing something trivial. "But she was not actually married. She worked here for many years, then she too died. But it was her time. She was old, and ready to continue her journey towards God."

"Old?" Emily was surprised. Was she Padraic Yorke's sister? Then she had to be considerably older than he. Or perhaps she was no relative. It was not a common name, but not unique by any means. "Might she be a relation of Mr. Padraic Yorke, who lives in the same village as Mrs. Ross?"

"Yes, yes," the matron said with a sigh. "That she was. Though it's a long time now, poor soul."

"A long time? But you said she was old!"

"So she was, not so far from eighty when she died. Must be fifteen years ago now, or maybe more."

Suddenly Emily was far colder than the room explained. Ugly thoughts crowded her mind, still shapeless. "She wasn't his sister then?"

"No, my dear, she was his mother," the matron said in surprise. "She came here before he was born. At first she said she was a widow, with child, but later she was honest with us. She was never married. A respectable girl to begin with, in service to a family in Holyhead, in England. When the master of the house got her with child she took ship and came to Ireland. She started in Dublin, but when the child began to show she was thrown out, and came west to Galway, where we took her in. She was happy here, and stayed with us for the rest of her days. A good woman she was, and we gave her the courtesy of a married title."

"So Padraic was born here?" Emily said incredulously. It was not that the shame of his early life appalled her, although it must have been hard enough, it was that in the eyes of the Irish he was an Englishman, by blood and breeding, if never at heart.

The matron nodded. "Of course he had to leave when he was fourteen, because we couldn't keep him any longer. There are no funds for children once they are old enough to work, and there was nothing here for him. He was a good student. He went to Dublin for a while, then up to Sligo, and at last to the coast, where he stayed."

"And Mrs. Riordan knew all this," Emily said slowly, as the ugliness inside her head took its shape.

Connor must have pieced it together, understanding exactly who Padraic Yorke was, not the Irish poet and patriot he said, but the illegitimate son of some rich Englishman and his cast-off maidservant. Would Connor have told anyone? Who dared take the chance that he would not?

"Thank you," Emily said to the matron, standing up with sudden stiffness as if all her bones ached. "I shall go back tomorrow to tell Susannah what I have learned. Then at least she will know. What she chooses to do about it is up to her."

She spent the rest of the day in Galway because she did not dare take the long road back when she would make the last of the journey in the dark. She paid her bill after breakfast and was on the road by nine, but it was with a heaviness inside her. She understood so easily why Hugo Ross had chosen to say nothing.

Padraic Yorke had killed Connor and it was probably murder. At the very best it was a fight that had gone disastrously wrong. But no one other than Yorke himself knew what had happened, the mock-

ery, the laughter, the humiliation he might have suffered. It could have been a lashing out at unbear-
able jeering, perhaps even an obscene insult to his
mother, surely a victim enough already. It could have
been at least half an accident, never meant to end in
death.

Or it could have been quite clearly a murder,
even a blow from behind delivered the coward's way
against a man who had come by information by
chance, and had never intended to use it.

Had Hugo Ross known? Had he spoken to Padraic
Yorke? Or had he kept silence as well? Did he even
know what he was concealing? She thought, from
what Susannah had said of him, that probably he
had known very well.

What he had not known was how the fear and the
guilt would slowly poison the very fabric of the village until it was withering, day by day, a new suspicion here, a fear awakened there, another lie to cover
an older one; Father Tyndale's self-doubt, and ulti-
mately his doubt even of God.

She was past the lake and heading towards

Oughterard, the wind tearing blue holes in a ragged sky and the sun brilliant on the hills. The slopes were almost gold, black stone ruins gleaming wet and sharp, when she saw a man in the road ahead of her. He was walking steadily, as if he were pacing himself to go far. She wondered if he lived in Oughterard. There was no house or farm anywhere in sight to either side of the road.

Should she offer him a lift? It seemed unwise. And yet it was inhumane to pass him and let him make his own way, against the wind on this rough road.

It was not until she was level with him that she recognized Brendan Flaherty. She pulled up the pony.

"Can I offer you a ride, Mr. Flaherty?" she said. "I'm heading home."

"Home, is it?" he said with a smile. "Sure, that's very good of you, Mrs. Radley. And I'll be happy to drive for you, if you like. Though Jenny knows her way as well as I do."

She accepted because she was tired, and although she was a good rider, she was completely inexperienced at driving, and she was sure Jenny was aware of it.

They had gone well over a mile before Brendan spoke.

"I shouldn't have run away," he said quietly, facing forward, avoiding her eyes.

"You're coming back," she replied. Now that she knew the truth about Padraic Yorke she no longer had any fear of Brendan.

He gave a little grunt, wordless, but heavy with emotion.

She felt the weight of sadness in him, as if he were returning to an imprisonment.

"Why are you coming back?" she asked impulsively. "Are you afraid that if you stay in Galway that you'll end up like your father, drinking too much, fighting, and in the end alone?"

"I'm not my father," he said, keeping his eyes on the road.

She looked at him and saw that it was not anger but apology in his face, as if he had failed, and somehow he had betrayed the expectations of his heritage.

"What was he like?" she asked. "Honestly. Not your mother's dreams, but in truth. How did you see him?"

"I loved him," he replied, seeking the words one by one. "But I hated him too. He got away with being lazy, and cruel because he could make people laugh. He could sing like an angel. At least that's how I remember it. He had one of those soft voices full of music that makes every note sound easy. And he told stories about Connemara, the land and the people, so real that listening to him seemed as if the past ran like wine in your blood, a little drunk maybe, but so alive. Actually I think now that most of them were Padraic's stories anyhow, but he never seemed to mind my father telling them."

"Did he know Padraic well?" she asked. There was a faint overcast coming across the sky, filling it with haze so the sun was no longer bright on the hills and some of the color faded from the grass. It was going to get colder. There was a veil of rain to the northeast over the Maum Hills.

"I don't know. I don't think so. But it wouldn't have made a difference. He'd have told the stories anyway. I asked Padraic one day if he minded, and he said my father only made them richer, and that was a good thing, for all of us, for Ireland."

"He loves Ireland, doesn't he." It was an observation; she intended no question in it.

Brendan looked at her. "You didn't come to Galway looking for me, did you? I thought at first you did. I thought you might have wondered if I killed Connor Riordan . . . over Maggie. I didn't." He said it vehemently, as if it were still somehow open to question.

Emily realized that that was what his mother was afraid of. She knew the violence in Seamus, perhaps she had even been a victim of it at times, and she imagined it in Brendan too, as if even Seamus's faults, repeated, could somehow keep him alive for her. No wonder Brendan had fled to Galway, or anywhere, to be free of the imprisonment of her dreams.

"I know you didn't," she answered him.

He swung around to face her. "Do you? Do you know it, or are you afraid to let me think you suspect me, in case I hurt you?"

"I know you didn't," she told him. "Because I know who did, with a far better reason than you have."

"Do you?" He searched her face, and must have seen some honesty in it, because he smiled, and his clenched hands on the reins eased.

"You should say good-bye to your mother properly, and then go back to Galway, or Sligo, or even Dublin. Anywhere you want to," she said.

"What about the village?" he asked. "We're deceived by our own dreams. Padraic has taken our myths and polished them until they look the way he thinks they should, and we've come to believe it's the truth."

"And it isn't?" Although she knew the answer.

He smiled. "He makes it more glamorous than it was. He creates saints that never existed, and making ordinary men with faults that were ugly and selfish into heroes with flaws that you love as much as their virtues. Then we've looked at the delusion because no one dares break the reflection in the glass."

"And Connor Riordan saw that?"

He looked at her, a flare of understanding in his eyes. "Yes. Connor saw everything. He saw that I love Maggie, and that Fergal doesn't know how to laugh and cry, and win her. And that my mother can't let my father lie in his grave as who he really was. And Father Tyndale thinks God has abandoned him because he can't save us against our will. And other things. I daresay he knew Kathleen and Mary O'Donnell and little Bridie, and everyone else."

He did not mention Padraic Yorke, and she did not either. They drove the rest of the way in companionable silence, or speaking of the land and its seasons, and the old tales of the Flahertys and the Conneelys.

*E*mily set Brendan down in the middle of the village, then took Jenny and the trap back to Father Tyndale. He did not ask her what she had learned, and she did not tell him. Daniel walked back home with her, carrying her bag. He looked at her curiously, but he did not ask. She thought perhaps that he already guessed.

She finally sat alone with Susannah in the evening, when Maggie and Fergal had left, and Daniel was in the study reading. Susannah had a little color back in her face, and she seemed briefly recovered again, though the faraway look in her eyes was still there, as if she were preparing to leave. Soon it would be Christmas Eve, and she was longing for the gift that Emily had for her.

"Hugo did know the truth," Emily said gently, placing her hands over Susannah's thin fingers on the coverlet. They were upstairs, where Daniel could not possibly overhear them. "Possibly more than we ever will. He did not tell it because he did not realize that the village's own fear would poison it, eating away its heart. If he had understood, I believe he would have told Father Tyndale, and let him see justice done."

Susannah smiled slowly and the tears filled her eyes. "Did you tell Father?"

"No. I will tell you, and you can do as you think best, whatever you think Hugo would have done, were he here," Emily replied.

Then she recounted what she had learned in Galway, and added a little of her certainty about Brendan Flaherty also.

"I was afraid it could have been Brendan," Susannah admitted. "Or Fergal. He thought Maggie was in love with Connor."

"I think she was in love with Connor's ideas, his imagination," Emily said.

Susannah smiled. "I think we all were. And afraid of him. He could sing too, you know, even better than Seamus. Colleen Flaherty hated him for that. I think he knew what a bully Seamus was too." She sighed. "Poor Padraic. Could it have been a fight, or an accident?"

"I don't know. But even if it was, Padraic let the village be poisoned by it."

"Yes . . . I know." They sat in silence for several moments. "Father Tyndale has been to see me every day. He'll come tomorrow, and I'll tell him. Hugo would have." Her fingers curled over Emily's and tightened. "Thank you."

❦

*T*he next day when Father Tyndale came in the morning, Emily left him with Susannah and she walked alone along the shore towards the place where Connor Riordan had died. The marker stone was higher up, beyond where the sea reached, but she wished to stand where he had been alive, and tell his spirit that the truth was known. It could hardly matter, except to the living. Even Hugo Ross would know without her telling him. It was simply a sense of completion.

The waves were strong, hissing up the sand, gouging it out, sucking it back in again, and burying it under with deceptive violence. She could see how easily a slip of the footing could be fatal. No one would walk close to the waves' edge. Only emotion powerful enough to destroy all attention would lead anyone to be so careless. Had it been a fight?

She looked up across the dune and the tussock grass and saw Mrs. Flaherty striding towards her, head forward, arms swinging purposefully. Emily kept on walking. She did not want to speak to Colleen Flaherty now, especially if Brendan had told her he was going to leave the village, perhaps never live here again. It would be a relief for Fergal, in time even for Maggie.

She walked on towards the place where Connor Riordan had died. The sand was softer under her feet. The last wave hissed, white-tongued, up to within a yard of her.

Colleen Flaherty was gaining on her. Emily felt a sudden flicker of fear. She glanced landward and saw that the dune edge was too steep to climb here. The only way back was to retrace her steps. She was at the end of the open sand. She could see the grave marker. This was where Connor had died. The sea that was creeping upward, this wave wetting her feet, was the same undertow that had pulled him in, burying, drowning, giving him back only when the life had been battered out of him, as if rectifying what the storm had left undone. Now she was frozen, shivering, wet up to her knees, the heavy skirts dragging her down into the hungry sand.

Colleen Flaherty stopped in front of her, her face gleeful with a bitter triumph. "That's right, English-woman. This is where he died, the young man from the sea who came here intruding into our lives. I don't know who killed him, but it wasn't my son. You should have left it alone and kept your prying to yourself." She took another step forward.

Emily moved back, and the next wave caught her, almost taking her balance. She teetered wildly, waving her arms, and felt the sand suck her down.

"Dangerous seas here," Mrs. Flaherty said. "Lots of people drown in them. You shouldn't have told Brendan to go away. It isn't any of your business. This is his land and his heritage. This is where he belongs."

Emily tried to pull her feet unstuck and go towards her. "It's time you let him go," she said angrily. "You're suffocating him. That isn't love, it's possession. He isn't Seamus and he doesn't want to be."

"You don't know what he wants!" Mrs. Flaherty shouted, taking a huge step towards Emily.

Emily struggled desperately and another wave washed in and raced up the sand, catching her well above the knees and sending her flying, drenched in ice-cold water, fighting for breath. This is how it must have been for Connor Riordan, like the shipwreck all over again.

She saw Colleen Flaherty looming over her, then felt arms pulling her, and she had barely the strength to fight. There was another wave, burying them both, robbing her of breath. Then suddenly she was free and Padraic Yorke was holding her up. Mrs. Flaherty was yards away. Emily gasped in the air. She was so cold it seemed to numb her entire body.

Another wave came and Padraic Yorke pushed her forward, towards the shore. She took another step. There were more people there but she was too battered to know who they were. Her lungs ached unbearably. Someone reached for her. Another wave came, but this time it did not take her. She was faint, stumbling, and then she pitched forward into darkness.

*S*he awoke in her own bed in Susannah's house, still fighting for breath, and deathly cold inside.

"It's all right," Father Tyndale said gently. "It's all over. You're safe."

She blinked. "Over?"

"Yes. Colleen will be ashamed for the rest of her life, I think. And Padraic Yorke has made his restitution, may he rest in peace." He made the sign of the cross.

She stared at him, understanding filling her slowly. "Is he alive?"

"No," he said softly. "He gave his life to save you. It was what he wanted to do."

She felt the tears prickle her eyes, but she did not argue.

"Thank you, Mrs. Radley," he said softly, touching her hand. "You have ended a long grief for us. Perhaps in a way you have given us a second chance. This time we will not turn away a stranger who brings us truth about ourselves that we might prefer not to know."

She shook her head. "It wasn't I, Father, it was circumstances that brought Daniel to the village, and gave us all an opportunity to face ourselves, and do it better this time. For me also. Perhaps that is what Christmas is, another chance. But it won't work if you don't tell everyone who killed Connor Riordan, and why."

His face pinched. "Can't we allow Padraic to die with his secrets? The poor man has paid. It might have been an accident. Connor was not Daniel, you know. He had a cruel tongue, at times. It may have been the blind cruelty of youth, but it hurts. The words cut just as deep."

"No, Father, if they don't know who killed him, they will not lay their own suspicions away, and realize that it was the lies that hurt. No one needs to know what secret Padraic Yorke had, but we need to know our own."

"Perhaps so," he said reluctantly. "If I had been honest with myself maybe all these bitter years need not have been. I wanted to save pain, but I only added to it. It was Hugo's debt too. I must thank Susannah for paying it."

*W*hen, on Christmas Eve, the church bells began at midnight, Emily and Susannah sat before the fire listening to the wind in the eaves. Daniel had decided to walk to the service, and they were alone in the house.

Susannah smiled. "I'm glad I can hear them," she said gently. "I wasn't sure if I would. Tomorrow will be a good day. Thank you, Emily."

ANNE PERRY is the bestselling author of two acclaimed series set in Victorian England: the William Monk novels, including *Execution Dock* and *Dark Assassin*, and the Charlotte and Thomas Pitt novels, including *Buckingham Palace Gardens* and *Long Spoon Lane*. She is also the author of the World War I novels *No Graves As Yet, Shoulder the Sky, Angels in the Gloom, At Some Disputed Barricade,* and *We Shall Not Sleep,* as well as seven holiday novels, most recently *A Christmas Promise.* Anne Perry lives in Scotland. Visit her website at www.anneperry.net.